Teen (Adult fiction)

Ebonics Included

Camille

-It's Goin Down-

Series 2 Book 2

Author & Publisher

Kelonda Isom

To my younger self

…and to anyone

who feels they need a positive escape or distraction from life or reality, in order to make it through while avoiding the negative things and the negative people of this world. No matter how hard it gets, you'll come out on top.

The positive road you're taking will not be in vain. You do it effortlessly! Everything will turn out great! Everything will be okay. Be proud of yourself. You will come out on top. God will guide you and will never leave you. Keep your faith in God as strong as you've always had. Listen when God speaks and obey his commands.

God loves you…. he always will.

Table of Contents

Chapter 1

Bump in the Road

After that second beating, I didn't clearly understand what was happening. Was I getting in trouble for mouthing off? Was I getting in trouble because of this boy again? Or was it both? My mom never had to beat me growing up. Those pops I got for the things I did here and there to my grandmas, didn't compare to how my mom beat me now.

My mom warned me about that boy, but she knew it wasn't my fault…or so I thought. But she is very big on respect, and I know for sure my mouth got me in a lot of trouble. So I figured, as long as I keep my mouth shut, I could get around being in trouble so much. When I went back to school, that's exactly what I did. Having to keep my shut and holding back things to stay out of trouble, taught me that I can keep a secret.

So many things happened at school, and as long as I kept that good girl persona in front of the adults, I was able to get away with practically anything! I always talked to my mom and told her everything. Some days I couldn't wait to get back home just to tell her how my day went. But after I kept getting in trouble for something I didn't do, our conversations changed.

I knew my mom very well, just as she knew me very well. I knew that I couldn't stop talking to her about things cold turkey, so I kept it at a minimum. I told her just enough to keep her off my back and to keep her from assuming. Once I mastered that, I was ready to take things to a whole different level. Although the world didn't know we existed, me and my cousins knew there was a whole different life we craved as kids.

We were very sheltered and had a lot of security to protect us for as long as we could remember. We were so closed in and could not do things or go places other kids could. But by us being in school, we met other kids who talked about a life we could only dream of. The more they talked about it, the more we became interested. This also frustrated us because we knew it was something we could never have.

We listened to our moms and obeyed them 100% of the time. They never had an issue out of us. But the older we got the more we craved freedom. They thought it was bad when I first got in trouble for that boy, but things got a lot more interesting once I started to pay attention to him. Things got quiet for weeks. Everyone thought I straightened up because of the beatings.

Little did they know, this boy showed me how to navigate around anything and anybody. He showed me how to not get caught and how to act if I did get caught in order to get out of trouble. We spent a lot of time together in school. He has ways of getting me out of class without the teacher knowing it was him. Sometimes, I thought it was real when someone would come to class with a pass saying that the office sent for me.

When I would come out of the classroom, I would look lost until I walk away from my classroom door and run into him. Then we would laugh, hug, he would grab my hand and we would run off to a spot in school where no one would find us. This lil boy had connections at school! Lol. After going to that spot with him a few times, he deemed it our secret place.

I still didn't know this boy's name! All I knew was that he looked out for me, and I always had a lot of fun with him. The next time we went to our secret place, he said, "I have something to ask you." I looked at him and smiled with my mouth closed, while I looked at him slightly confused. I said, "Okay?" He looked at me and smiled fully. Then he said, "Camille…can we be best friends?"

I smiled fully and said, “What?” As he played with a few rocks throwing them, he said, “Can we be best friends? I’m a loner, I don’t take to many people, but you different. I like you. I like you a lot. I only come to school for you.” I chuckled a little bit and said, “Wait what?? What would you do if I wasn’t in school?” He looked at me and said, “Drop out.” I blinked a couple of times looking confused. Then I said, “Drop out? What’s that?”

He stopped throwing rocks and walked closer to me. Then he said, “I don’t know, I heard my older cousin talking about it. He said after he drop out, he’ll be free, and he can do whatever he want because he won’t go to school.” I said, “Oh, well don’t drop out even if I’m not in school. It’s good to be in school. It gets you out of the house, plus you meet people.”

He looked at me sarcastically and said, “You don’t get out much, do you?” I smiled with my mouth closed and said, “No.” He said, “Why you said if you not here to stay in school? Where you goin?” I said, “Nowhere now, but wherever my mom takes me.” He said, “Oh, I wouldn’t want you to leave. I’ll be sad. What yo mom do?”

I looked at him and my facial expression dropped as I said, “A lot. But I don’t wana talk about it.” He said, “I respect that. I’ll be sad if you leave. You my only friend here. I been on the move a lot lately. I got a lot of stuff I’m starting to do. Since I move a lot, I don’t make friends. I don’t wana lose’em.” I looked at him curiously. I said, “Then why did you befriend me?”

He looked up at me and said, “You different Camille, just like I said. People like you only come around once in a lifetime if we lucky. That would’ve been stupid for me to not act on it…. So, can we be best friends?” I smiled again and said, “Yeah sure, we can be best friends.” He got so happy. He jumped up and down and yelled, “Yes! Yes!”

We both laughed and I said, “Shh.” I didn’t want anybody to hear him. He stopped quick and put his finger over his mouth as he repeated me, “Shh.” Then I said, “I have to tell you something though.” He smiled and said, “What?” I said, “I have a best friend already.” He said, “Where?” I said, “Down in Miami.” He was shocked as he said, “Miami?! You be down there too??” I looked at him curiously and asked, “Too?”

He then revealed to me, "I be down there sometimes too." I smiled and said, "Are you lyin to me?" He said, "No, I wouldn't lie to you Camille. I work down there often. I'm just up here for a minute too." I was shocked to hear him say that. I said, "You work?" He looked at me and said, "You don't?" I was looking confused and said, "No."

He said, "Is it a girl?" I said, "Huh??" He said, "Your best friend, is it a girl?" I said, "Oh yeah, her name is Que." He said, "Oh okay, I can be your boy best friend then." I said, "I guess you can." He said, "Let's take a picture." I said, "Where you gone put it?" He looked and me, smiled, and then said, "Camille, you sure you not a celebrity??"

I was on edge at this point. I said, "Yes, why you ask?" He said, "You move like one. The way you handle yoself and the questions you ask. I never see you around town outside of school, so you must be kept inside a lot. I bet you got a bunch of security that's hiding you from the world. Trust me I would know." At that point I tucked my lips in mouth as I looked off to the side thinking.

He laughed and said, "Relax. I'm playin with you." I nervously laughed and said, "Oh." Then he said, "The picture is just for me. I'ma keep it forever. This is the start of something great." I said, "Okay." He set the phone up for the camera to take our picture. I was sitting on the wall, and he stood in front of me slightly off to the side. I had one leg up on the wall leaning on it, and the other leg hanging off the wall.

He had his feet spread apart with his arms crossed. Once the camera took the picture, he said, “Alright let’s get you back to class.” As he held my hand to help me off the wall, I said, “So best friend, what do I call you?” He looked at me, smiled as he put his other hand on his chest, and said, “Shaun, my name’s Shaun.”

I smiled looking relieved. Then I said, “Shaun…I finally know your name.” He looked at me and said, “I hope you never forget it.” I smiled and we started to walk back inside hand in hand. No one caught us, he got me back to class without anyone knowing I was with him. I sat in class just smiling with my mouth closed throughout the rest of the day. All I thought about was how much fun he cared to let me have.

When I got home my mom asked me, "How was your day?" I smiled as I replied, "It was fun." She smiled a little with her mouth closed and said, "It seems like you had a lot of fun." I laughed and said, "Yes. I just had fun with my friends. That's the only time I get to interact with other kids here, so I enjoy it."

My mom said, "Well, you been stayin out of trouble so I can't complain. Whatever happened to that boy? Has he been talking to you in the hall?" I said, "No. I still see him, but I told him he kept getting me in trouble. So he doesn't talk to me anymore when he sees me in the hall." My mama sternly said, "Good." A little bit more time went by, and I got used to Shaun's routine.

I learned when he was coming and going. I knew when he was bothered or happy. We spent so much time together to where I started to understand and know how he was thinking. I was able to tell him how he was feeling based off of his body language and facials. I was even able to tell him what he was thinking at times.

This wowed him. He never knew anybody that paid him that much attention to where they knew his every move…well besides his mom. One day at school, he asked me to meet him at our secret place. He said it had to be at noon. I was watching the clock that day. So a few minutes before 12, I raised my hand and asked for a bathroom pass. My teacher gave me one and I left the classroom.

The advantage of this was the bathroom wasn't too close to my classroom. This gave me a little bit more time to linger. Besides, I knew it shouldn't have been too long because Shaun didn't use one of his help Camille escape class plans that day. I got to the secret place and saw him sitting on the wall. When he saw me, he looked at his watch and said, "Right on time."

We gave each other a closed mouth smile as he jumped off the wall. Once he was in front of me, he said, "Camille, thanks for coming." I said, "You're welcome. What's up?" He then took a deep a breath slightly looking to the side. I started to read his body language. I knew something was bothering him. I immediately said, "You're nervous, what's wrong?"

He looked at me as he took another breath and rubbed his hand over his hair. Then he said, “You really do know me better than anybody.” I smiled and said, “Duhh! Now tell me what’s the matter.” He gazed at me as he said, “Wow, you truly are amazing.” I smiled and replied, “Thank you…Now what’s on your mind?”

He said, “Camille, I have something to ask you.” I squinted quickly looking confused. This sounded awfully familiar. I replied, “Okay?” Then he said, “Well Camille, you’ve been an amazing best friend. We have a lot of fun together. We laugh together, we talk about how we feel about certain things we go through, although we only see each other in school, you still meet up with me no matter how many times I ask…you a rida.”

I chuckled a bit and said, “Yeah, I’m loyal.” He shook his head in a yes motion. He was overwhelmed by my response because he agreed with it. He said, “I really like you, Camille. I don’t ever wana lose contact with you. You all I got, and I appreciate you.” I smiled and said, “Aww, you were there for me when I needed someone the most. So I’ll always be there for you no matter what.”

He looked at me as if he was shocked and touched by that. Then he said, “I appreciate that.” I said, “You’re welcome. What’s your question?” He rubbed his face and turned his head for a second. When he turned his head back to me, he said, “Camille I just wana ask you…would you be my girlfriend?” My eyes got so big. I was taken by surprise. My mama never said much in particular about boys to me.

But I knew I wasn't allowed to have a boyfriend. I was speechless. I felt so indifferent. Shaun noticed and said, "I'm sorry. It's probably too much to ask. We best friends, I don't wana ruin that. You probably don't look at me in that way, but I understand." I broke my silence and slowly responded, "No, that's not it."

He was surprised. He said, "So you do look at me like that?" I said, "Huh?" He said, "Am I your type?" I said, "Um." I was so confused. I had no idea what he meant by my type. I was very much a rookie. Then he said, "Do you like me, like more than a friend? Like do you think I'm cute?" I said, "Oh!" He said, "If you think I'm ugly that's fine too, I just wana know what you think."

I said, “Yes I think you’re cute.” He got excited and said, “For real?!” I said, “Yes.” He said, “So why you looked so devastated?” I said, “I’m sorry, you took me by surprise. I’ve never dated anyone before. I’m not allowed to have a boyfriend.” He looked down and said, “Oh.” I felt kind of bad for him and said, “But if I was, I would say yes.”

He looked up at me so fast as he smiled. Then he said, “I don’t wana get you in trouble anymore. I was gonna say we would do the same things we do now. See each other in school and not tell anyone, that way you wouldn’t get in trouble. But only if you okay with it…I never had a girlfriend either. I wanted to wait for someone special. I thought I would find her later in life, but you came early.”

Now I was sassy enough to catch a line when I heard one. I chuckled and said, "That's the best you got?" Shaun looked up with a shocked look on his face as he smiled with his mouth open. Then he said, "What??" I said, "Is that your pickup line?" He laughed and said, "No, I was being truthful. But where did you learn that? About pickup lines?"

I said, "I said I never had a boyfriend. I didn't say I never witnessed pickup lines people tried to use on my mom and my aunties." We both laughed so hard. He said, "See?! That's one reason I really like you, Camille. You tell it like it is. Well, at least we'll still be best friends." He turned to walk away. As he did that, he heard me say, "About that…"

He turned around and he was so uneasy. He said, “Don’t tell me you can’t be my best friend no more.” I said, “I have to tell you something.” He was so scared, I saw it all in his face. He nervously let out a, “What?” I was looking down as I said, “I changed my mind.” He took a deep breath and said, “I messed it all up, didn’t I? I made you feel uncomfortable, now you don’t wana be my friend anymore, right? I’m so sorry Camille.”

I said, “No it’s not that.” There was a pause. I looked up at him and calmly said, “I’ll be your girlfriend.” It took a couple seconds for it to register in his head. As it registered his smile got bigger. Then he jumped up and down screaming, “Yes! Yes! She said yes!!” I laughed as I smiled at him. He ran back to me and hugged me so tight. He lifted me up and spun around in a circle as I hugged him back.

After he put me down, we looked at each other smiling for a couple of seconds. Then he said, “Let’s put our initials on this wall.” I said, “Wait, why?” He said, “Because this is where I asked you to be my girlfriend, and this is where you said yes. This is a special memory.” I had my arms crossed as I laughed. Then I said, “Okay.” I watched as he tried to carve our initials in the wall with a rock. It wasn’t working.

Then he pulled out a permanent marker from his pocket and said, “I forgot I had this!” I didn’t think anything of it. I watched him write his initial and the and symbol. Then he looked at me and said, “You have to write your initial.” I took the marker and wrote my initial. Then he came up behind me and said, “Now we have to draw a heart around it together.”

I slightly looked over my shoulder at him and asked, “Why?” He said, “Because it’s more special.” He put his hand over mine and we began to draw the heart around our initials. Too bad I was on a bathroom pass. As soon as we finished the heart all I heard was, “Camille Lockhart!” Me and Shaun turned around quick as we gasped. We saw my teacher and the principal.

When Shaun turned around, the principal said, “Shaun Mace!” My teacher looked at the principal and said, “So that’s his name!” The principal said, “He’s no stranger to my office.” Me and Shaun slowly looked at each other. We knew we were in big trouble. My teacher said, "Camille, I thought we worked through this. You were on a bathroom pass. You said you didn't know him or his name, and now you're defacing property with him??"

I remembered to not mouth off no matter how much trouble I was in already. I did good until she said, "You're a good kid. This is why I call your mom. I refuse to watch you allow some delinquent to bring you down." Shaun looked as though he heard that before, as if people talk down on him all the time. I wasn't gone stand for it. But as soon as I opened my mouth, Shaun covered it with his hand. I looked at him as he still had my mouth covered, and he shook his head no.

The teacher's mouth dropped. She was even more offended than she would've been if I had said something. She knew because he covered my mouth and told me no, I was gone really let her have it. She was speechless as she stared at the both of us. He finally took his hand off of my mouth. Then the principal said, "Both of you, my office."

We took a deep breath as we followed him back to his office. Once we got to the office we sat down. I seemed very calm, but I was terrified inside. As we watched the principal move around the office, I whispered to Shaun, "This is the most trouble I've ever been in before." He whispered back, "I'm so sorry." He then held my hand and said, "No matter what happens, I'll always be here to make you feel better."

I smiled at him. At that moment the principal turned around and saw us holding hands. He yelled, "Let go of her hand!" We both jumped as we quickly looked at the principal. Then we let each other's hand go. The principal then said, "Just so you know, defacing property gets you suspended." Me and Shaun looked at each other as we let out a silent deep breath.

Shaun then did something that took me by surprise. Something I'll always remember. He turned back to the principal and said, "Sir, please. Camille had nothing to do with it. It was me. She didn't want to write on the wall. I grabbed her hand and made her do it. If you have to suspend someone, suspend me. It was my idea anyway." I was so shocked he did that. I looked at him shocked.

The principal was intrigued Shaun said that. So he looked at me and asked, “Camille? Do you understand what just happened?” I said, “No sir.” He shook his head in a yes motion. Then he said, “Camille, you’ll be excused from suspension. But we’ll still have to call home.” I humbly said, “Okay.” The principal then said, “You can go back to class.”

I turned to Shaun and whispered, “Thank you.” He smiled and said, “You’re welcome.” We both gave each other a long hug. My head was rested on his shoulder. I didn’t understand what suspension was, but I had a feeling I wasn’t going to see him for a while. The principal watched us for a while and then he said, “Okay, okay, that’s enough.”

We stopped hugging. I was so moved by the way this boy looked out for me, that I cried. When we stopped hugging, we looked at each other. He saw me wiping my ongoing tears away with the sleeve of my sweater, the part on my wrist. That made me emotional. He didn't cry but he immediately went into comfort mode.

He moved my hand from my face as he started to wipe my tears away. Then he said, "Don't cry, everything's alright. We'll be okay." I tried to calm down, but my emotions got the best of me. I guess the emotions of everything I was dealing with in my life and the thought of what I was about to deal with when I got home that day, was getting the best of me in that moment.

As Shaun said everything was okay, I begin to repeat, "I'm sorry." He stopped me as he held both sides of my face with his hands. He looked at me in my eyes and said, "Hey. Don't ever be sorry for something you didn't do. I'm a man, I'll always take the wrap for you." I started to calm down as I smiled at him with my mouth closed.

He said, "I never wana see you cry. I only like it when you smile and when you happy…Everything is okay, alright?" I shook my head in a yeah motion as I smiled fully. He wiped away the last of my tears. Afterwards he rubbed my chin as he said, "I'll see you when I get back." I smiled and said, "Okay." We hugged one more time.

Then I heard the principal say, "Camille?" We stopped hugging. I looked at the principal and he said, "Be on your way." I looked back at Shaun who was holding my hand and said, "Bye." I turned around as I started to walk away, he still had my hand. Shaun then said, "It's never bye…" I turned to look back at him. Then he said, "This is see you later." I smiled and said, "See you later." Shaun smiled and let my hand go.

I walked out of the office. The principal rolled his eyes up to the ceiling playfully as he shook his head in a no motion. He couldn't believe he was seeing kids act like adults would in a relationship. Of course he knew nothing about us dating. He just thought oh she's going to miss her friend. Once I got to class, I could tell my teacher was mad at me. But I didn't care.

All I could think about was Shaun. I felt bad that he took the blame for it all. But he seemed to not worry about it. I was so concerned for him, I forgot about what I had to deal with when I got home. Soon school was over. I didn't see Shaun after I left the office. I have to say, I felt really sad about it.

In school I eventually made a lot of friends. But I didn't take to any of them on a personal level. Shaun was the only friend I met that I really cared for on a personal level. I never felt that way about anybody before. It was so new to me. I felt happy and protected whenever I was in his presence. He was the only person besides my family, that I was allowed to be myself around.

I knew I couldn't expose who my parents were, but other than that I hadn't a care in the world when I was with him. This feeling was new. I didn't know what it was, but I loved it. Without him there I wasn't sure what I was going to do. After school me and Crystal got picked up per usual. When we got home, my mama wasn't in the living room.

I took Crystal up to her room, gave her a snack, turned on her tv, and made sure she was comfortable. She noticed something was off about me. Before I walked out, she asked, "Camille?" I turned around to her and answered, "Yes Crystal?" She looked concerned as she said, "What's wrong?" I looked at her for a second and took a deep breath. Then I slightly grinned and said, "I'm okay."

Crystal kept looking at me and said, “You don’t look okay.” I said, “Everything is okay Crystal, don’t worry.” She then looked at the tv as I walked out of her room closing the door. I knew from the last time I got in trouble, that my mom was waiting for me in my room. I wasn’t ready for that again. So instead of going to my room, I quietly went back downstairs and hid in a place I knew my mom wouldn’t find me.

When I didn’t come in my room like I normally would, my mom went looking for me. She first checked in Crystal’s room and then she checked the bathrooms upstairs. After that she suspected that maybe I went to get a snack or something. She decided to wait in my room a little while longer. After about 20 minutes, her motherly instincts kicked in. She knew something was off.

She got up and went downstairs to look for me. She searched everywhere! She could not find me. The way my mom is, she goes into panic mode when she can't find me after a while. She double checked everywhere again before she lost her cool. She didn't find me. She didn't want to scare Crystal, so she started to go through it quietly at first. After a while she couldn't take it anymore.

She ran to Crystal's room and calmly asked, "Crystal where is Camille?" Crystal looked up at her and said, "I don't know." My mama asked, "When did you see her last?" Crystal said, "When we got home, she gave me a snack." My mama started to panic as she said, "And that's the last time you saw her?!" Crystal shook her head yes as she stood up still looking at my mama.

Then she said, “Mommie, is everything okay like Camille said?” My mama paused as she looked at Crystal shocked and speechless. Then she eagerly said, “What did Camille say to you?” Crystal looked confused as she held out her hand and said, “You and Camille are acting the same. But Camille was much calmer.” My mama said, “Acting the same?? Crystal baby, what do you mean we’re acting the same?”

Crystal said, “Something’s wrong but you both say everything’s okay. I can tell by you and Camille’s faces that ya’ll are scared of something.” She looked at my mom and innocently asked, “So Mommie, what is it?” My mom was taken back by what she had just said. She was shocked at how much Crystal noticed too. I don’t see why, after going through life with me and how I always knew what was going on around me.

My mama took a deep breath as she bent down to Crystal's height. She held both sides of her face gently and then slowly said, "Crystal, what did Camille say to you?" Crystal said, "She said I'm okay. I told her she don't look okay, then she said everything is okay Crystal, don't worry. Then she walked out of my room." My mom was confused.

She asked, "How did Camille look when she said it?" Crystal said, "I think Camille wanted to cry. She was sad when we were leaving school." My mom thought for a second and then said, "Okay. Thank you baby." Crystal said, "You're welcome Mommie." Latoya left out of her room. When she got in the hallway, she said to herself,

"Oh no." She thought I was so scared of getting in trouble that I went somewhere.

She was so nervous, and she felt indifferent about beating me the two times she did. She knew I needed to be disciplined during those times, but now she was wondering if it was worth it. She ran to the phone and called Grandma Tam. Once Grandma Tam picked up, my mama was talking a mile a minute. My grandma said, "Toya, Toya hunney calm down. I can't understand what you're saying."

My mama took a deep breath and said, "Ma, I can't find Camille!" My grandma got quiet for a second. My mama said, "Ma??" My grandma said, "I'm on my way over." Then she hung up the phone. My mama nerves was so wrecked she had to talk to someone. So she called Alexi. Alexi picked up so cheerfully and happy. Then my mom said, "Lexi, Camille is missing." Alexi smile quickly went away as she responded with, "What?!" There was a pause.

Alexi asked, "What do you mean Camille is missing??" My mama said, "Camille got in trouble in school today, she came home and put Crystal in her room. But now Camille done went somewhere, probably to avoid getting in trouble and I can't find her nowhere!" Alexi was so scared, she started to take in multiple breaths. Before it got worse, she asked my mom, "When was the last time Camille was seen?"

My mama said, "Um, when her and Crystal got home so a couple of hours ago." Alexi said,

"And you can't find her?! Have you checked everywhere?" My mama said, "Everywhere Lexi. I'm panicking, I don't know what to do!" At that point Alexi started to hyperventilate. She was backstage at one of her shows too. Her team rushed to her to help her. She dropped her phone as she hyperventilated, so everybody around her got scared.

My mom heard the commotion and was yelling her name, "Lexi?! Lexi!" It scared my mom. Someone got on the phone and told my mom what was going on. My mama started to freak out more. Alexi's manager got on the phone with my mom to figure out what happened to Alexi. My mom said, "We're going through a family crisis right now…oh my gosh!" The manager felt bad for both of them.

Just then my grandma got there, and she was concerned after seeing my mom freaking out. She saw her phone in her hand. She took the phone and spoke to Alexi's manager to figure out what was going on. When she found out that Alexi was not doing too well, she went into a panic and asked to speak with Alexi's mom.

When she did speak with her, Alexi's mom told her, "The emergency team is here. They're trying to help her breath properly." Just then my grandma said, "Toya hunney don't do that!" My mom had picked up the house phone and called Trinity. My grandma didn't want to worry everyone, but it was too late. Trinity freaked out.

My grandma and Alexi mama hung up with each other after that. Trinity said to my mom, "How did you lose her?! I'm on my way." When she hung up my mama called my other aunties. Since my grandma was trying to stop her from telling them, they heard the commotion and got scared. Everyone was at my house no more than 10 minutes later. They all rushed inside still freaking out. By this time my mama had already cried.

She scared them. After they all searched the house and outside, they cried too. It was a scary moment for them. The emergency team where Alexi was, finally got her to breathe correctly. She kept requesting to call my mama back, but her mom and everyone else there didn't think that was a good idea. They kept the phone away from her, which did not make matters better.

Being that Alexi didn't know what was going on, she couldn't function right. The full stadium she was performing for that day was waiting for her to come back out. People had to go out there and stall by putting other performers on stage while they tried to get her back together. At one point she was sitting there staring into space. She didn't respond to anybody when they spoke to her, not even her mom.

She was in deep thought. Everyone was okay because at least she was breathing correctly. Just as everyone got comfortable with how she was, Alexi went back into a panic, it came from nowhere. She started to breath crazy again as she fell back in her chair. Everyone jumped up yelling, "No!" They were also yelling her name, "Lexi!"

But she just laid back, appearing to be too weak to do anything.

This time the emergency team rushed and kicked just about everybody out of the room. Her mom and her sister was allowed to stay. Meanwhile back at my house, my grandma called my aunties mamas to help her. She couldn't handle all of them in a crisis like this on her own. Their moms freaked out too and wondered why no one told them. They rushed over to my house.

When they got there, they questioned everyone about what was going on. Between them all they were able to tell them everything. At that point they looked for me too. When they couldn't find me, Grandma Tia asked, "Should we do a missing person's report?" That triggered all of my aunties and my mom. They paused and then started to cry.

My grandmas tried to calm them down. As they did that, my mom's phone rung. My grandma looked at it and said, "Alexi's calling." My mama looked at her so fast. As she reached for the phone, she quickly said, "Ma give me the phone please." My grandma passed her the phone. My mama picked up and eagerly said, "Hello?" But it wasn't Alexi, it was her mom.

My mom asked, "Oh, how is Alexi?" When Alexi heard her mom say my mama's name, she reached for the phone and said, "Ma, please give me the phone." Her mom told my mom, "Hold on." Once Alexi was on the phone, she said, "Toya what's going on?" My mama asked, "What happened to you?" Alexi said, "Panic attacks. Did ya'll find her yet?" My mama didn't want to tell her because she didn't want her to have another panic attack.

But Alexi wouldn't allow her not to. So my mama calmly said, "Not yet, we still looking." Alexi took a breath as she laid back on the stretcher they had her on. She put her arm over her eyes as she quietly said, "Oh my gosh." My mom was happy she didn't have another panic attack. Alexi said, "Well did you ask security? If she left, they would have seen her, they actually would've stopped her."

My mama gasped and said, "You're right!" My aunties and grandmas were looking at my mama crazy as she got up to run out the front door. She went to multiple security guards, but they all said they saw me go in but never saw me come out. This confused my mom. She went back in the house looking crazy. Grandma Tam slowly asked her, "Toya, what the matter baby?"

My mom said, "Alexi's right. Security would've saw her. There is no way they would've let her leave. They saw Camille come in, but she never went back out the house…Camille is still here." That spooked everybody! Trinity said, "Well then where the h*ll is she?! We looked everywhere." Latoya started to think. She started to pace as she pointed her finger.

She then said, "I haven't been thinking logically. Camille has always been a pro at hiding since she was little. Her favorite game has always been hide and seek. Most of the time I couldn't find her no matter how much I looked. Camille is somewhere in this house. We just haven't looked everywhere." Beonca was confused. She said, "But we have." Latoya asked, "Did we look under counters, in the closets, the garage, weird spaces that she can crawl into?"

Everyone was in awe. They couldn't believe they didn't think of that. Alexi stayed on the phone while they looked in those places. They still had no luck. Then Alexi said, "Where are her cousins?" Latoya said, "I guess at home, why?" Alexi said, "If Camille is hiding, if anybody could find her it would be them. They play hide and seek with her all the time. They have for years. They should know some of her patterns."

My mom gasped, then she told my aunties and my grandmas what Alexi said. They all wanted to know how she was thinking so rationally. But truth be told, Alexi was the most relaxed because she was forced to be by the emergency team. They had her on the stretcher already and she knew if she had another panic attack, they were going to take her from her show to the hospital. She didn't want that, so she tried to keep herself calm.

She only had time to think, plus her mom was helping her to stay calm. My mama asked her sisters, "Where ya'll kids at?" They all said, "At home." My mama said, "Get them over here but don't tell them Camille is missing." They had their security to bring my cousins over. Once they got there, Alisha asked, "Where is Camille?" My mama said, “That’s a good question. I think Camille is hiding and we can’t find her.”

Carmen got excited as she smiled and asked, “Camille is playing hide and seek?!” They all were shocked to hear her say that. Latonya said, “We think so, but we can’t find her.” Cashae asked, “How long have ya’ll been looking for her?” Grandma Tam said, “It’s been a few hours.” My cousins all smiled and looked at each other confused as they said, “A few hours?!”

Then Alicia said, “Come on ya’ll let’s find her.” Carmen said, “Yeah, we the experts.” They walked off quick going their separate ways. Our moms and grandmas were so happy they started to look for me. They were even more happy at how confident my cousins were that they would find me.

The adults didn't follow them around, but when my cousins looked for me near the adults, the adults were shocked at the places they looked for me at.

Cashae used Camieka to crawl into the smaller places. She would even lift her up to look over things they couldn't see. Alisha even went to get Crystal out of my room. When they saw her carrying Crystal, Alisha asked, "Auntie, can we use her?" Latoya said, "Yes that's fine." Alisha said, "Yes!" She had Crystal go to hiding places she's found me in before or saw me come out of before.

After about 30 minutes my cousins came back to our mamas shaking their heads in a no motion, looking defeated. Carmen had her hands on her hips as she said, "It makes no sense, we would've found Camille by now." Cashae said,

"Unless she cheated." Alisha said, "Camille never cheats." Alicia asked, "Did Camille leave the house?"

My mama explained what the security told her. Carmen immediately went into deep thought as they all kept talking. Alisha said, "So, nobody can find Camille in the house and security said she came in, but she never came out?" At that point Carmen lightly gasped as she looked up surprised. Her mouth was wide open, and she had her pointer finger up.

She quickly said, "Wait a minute." Then she ran off towards the kitchen area. Everyone was confused. Cashae even asked, "Where she goin?" My cousins shrugged their shoulders as they said, "I don't know." Everyone just kept talking. About 5 minutes later, Carmen came running around the corner. When everyone looked up, they all got quiet, and their faces dropped.

They were shocked to see Carmen running around the corner hand in hand with me running behind her. There was a pause. Carmen said, "I found her!" Due to the silence, Alexi asked, "What happened? Hello??" While still looking at me and Carmen, my mama said, "I can't believe it. Carmen found her." Alexi screamed short and loud. She scared everybody in the room with her.

She even scared some people that were outside the room waiting to see how she was doing. Her mom said, "What happened?!" Alexi said, "They found Camille!" Her mama got excited and said, "They found Camille?! They found Camille!

Oh thank God!" My mama them was still quiet. Then Latoya said, "Lexi, I'll call you back." Alexi said, "Alright." Alexi was so relieved, she took a deep breath and started to recover easily.

She was weak and needed some time before she went back on stage. After hanging up the phone, my mama asked Carmen, "How the h*ll did you find her??" Carmen said, "We play hide and seek all the time. Camille never cheats. We looked all over the house but couldn't find her. Camille never left, so the only logical place was the backyard." She was tapping her chin when she said that last part.

Our moms and grandmas mouths dropped. They felt so dumb for not checking the backyard. Carmen said, "We never reveal her hiding places just in case she wants to use them again. But I can tell under the circumstances and tension in this room, that ya'll wana know where she was, and she probably won't be using that hiding place again." Once again, the adults were shocked at how Carmen knew it wasn't a game and it was something more serious than what they presented to them.

Yet again, I don't know why they were so shocked. They know us better than that. After the shock, my mama asked, "Camille, where were you? We've been looking all over for you for hours." I said, "I was sitting on the side of the house. Carmen ran around the corner and grabbed my wrist. She snatched me up fast. I didn't know what was happening, so I just followed her."

My mama said, "Is that where you were this whole time?" I said, "Yes." She zoned in on me and asked, “Why?” I looked at her nervously biting my bottom lip. The room was quiet. At this point, my cousins knew something really bad must have happened. My mama knew I wasn’t gonna answer her easily with everyone else there. So she asked, “Did you know your principal called me today?” Everyone including my cousins gasped.

My cousins gasped lower than the adults. They were shocked but didn’t want to make it worse. I was looking scared as I lowly answered, “Yes ma’am.” She then asked, “Is it safe to say that’s why you were hiding?” It was hard for me to answer that, but I managed to let out a low, “Yes ma’am.” That shocked everyone in the room, now they all wanted to know what happened with me in school.

They all waited for a few seconds, then Beonca said, “Principal? What the h*ll happened with Camille that the principal had to call home?? She don’t get in trouble like that.” Latoya was still looking at me and said, “That’s what I thought.” I was quiet. Latoya continued, “But apparently a boy at her school keeps getting her in trouble. But I can’t put all the blame on him, because Camille has her own mind, and she knows she does not have to include herself in things she has no business doing.”

Everyone was tuned in. My mama then said, “Yet you still chose to…why??” Now all eyes were on me. I got very shy when I knew a lot of people were paying attention to me at once, family or not. They all can tell I was embarrassed. I didn’t know what to say. Just then they heard my grandma say,

"Hey, uh no we're trying to figure that out now Lexi… we'll keep you on the phone."

My grandma put the phone on speaker and placed it on the living room table. The table that everyone was sitting and standing around. My mama said, "That's Lexi?" Alexi said, "Yeah it's me, hi everybody." Everybody said, "Hey Lexi." My mama said, "She really ain't gone wana talk now." Alexi said, "What happened?" My mama said, "Camille was hiding from me because the principal called me today."

Alexi said, "Principal?? What?" Latoya said, "Yeah, she got in trouble with the same lil boy again." Alexi said, "Ah! What?! Didn't she say he was getting her in trouble?" Latoya said, "Yeah, but I think it was different this time. Camille almost got suspended." Everybody including Alexi gasped really loud. The ones that were able to see me looked at me shocked. Alexi said, "Suspended?! What did she do?!"

Latoya said, "That's what we waiting for her to tell us." Alexi said, "Wait, Ma, I'ma video call you I gotta see her." She called my grandma phone because my mama told her she would call her back. So she turned the call into a video call. My grandma picked it up. Alexi said, "Thanks Ma." My grandma said, "You're welcome." She propped the phone up on the table facing me.

Alexi had a clear view of me, and she looked pissed. She had reason to be. I mean, I did scare her half to death, and she was missing some of her concert because of me. I tried not to look at the phone, I looked down mostly. Then she said, "Camille?" I looked up at her with my eyes. When I did, she said, "Why did you almost get suspended?" I was messing with my nails as I timidly said, "I don't know."

All of the adults, especially my mama, looked at me like, What?! How you don't know?! I looked around at them for a second, I was scared. Then Alexi said, "How you don't know?? Matter fact, start over, just tell us what happened from the beginning, and we can tell you why you almost got suspended." All of the adults agreed saying, "Right!" I took a deep breath and said, "I guess because we wrote on the wall?"

They all said, "Uh un nope! Tell us from the beginning." My mama said, "Now you magically remember when we ask for the whole story. Uh un what happened from the time this started at school?" I started off slow telling them how he asked me to meet him somewhere. Then I told them that he wanted to write our initials on the wall. I let them know how he wanted me to write my own, so I did. Then I told them that's when we got caught.

The adults were pissed off at me. My mama said, "Initials? For what?" I slowly said, "Because he said we're best friends." That was the first time I lied to my mom. I didn't want to, but I was scared that I was gonna get jumped on by all of them if I admitted that Shaun was my boyfriend. My mama said, "Hmm." Alexi said, "So that means you know his name now, right?"

My mom and aunties all said, “Oh yeah! What’s his name??” I looked down and said, “Shaun.” My mama said, “Shaun, when did you find that out?” I said, “A couple of weeks ago.” My mama said, “How did you find out?” I said, “He told me.” My mama said, “You haven’t been getting in trouble, but you also told me you haven’t been speaking to him in the hall. That’s the only place you see him.”

I said, “I didn’t see him in the hall when he told me.” My mama said, “Something not adding up.” I said, “I saw him on my bathroom break, and he told me. But it wasn’t in the hallway. The bathroom is not that close to my classroom.” My mama said, “Do you understand what defacing property is Camille?” I shook my head no, as I answered, “No.”

She said, “That’s a crime Cee Cee!” I gasped as my mouth dropped. She continued to say, “When you mess up somebody’s property by writing on it, you get in trouble with the law. You can go to jail for that.” I gasped again. I started to think and then I got mad. I looked off to side as I was in deep thought. I couldn’t believe Shaun would do something so bad that could get me in so much trouble.

The one person who I thought I could trust was the same person that could have put me in jail. Where was the trust in that?! I was so confused and upset I agreed to be his girlfriend after he did that to me. I felt like that was a mean thing to do to someone you claim to be the only person you have. I couldn’t wait to see him again to give him a piece of my mind.

They all saw my face and knew I was thinking about something. My mama asked, “Camille, what you thinking bout?” I came out of it and looked at her. I tried to answer but all I could do was take in deep breaths. She said, “I know…that’s why you don’t do things people tell you to do. Especially if you don’t know what you doing.” I said, “I’m sorry, I didn’t know. I didn’t wana do it. He grabbed my hand and made me do it.”

Once I said that, they got mad. Trinity asked, “Why you didn’t say that before Camille?? Why you protecting this boy??” I was looking sad. My feelings were hurt, I really trusted him. I closed my eyes as I shook my head in a no motion. Tears fell from my eyes as I said, “He said I’m all he got.”

They said, "What?!" Alexi sarcastically laughed and said, "Uh un who is this boy?!"

My grandma looked at my mama like, girl I told you. They all were so shocked, because they knew they were told this by a guy at some point. Even in their adult years. My mama said, "No, uh un ya'll too young for all this. Camille that sounds like someone that's trying to be your boyfriend." I was surprised she said that.

I looked at her confused and said, "Huh?" Alexi said, "Camille, you can't always believe what these boys tell you. Sometimes they tell you things just to get you to do whatever they want." At this point I held my head as I put my head down. I was so confused. Did he lie to me? Or was he really telling the truth? My grandma and my mom looked at each other. My grandma lowly said, “I think you and Camille need to have a talk.”

My mama was not prepared but she agreed that she should. If I learned anything about dating and the real world, she wanted to be the first to tell me so no one can tell me anything wrong. She was just hoping what she was thinking was not true, because I was only 10 years old. In her head she was thinking, please God not my baby.

They all talked to me and gave me advice on boys and people in general. They were all happy I wasn’t missing. Soon they all left our house and Alexi went back to her show. Later that night, my mom spoke to me about a lot of things she didn’t think she would have to speak to me about until I was at least 13. But I was so sheltered, I knew nothing about boys, dating, or the real world.

I just knew what went on around me and she managed to hide that well since I was like 5. After she spoke to me about boys and precautions I should take to stay out of trouble, I felt like I knew a whole lot more. I was happy she talked to me about that stuff, now I felt better prepared to face any boy that tried to approach me in that manner.

Towards the end she told me, “You do understand that you’re too young to date, right?” I said, “Yes.” She said, “Okay. I know you’re in public school, but I don’t want you to run into the wrong crowd. Always have your own head, don’t follow behind anybody.” I said, “Yes ma’am.” After we were done, I started to walk out of her room. I didn't get a beaten this time which was great, but I couldn't help but feel bad for lying to her earlier.

I knew this could cost me everything, but I couldn't sleep with that on my head. So I turned back to her and said, "Mommie?" She said, "Yes?" I said, "I'm sorry." My mama said, "For what?" I said, "I lied earlier." She looked at me like she saw a ghost. She nervously said, "About what??" I said, "About the reason why I wrote on the wall." She said, "You told me he grabbed your hand and made you write on the wall."

I said, "Well, I was scared to admit it in front of everybody. I didn't want to write it, but after he asked me twice, I wrote my initial. But he told me we have to draw the heart around it together. That's when he grabbed my hand and drew it with me." My mama almost choked. She said, "What?! There was a heart around the initials?? For what??"

I said, "He asked me to be his best friend a couple of weeks ago…" She said, "Yeah, you told me that." Then I said, "But today, he asked me to be his girlfriend." My mama said, "Camille!" I said, "That's why it seemed like a boy trying to be my boyfriend. Ya'll was right, he was, and he did." My mama said, "Wait a minute. Are you telling me that the reason ya'll wrote ya'll initials on the wall, is because he asked you to be his girlfriend and you said yes??"

I said, "Yes. I told him I'm not allowed to date but then I felt bad, because he said I'm all he has. So I said yes." My mama flipped out. She said,

"Mommie was right, she's only 10. No, Camille! You are not dating anybody. You are only 10 years old, you are too young to have a boyfriend! When did this even happen?? You didn't know him remember?" I said, "He kept protecting me. He protected me when no one else did. I never had that."

My mom looked at me so shocked. She couldn't believe she was hearing this from her 10 year old's mouth! She said, "Camille, what do you mean? I protect you all the time." I said, "Yeah, but when I'm out there without you, he was the only one that protected me. Plus he's a guy." My mama paused and said, "A guy?" I looked at her and said, "I don't know how it is to have a guy protect me…Andre never did."

My mama's eyes closed slowly as she took a deep breath. Then she said, "Listen, you never have to go out there to try and find any boy or man to protect you. I don't want you to feel that you have to look for protection or love in other places because of what Andre lacks. We are all here for you, you don't have to run to nobody in the streets for anything. You'll always have it here, do you understand that?"

I said, "Yes." Then she said, "Good. Now when you see this boy again, I want you to correct what happened. You not allowed to date anybody, ya'll are still kids. Take time and be kids, you'll have plenty of time to date later in life, trust me. I don't want you to go through what I've been through. It wasn't easy at all." I said, "Okay." She said, "I appreciate you being honest with me. Never forget you can come to me and talk to me about anything. I rather you talk to me than to somebody out in the streets that can tell you what they wana tell you."

I said, "Yes ma'am." She gave me a hug and kissed my forehead. After I went to bed, she called her sisters and Alexi. She told them what I admitted to, and they were all shocked. They couldn't believe little Camille did all of this and was hiding it. They all decided to start keeping a closer eye on me and all my cousins. They thought us being into boys would come later in life, not now.

They started to think about when they were young. They knew what they did to their moms and now they were scared. They were taken off guard and didn't know how to feel or how to handle the next phase of life with us. They all spoke for hours about it before they went to sleep. They all hoped for the best.

Chapter 2

Bonded

As the days went by in school, I felt alone again. Although I was upset with Shaun, I still wished he was there to make my day better. I found myself back at square one. School was a drag without him, and I had no idea why. I stayed out of trouble because I was sad and stayed to myself.

Without Shaun there to cheer me up, I closed up again. Most days I would sit there leaning my head on my hand with my head down. I didn't know how long Shaun was gonna be gone or if he was coming back at all. He did say he goes to

Miami for work, and he didn't seem to care that he was getting suspended. All I could do was wait.

My mom and my teacher noticed how I didn't get in trouble during the time Shaun wasn't around. My mom started to believe that it was Shaun getting me in trouble. She would ask me if he was back every so often. She asked because she wanted to make sure I told him I couldn't be his girlfriend.

After a while she questioned me because I kept saying he wasn't back. She thought I was just saying that to avoid telling him. But I explained to her that I didn't know how long he was going to be gone. I also told her I think they suspended him for a lot of days. After I explained that to her, she believed me again. I didn't know how to handle this new interrogation from her.

I always answered her questions respectfully. But I grew tired of the daily interrogations. I started to think of ways to get around it. Sometimes, I fantasized about the day I wouldn't have to deal with so many questions, and be able to feel somewhat worried free. It didn't help that I was already afraid of getting in trouble with my mom.

I didn't know how to handle all of this pressure. Just as I felt like I was about to lose it, I went to school and guess who I saw? It was Shaun! I couldn't believe he was finally back. I stopped in my tracks immediately. I wanted to be happy because I missed him, but I was upset because I felt like he lied to me just to make me his girlfriend.

When he saw me, he spread his arms out and smiled. He was about to say hi. Instead of embracing him, I crossed my arms, squinted my eyes as I gave him a death stare, and then I sucked my teeth and walked away in the other direction. I walked away while I was a distance from him. After I walked away, he looked confused and disappointed.

He didn't know what happened to me. All he knew was, this wasn't the Camille he last saw before he got suspended. It bothered him all day, especially because now my teacher was on to him. He couldn't get close enough to me to get me out of class anymore. He wanted to talk to me so bad. I avoided him all day. I even held my bladder so I wouldn't run into him in the hallway.

Only problem is, after lunch and towards the end of the day I couldn't hold my bladder anymore. I raised my hand to get a hall pass. My teacher looked at me for a second before handing the pass to me. She thought about what me and Shaun did before. But then she remembered how well I was behaving since he got suspended. So she figured she wouldn't have a problem with me going to the bathroom.

What she didn't know was that Shaun was back. I went to the bathroom. I used it and after washing my hands, I took a deep breath as I glanced in the mirror. I assumed that Shaun wasn't in the hallway and that he got the point. I confidently opened the bathroom door to head back to class. When I opened the door, I saw Shaun leaning on the wall right next to the opening of the bathroom.

He looked up at me and I instantly closed the door. He scared me! My mouth was wide open. How did he know I was in the bathroom? Better yet, where did he come from?? Because he wasn't in the hallway. He must not have told me all his tricks of the hallway. I didn't know what to do. Then I heard him say, "Camille, what's wrong?" I covered my mouth still shocked that he was right there.

I didn't want to get in trouble again if the teacher saw us together, so I stayed in the bathroom. Since I didn't answer him, he said, "Camille, I don't know what I did but whatever it is, I'm sorry. Can you please talk to me?" There was a pause. Then he said, “Camille come on, talk to me. I’m not going nowhere until you say something.” I couldn’t find the words, but I had a lot to say.

I never thought I would say anything, but then without warning I blurted out, “Shaun I can’t be your girlfriend.” I covered my mouth quick right after. Then he said, “What?! …Camille what you mean?? I only left for 10 days and now you can’t be my girlfriend?? Did you start dating somebody else while I was gone? Tell me who it is so I can…”

I interrupted him and said, “Shaun!” He stopped talking and said, “Huh?” I said, “I’m not dating anybody, and I can’t date you.” He was sad and asked, “Why?” I took a deep breath and said, “Did you lie to me?” He said, “Never.” I said, “So when you said I’m all you have…were you telling me the truth? Or were you just saying that so I can say yes, I'll be your girlfriend?"

He was shocked to hear me ask him that. He said, "No, I would never trick you, Camille. Everything I told you is true, you are all I have. Even when you told me you couldn't be my girlfriend, I was sad, but I was okay with being your best friend remember?" I started to think and realize that is how it went. Then he said, "I would never make you do anything you don't want to do."

I said, "So why did you make me write on the wall?" He said, "I'm sorry. I didn't know that was a bad thing. I did grab your hand, but that was because I wanted it to be special. I wanted us both to draw the heart, that way we'll always remember one of the best days of our lives." I smiled as I quietly chuckled a little.

Then Shaun asked, "So we cool?" I said, "Yeah." He said, "Can you still be my girlfriend?" I said, "No, I can't." I heard him take a deep breath, then he said, "Camille, I would hate for you not to be my girlfriend. But if we're friends, at least I'll have you in my life. I can take disappointment real good, I'm kind of used to it." That caught my attention when he said that.

I immediately asked, "What do you mean?" As he played with his fingers he humbly said, "I never told nobody this but, I don't feel complete. I have daddy issues, you know? I have my mom and she do a good job with me, but I don't think she understands what it means for me to have my dad around." I grabbed my shirt where my heart was. I got teary eyed, and my mouth was wide opened.

Then he continued, "I guess this is why I'm always in trouble. I don't have my pops around to correct a lot of things I do. My mom feels bad for me, so I get away with a lot. The love I wanted from my dad I don't get. When I met you, you showed me love. You genuinely showed me you cared for me even as a friend. With you around, I don't feel that I need that love from my pops. You make me happy, you make me forget about the love and attention I lack from my dad. I never want that feeling to go away."

At this point tears were falling from my eyes. I couldn't believe he was going through the same thing I was going through. I understood exactly where he was coming from. He even said it as if it didn't bother him as much as it really did. He was covering up his emotions, like I did often whenever I talked about my dad to my mom and other people.

I never wanted other people to have a negative reaction to what I felt towards my dad. I never wanted them to be upset, especially my mom because she would confront him. So I always downplayed the way I really felt towards my dad. Then I heard Shaun say, "I don't like to tell people how I really feel, because I don't trust them. But for whatever reason, I trust you. You the first person I feel understand me, and I don't know why."

At that moment I broke my silence, through the light crying I said, "Because! I feel the same way. Nobody besides my family knows I have daddy issues. The way you explained your dad sounds just like mine. But my dad pops in and out of my life whenever he wants to and that makes it worse. If he wasn't there at all that would be better than him continuously hurting me." Shaun was so shocked.

He felt bad for me. I continued to say, "I'm taught to be quiet and never speak of family business, but that's hard when you feel like you have no one to listen to you. My mom is great, she does everything she possibly can to protect me and help me. But she feels so bad for everything I go through and been through. She blames herself and it's not her fault, it's his!"

Shortly after saying this, I broke down in that bathroom. Shaun said, “I’m so sorry Camille.” I started to wail loudly. Shaun immediately went into protection mode. He yelled, “Camille! Camille?!” The only time I’ve ever had a break down like this was at home. Whenever this happened, the only person that was able to calm me down was my mama and she was not there.

This was not good at all. After he called out to me for the third time, he couldn’t take it no more. He burst into the bathroom and saw me fall onto the wall. He ran to me and caught me just as I was falling to the ground. He refused to let me hit the ground. Once he was able to hold me up comfortably, he started to redirect my attention to him.

He said, “Hey, Camille it’s okay. It’s okay, you’re not alone, I’m here Camille.” He said that about three times before I looked at him. Once I did, he knew he had the potential to bring me out of what I was going through. He said, “I got you. It’s okay to cry, it’s okay. Take a breath, calm down, you alright. You need a hug? Can I have a hug? I need one too.”

When he said that, I zoned back in and hugged him so tight. He hugged me back tight as well. A few tears still fell from my eyes. But for the most part I was calming down. I know Shaun and I were the same age, but his hug felt different. I don’t know if it was because he was a boy and I was a girl, but it felt like something I never knew I needed. Something I never got before.

Strangely I felt secured and protected in his arms. I wasn't sure what this feeling was, but I loved it. He hugged me until I calmed down completely. He literally did not let me go. We stayed in that same position this entire time. Although I know my mom and her family loves me, this was the most loved and protected I've felt in weeks!

This was different for me. I never wanted this feeling to go away. I'm not sure what was going on, but for the first time I think I really fell for Shaun. I didn't know anything about crushing on a boy, liking a boy in a different way, or dating a boy. But I did know that my stomach fluttered. I felt warm inside and all I wanted was to be around him all the time.

He made me feel a way I never felt before and it was an amazing feeling. I wasn't willing to let that go easy. Once I got quiet and finally stopped sniffing, he asked, "You okay?" I lowly answered, "Yes." He said, "Good. Your happiness is what matters most to me." I just melted when he said that. I know what my mom told me about people saying things just to get me to do what they want, but I felt that Shaun wasn't lying.

I just knew he was being truthful and that he really cared for me. We were still hugging, my head was leaning on his shoulder. I was comfortable there. In that moment we shared something so special between us, I think it might have bonded us for life. Even if we remained just friends, I knew we would always be a part of each other's lives. I never shared a bond like this with anyone outside my family.

Shaun then asked, “So, why you say you can’t be my girlfriend?” After a slight pause, I said, “I changed my mind Shaun…I’ll still be your girlfriend.” He was so happy to hear that. He took a breath of relief then said, “You change your mind a lot.” We both laughed. I said, “I’m sorry. It’s not my fault.” We stopped hugging and looked at each other. He said, “I was sad earlier when you walked away. But I’m happy you still my girlfriend.”

I said, “I cared for you before you told me what you were going through. But now that I know, your happiness matters most to me too. I’m a girl, but I feel like I want to protect you now. I understand what you’re going through and how you feel because I go through it too." I can tell Shaun was touched by it. He tried to keep his tough boy persona on, but he was falling through the cracks. He pinched the top of his nose with his thumb and pointer finger. He was trying to stop the tears before they came full on.

He looked at me and said, "Nobody ever cared about me that much. Thank you, Camille. I think I just fell for you a whole lot more." We both laughed again. I said, "You're welcome. But thank you, you have no idea how much you've helped me out already." Shaun said, "I'll always be there for you Camille. You the first girl besides my mom that I ever cared for."

I smiled and we hugged again. We had a nice moment and for that I was thankful. As we took it all in. The bathroom door opened. All we heard was, “Excuse me!” We both looked quick. It was a teacher. Her mouth was to the floor. I could only image what was going on in her head. Shaun’s hands fell to my waist and my hands were on his shoulders, my arms were relaxed in front of his chest. My elbows were almost touching his chest.

We didn’t even realize it. Since she yelled excuse me so loud, a couple more teachers ran to the bathroom and saw us. They couldn’t believe what they saw. Me and Shaun were just stuck. Then the principal pushed his way through them. When he saw us, he gasped so loud, and his mouth dropped. They were all silent just staring at us.

Then the principal said, “Shaun Mace and Camille Lockhart!... Again?! Take your hands off of each other!" Me and Shaun gasped as we looked at each other, then we let go of each other fast. We looked back at the principal. He said, "Both of you, in my office now!" We were both scared but tried not to show it. We walked to his office and sat down. He just looked at us in shock at first.

After he sat on his desk, he said, "Why? Why would you two be in the bathroom together against a wall hugging??" Me and Shaun looked at each other then back at him. The principal then said, "I believe you are the influence, Shaun. While you were gone, we had no issues out of Camille. Before you came out to the school, Camille managed to make it through almost 6 years at this school without a peep…and once you appeared, her name has been one of the most I've had reported to me this year!"

Shaun let out a breath of disappointment. He was beating his self up about it and I didn't like that. Shaun then said, "I'm sorry. My intentions are never to get Camille in trouble. I was only in the bathroom because Camille needed help. Nobody was around and I had no choice." The principal was curious, he asked, "What could she possibly need help with in the bathroom?"

Shaun didn't want to put my business out, so he stopped talking. This made the principal think that he was lying. When I noticed that, I chimed in and said, "I was having a meltdown. He heard me in there. He called out to me a few times, but I didn't respond. I just kept crying. When he heard a loud sound, he ran in and caught me before I fell. Shaun was hugging me to stop me from getting hurt and hitting the floor."

The principal was shocked. He said, "Camille, that's the most I've ever heard you speak." He then looked at Shaun and said, "Is this true?" Shaun said, "Yes, it's true. I ran to three different classrooms trying to get a lady teacher, but they never came until after I went in the bathroom." I looked at him so shocked. I didn't know those teachers came because he knocked on their doors to get them to help me.

This boy was truly something else. I was thankful to him for trying. The principal took a deep breath. He called those teachers to find out if Shaun knocked on their classroom doors. They all confirmed he did. Those teachers didn't understand why he knocked on their classroom doors just to get caught in the bathroom with a girl. But they didn't know what was going on. After they confirmed it, the principal took another deep breath.

He looked at us and said, “We’re at the end of the day. I don’t know what the truth is here, but we would normally call your parents.” As he spoke, the bell rung. He let out another breath, then he said, “Go home and stay out of trouble.” We got so happy. We jumped up smiling. As we ran out the office the principal yelled, “And stay out of my office!” We both shouted, “Okay!”

I never walked with Shaun at school, but since we were just leaving the principal’s office, we both were going to the front of the school. I told Shaun 3 times he didn’t have to walk me out, but he insisted. I didn’t want him to see our security. Although we trusted each other, I still wasn’t supposed to expose who our parents were. He walked me out the front door.

As we stepped down the first step I stopped and said, “Oh my gosh!” He said, “What??” I said, “I’m sorry I forgot something. I gotta go back. I’ll see you tomorrow.” He said, “Okay.” He gave me a quick hug and left off the steps. I ran in the school and 5 minutes later I came rushing out the school holding Crystal’s hand. I forgot Crystal! Crazy part about it, security saw the whole thing.

When they saw Shaun hug me, they took their shades off to get a better look at him. Once they noticed I forgot Crystal and came back out with her, they said, “Uh oh.” They already knew the boy they saw must have had my head distracted. They just chuckled a little. Once me and Crystal approached the car the security got out and opened the door. We got in the car and to my surprise that day out of all days, no one else was in the car!

My mom always made sure a family member was in the car too, but that day none of them were there. I was happy they wasn't though because they would've saw Shaun. They would've also saw how I forgot Crystal. I was very happy my mom wasn't in the car. When we got home, everything seemed normal. Nobody called my mom from school to tell on me, it was weird.

I even went to my mom and asked, "Why was nobody in the car with security today?" She answered, "I wanted to test things out and see how everything worked out without a family member in the car. You're responsible already and I want you to practice being responsible. You never know when you'll have a lot more responsibility one day." I said, "Oh."

She asked, "How was it?" I answered, "How was what?" She said, "The ride home?" I said, "Oh! It was fine. It went how it normally goes." She said, "Good." Once I left from around her, all I could think about was Shaun. This was so new to me, I didn't understand it. After that day, Shaun wanted to make walking me out to the front, a thing. Whenever I rejected his offer, he would wonder why, and I would end up letting him walk me out to the front anyway.

The next time, I didn't forget Crystal. I told him, "I have to go get something." He said, "Again? I'm going with you." I said, "Okay." He followed me to the back of the school. Just as he asked, "Why you coming all the way back here?" Crystal yelled, "Camille!" She ran towards me with a big smile and her arms wide open. I knelt down with a big smile. I held my arms open until she ran into my arms and gave me a hug.

After she hugged me, I said, "You had a good day?" She smiled and said, "Yes." I have to say, Crystal has to be the most energetic when she sees me picking her up from class. That's probably only because she knows I'm taking her home lol. Once we get home she stay in her room and be to herself. Shaun was amazed. He asked, "You have a sister??" I smiled and said, "Yeah."

He said, "You never mentioned that to me." I looked at him and smiled as I said, "Family business." He playfully asked, "Who are you??" I laughed. We started to walk to the front of the school. I can tell he was intrigued that I had a sister. He kept looking at her and said, "Hi." She looked up at him smiling and said, "Hi."

He asked her, "What's your name?" Crystal replied, "My name's Crystal…what's your name?" I looked at Shaun quick. My eyes were big as I quickly shook my head in a no motion. Shaun glanced at me. He looked back at Crystal and said, "Jeremy. My name's Jeremy." I looked at him so quick and confused. When we got outside, he leaned over Crystal and whispered in my ear.

He whispered, "Jeremy is my middle name. Don't worry I won't lie to your sister, and I won't let you get caught up." After he whispered that, I looked at him impressed. I smiled and said, "Wow! How did you know…" He cut me off and said, "I'm beyond my years." He left me standing there with my mouth wide open while I smiled. He took me by surprise. I've been told all my life I was beyond my years, and now he is too?

This was too good to be true, me and this boy have so many things in common. The more I found out about him the more I liked him. Once me and Crystal got in the car, the security asked, "Camille, you made a new friend?" I said, "Huh?" He said, "Who is that young man I keep seeing with you?" I calmly said, "Jeremy." I was too keen to say his first name.

My mama speaks to security every now and then. I didn't want them to mention Shaun's name to her, that would drive her up the wall. If she knew I was spending more time with him at school, she would probably show up out there herself. I couldn't chance that. Security said, "Jeremy. Okay." I was quiet the rest of the ride home. Security never got in our business, but it was their job to protect us.

When they feel that we are at risk or see us getting close to someone outside, they're supposed to investigate it. By him asking me that I knew they were watching and were concerned, because that could jeopardize their job if they asked us kids questions like that. I knew better than to tell my mom they asked me that. They wouldn't have lost their jobs in this case, but I would've got in a lot of trouble.

When I did get home, my mom came to me. She said, “Camille, I forgot to ask you. It’s been a few days now. Has Shaun come back to school yet?” My body got warm, and my heart dropped. I was so scared. I calmly answered, “Yes.” She said, “Oh he did! When did he come back?” I said, “A couple of days ago.” My mama looked at me for a second and then she said, “Why didn’t you tell me?” I looked like I was thinking.

Everything was quiet, then she asked, “Did you tell him?” I looked at her and said, “Yes.” She asked, “What did he say?” I said, “He asked why I couldn’t be his girlfriend. Then he said it’s okay we can still be friends.” My mama said, “Good! I understand boys will like you, and there will be a day where you would like boys too. But right now both of ya’ll are too young. You didn’t even know what it was to date a boy. When you're older you'll understand. Until then you are not allowed to date."

I lowly said, "Okay." I was happy the conversation ended there. I was so scared. Normally my mom would pick apart what I say to her and would always find out the truth. This was a reason I always told her the truth. If I ever got caught lying to her, I don't know what would happen and I wasn't trying to find out.

I know it went a lot different than what I told my mom, but I didn't have the nerve or courage to stop her and tell her that I never broke up with Shaun. I wanted to tell her what happened, but I was scared to get in trouble. I knew I would get a beating for disobeying her. Judging from the two beatings I did get so far, her beatings hurt! At this point for the first time ever in my life, I guess I figured what she didn't know wouldn't hurt her.

Chapter 3

Losing Control

I never said a word about me still dating Shaun. I was willing to wait to see if she would find out on her own or not. As far as she knew, I told him I couldn't be his girlfriend no more and that settled that. I didn't feel good about keeping this away from her, because we were always able to talk about everything.

But somehow talking to her about boys was different. She had no tolerance for it at all and I didn't understand why. She always said she didn't want me to go through what she went through. I know she had me young because she told me, but I guess I didn't understand the severity in it. She didn't go into details, she only told me she had me young and she wants better for me.

What I did know was that she paid a lot more attention to me. She even asked me a couple of times, "Why you so quiet lately?" She knew I was a talker, especially around her. I would talk my mama ears off, and she would sit there and listen to every word I had to say. But since Shaun came in the picture, I was more stand offish.

Another few weeks passed by, and Shaun walked me to the front of the school every day. The day that I forgot Crystal, Shaun gave me a hug goodbye. But since Crystal was present, he didn't want to hug me out of respect of Crystal. So we would just say goodbye and go our separate ways.

Security saw this every single day. They never asked me about Shaun again, they just watched and observed.

One day I went to school, it was a Friday. My mama set up a playdate for me and my cousins. It wasn't a playdate just for us, we were allowed to invite two friends. Our parents of course would not be there, in order to keep us a secret. But security and our nannies would be there. They scheduled our playdate at a public inside amusement place.

We were excited. The only thing is, we had to get our friends to say yes on a short notice. I talked to a lot of people, but there was none I cared to invite out with me. Well except one person…Shaun. But I wasn't sure if that was too risky or not. I gave it a lot of thought. By the time I got in front of Shaun all of that thinking went out the window.

I immediately opened my mouth and said, “Shaun, what are you doing tomorrow evening?” He looked at me with his eyes lit up. He smiled and said, “Nothin if you need me.” I smiled and said, “Well, me and my cousins have a playdate scheduled tomorrow. You think you’ll be able to make it?” He took in a deep breath and was so happy that I asked him that.

He then smiled and said, “Of course! I’ll be happy to come.” I smiled and said, “Great!” He said, “Where is it?” I pulled out the invite and handed it to him. He looked at it, then I smiled and said, “Don’t be late.” He smiled and said, “I won’t.” After walking away from him, I wondered if I should have just invited a girl. I knew our moms expected us to, but they never said we couldn't invite boys.

After school I didn't see Shaun. I had no idea where he was. I got Crystal like normal and went to the front. When we got out there, I saw him by the road. I was surprised. I yelled out, "Shaun!" He turned to me, we both waved and smiled at each other. Me and Crystal went to the car and security opened the door for us to get in. Once we got in the car, the security said, "Camille?"

I responded, "Yes?" He asked, "What did you say your friend's name was again?" I answered, "Jeremy." He said, "Okay." I wondered why he asked me that again, but I didn't pay it any mind. After he dropped us off at home, my cousins came over. They were going to spend the night. During that night we asked each other about our friends we invited over. That conversation was interesting. We didn't know each other's friends, but I guess we were all gonna meet the next day.

I never told them I invited one person, and that person was a boy. I kept my mouth closed. Alisha however said, "I don't want to get in trouble, but I invited 3 people. I have three friends I want to come, and I couldn't leave any of them out." She knew the max was 2 for each of us. I told her, "Don't worry. I couldn't find a second person, so you can just say one of them is my guest."

She got so happy and said, "Thank you Camille!" I said, "You're welcome." Soon after we went to sleep. The next day came so fast! Before we knew it, it was time to go to the amusement place. Me and my cousins were so excited to finally get out the house. Not only were we going to play with other kids, but we were going to play with our friends!

When we got there, our friends were all on time. They greeted us and we started to play right away. Shaun was the only one I didn't see. My cousins said, "Camille, where is your friend?" I said, "I don't know, let's play." While we were playing, someone came up behind me and said, "Boo!" I turned around just to see Shaun smiling. I laughed. He ran away and I ran after him so fast.

We ran past my cousins. They looked like what the heck is going on?? So they ran after us. Once we got in this tunnel, Shaun was cornered. My cousins finally caught up. When they saw him facing me breathing fast, they said, "Camille who's this?" I smiled and said, "It's okay, he's my friend." Alisha asked, "From where?" I looked at her and said, "School, I didn't know he was here."

They all said, "Oh okay." I looked at him and said, "These are my cousins." He said, "Hi, I'm Jeremy." They all said, "Hi." Then they told him their names. Afterwards, I said, "Okay, now that we all know each other let's play." They agreed. I said, "Okay, well he's it." We all took off running fast and he was right behind us.

We all had so much fun! We introduced him to my cousins other friends too once we got back around them. We played for a couple of hours before our nannies came over to get us. When they got to us, they said, "Okay ladies, it's time to go." We were all kind of sad. One of them was on the phone, she said, "Hang on guys." Then we heard her say, "Okay…Okay…yes ma'am."

She then looked at us confused and said, "All of them??...okay yes ma'am not a problem." After she got off the phone she took a breath of relief, smiled with her mouth closed, and said, "Okay! Looks like the party is just getting started. Everyone who was invited here by the girls, pack up and let's go. This has turned into a sleepover." Everyone except me jumped up and down yelling, "Yaye!!

I looked over at Shaun with my eyes opened wide. I was so nervous. Our parents thought it was just girls, I'm sure. I whispered to Shaun, "Shaun!

You can't sleep over." He looked at me, smiled, and said, "I was invited. She said whoever was invited. I'm going to the sleepover." I took a breath as I held my hand over my eyes.

That's the reason the lady said all of them?? Because she saw Shaun standing there with us. Cashae came to me and whispered, "Camille, tell yo friend we gotta go." I was looking so crazy. She said, "What's wrong?" I said, "That's my friend…my friend that I invited." Cashae covered her mouth so fast. Apparently, the nannies were supposed to speak with the parents of our friends for permission.

They did and they all got permission. When they saw Shaun following us, one nannie asked, "Oh honey are you lost?" Shaun answered, "No,

I'm Camille's guest." Her mouth dropped. She asked me to be sure. After I confirmed he was, she told Shaun, "Okay…well I'll have to speak with your mom." He handed her his phone so fast so she could speak to his mama.

He was all smiles. My cousins was laughing so hard at him. The nannie took the phone slowly. Then she said, "What's your name?" He said, "Jeremy." She got on the phone because he had his mama's number on the screen ready to dial. Once his mom answered, the nannie introduced herself and ask for permission to have him over. The way she paused mid-sentence had us concerned.

But then she said "Okay, thank you. We'll have him home Sunday afternoon…okay thank you." When she handed him back the phone, she was still looking confused as she said, "She said it was fine with her." He smiled as he put his phone away and said, "I knew she would." I was still looking at him in shock. Then he said, "Well, what are we waiting for? Isn't it time to go?"

The nannies said, "Yes, it is. Come on everyone." We all followed them out. When we got outside, Shaun didn't see the car he always saw when we got picked up from school. Instead he saw an even more lavish limo SUV. He paused and his mouth dropped. His eyes were wide open. He said, "This is the car we gettin in?!" I smiled with my mouth closed and grabbed his arm as I lowly said, "Yes, come on."

He got in that car and like all of our other friends, he was going crazy. They were all excited and really enjoyed the car. Shaun said, "Wow! How much this set ya'll back?" We were confused. I said, "Huh?" He said, "Ya'll must've spent all ya'll money on this." We laughed and said, "No, our parents must've got it for us."

He couldn't believe it. Once we pulled up to my house, Shaun said, "Is this a pit stop?? Who castle this is?" We all laughed again. He appeared so hilarious to us. Alisha said, "Shaun, I like you, you so funny." He looked confused and said, "What? I'm serious. Where we at??" As we started to get out the car, Carmen said, "This is Camille's house." He looked at me with his mouth to the floor. Then he said "Camille?!" I looked at him quick.

Then he said, “I knew you was rich! I knew it!” I said, “Shaun stop it, come on.” We walked past security and went in the house. When we got in the house, all of our friends jaws dropped to the floor. While looking up and around, Shaun said, “There is no way this is not a castle.” He looked at me and said, “Camille, what do you do?”

I laughed a little and said, “I’m a kid.” He said, “Who are your parents?” I said, “That’s not important, come on.” We showed them around the house and then we started to do some activities around the house. We were all having so much fun. We had food catered to us, we had pillow fights and yes Shaun was in it too. He played with us as if he wasn’t the only boy there.

He didn't care, he just wanted to have fun and that he did. Since our parents were not going to be there, we were able to enjoy his company comfortably. We got in the pool, we watched movies in the movie room, we played games, our parents scheduled nail techs to come give us pedi's and mani's. They asked Shaun if he wanted his done.

As he stretched out both of his hands and looked at his nails, he smiled and said, "Of course. I like clean nails." He made us all laugh. I have to say by the end of the night, everyone liked Shaun. He was like the life of the party. Soon everyone laid down to go to sleep, that's when the nannies got confused. They knew that boys and girls should not have sleepovers together. But they were lost because it seemed as though my mom was okay with it.

The nannies didn't want to bother my mom, so they went along with it. Everything was set up for girls, but Shaun didn't care. I'm not sure what he was going through at home, but he seemed to be happy just to be away from it. When we all saw the sleeping arrangements we were in awe. My mom had everything decorated so nicely. It was every little girls dream to have a sleepover so extravagant.

We all slowly looked at Shaun. The nannies apologized to him and said they thought it would only be girls attending. Shaun smiled and said, "It's okay. As long as I have a comfortable place to sleep, I can get past all the pretty decorations." We all chuckled. The nannies smiled as they took a breath of relief. We all played some more and then it was time for bed.

Shaun was so happy to spend so much time with me outside of school. This moment made us bond even more. I never said a word to anyone about what me and Shaun had going on. Not even my cousins knew at this point, they still thought his first name was Jeremy. My grandma was right, I knew how to keep a secret. Which in some cases was not a good thing.

We slept the night away. The next morning, we all woke up and immediately laughed as we all stared at each other. I'm not sure why, it was just funny. We brushed our teeth, washed our faces, got dressed for the day, and headed downstairs. We had a full breakfast catered to us. Everyone enjoyed it.

After breakfast, we all started to play with each other again. The afternoon was creeping up and everyone was going to be taken home soon.

I kept watching Shaun that morning as we all interacted. I had to talk to him, but I didn't want to in front of everybody. So I pulled him to the side. Once we were alone, I said, "Shaun when we get back to school, please don't mention any of this to anyone at school." Shaun smiled and said, "Your secret's safe with me."

I took a breath of relief and said, "Thank you. The people at school, kids, and teachers, have been trying to find out more about me since kindergarten. I don't want them to know anything about me." Shaun said, "Those people so nosey. I would never tell them anything. All they ever want to do is get you in trouble." I said, "Exactly." We were whispering the whole time.

Just as I said exactly, a nannie and the security guard who picks me up from school walked in the hallway. They stopped in their tracks and stared at us. Me and Shaun stopped talking immediately and looked at them silently. Our mouths were wide open, and our eyes were stretched wide. After about 10 seconds, I lightly pushed Shaun back in the room with one hand and followed behind him.

The security guard was looking confused. The nannie said, "That was odd." My mom called the nannie to let her know she was on her way back to the house. That was the queue to take the kids home. The security guard wasn't paying attention.

Still in his confused state, he pointed as he asked, "What he doin here??" My mama heard him, she asked the nannie, "Who is he talking about?"

The nannie nervously said, "Oh, uh one of the kids." My mama said, "I heard Bernard say him. There should only be girls there." The nannie was really scared now. She said, "Uh yes ma'am. Well see the thing is, I tried to tell you, but I was in front of the kids and didn't want anyone to feel bad. Um, when you said a sleepover and I asked, all of them?? That was because there was a boy invited by one of the girls."

My mama was so confused as she said, "What?!" The nannie said, "Yes, he was invited. He's a friend from school." A lot of thoughts was going through my mama's head at this time. She couldn't imagine any of us inviting a boy to our playdate, more less going through with having them at the sleepover. After thinking for a few seconds, my mama asked, "Whose friend is he?" The nannie answered, "He says he's Camille's guest. She confirmed that she invited him."

My mama was outraged. She shouted, "What?! Camille?!" My mama knew what she had been going through with me lately. It was weird for me to up and invite a boy to a playdate, when normally I would invite a girl. I never did that before. But all of a sudden after meeting a guy, my plus one was a boy. She just knew I wasn't bold enough to invite the boy I had been getting in so much trouble for, and letting him stay the night.

She was on the verge of getting upset. But before she blew her top, she wanted to make sure it wasn't another little boy. She eagerly asked, "Who is this boy?" The nannie explained, "Uh, his name is Jeremy. He's in the same grade as Camille…" As she spoke my mom was relieved. She said, "Oh, okay. I never heard of a Jeremy. I'll have to talk to Camille about…"

As she was speaking, she heard the security guard say, "Jeremy?? That's not his name." The nannie was stuck. My mama said, "What did he say? That's not his name??" The nannie said, "Yes, but that's what I've been told by him and Camille. I even spoke to his mom and referred to him as Jeremy. She didn't correct me." My mama said, "Can I speak with Bernard please?"

The nannie passed Bernard the phone. Once he got on the phone, my mama asked, "If his name not Jeremy, what's his name?" Bernard said, "Shaun." My mama heart dropped. She was so shocked. She asked, "Are you sure? Why would him, Camille, and his mom refer to him as Jeremy if that's Shaun?" The security guard put his hand on his chest as he said, "I don't know Ms. Lockhart. But I assure you, that's Shaun."

He pointed in the direction of Shaun when he said that's Shaun. My mama said, "How are you so sure?" The security said, "I pick Camille up every day. I watched that same boy in the room walk Camille out the school every day. Sometimes they hug, sometimes they play, one time he kissed her goodbye." My mama said, "What?!" Bernard said, "On the cheek." The nannie gasped while covering her mouth every time he said how we said goodbye to each other.

Bernard said, "The reason why I'm saying something is because as a dad, that pissed me off. I asked Camille who her friend was, and she said Jeremy." My mama said, "So she been telling you Jeremy too." Bernard said, "From the gate. But a couple days ago, I was waiting out front for Camille. As I sat there, I saw the young man in front. He was playing with his friends, and they kept saying, Shaun, Shaun, Shaun. I was confused, I didn't know who they were talking to."

My mom listened as he continued, "I'm like yeah that's Jeremy. Then Camille and Crystal come out the school. Camille looking around frantically like she tryna find somebody. She didn't see me yet.

She looked over to where Jeremy and his friends were playing and then she yells out, Shaun! I looked at where she was lookin, because I kept hearing that name. Not one time did I hear Jeremy. When I looked up, the boy she told me name was Jeremy looked at her quick! They both waved at each other and then Camille came to the car."

My mama was so confused. Bernard said, "When she got in the car, I asked her again what's your friend's name? She said Jeremy and she knew who I was talking about." My mama said, "Are ya'll sure? Why would she be saying Jeremy if his name Shaun. Even his mom didn't correct the nannie when she referred to him as Jeremy. You sure it wasn't another boy in that group she was calling?"

Bernard said, “Ms. Lockhart, in no way shape or form am I calling Camille a liar. But Camille told me that her friend’s name is Jeremy, when she’s not around us she calls him Shaun and he answers to it. The way they both just jumped when we saw them talking in the hallway, I think Camille might be hiding something.” For him to say that and not know what has been going on with me getting in trouble for this boy, my mama knew it wasn’t far from the truth.

She immediately said, “I need proof.” Bernard said, “Okay. I’m gone put the earpiece in my ear and have you on video call so you can see him.” My mama said, “What’s that gonna prove?” Bernard said, “I’ma call him by his real name and watch he answer. I’m tellin you Ms. Lockhart, that’s Shaun.” She said, “Okay.” He got her on video call and put the earpiece in his ear so nobody could hear her response.

After he had that set up, he said, "I have the camera facing me, so they won't see you or know you on the phone." My mama said, "Okay." Bernard had the camera on us before he walked in the door frame. He did this in order for my mama to get a good look at how Shaun looked. He whispered, "You see him?" My mama said, "Yeah." We were all into what we were playing, we didn't notice the camera. We were playing with toys. Shaun was sitting closer to me than anybody.

Right before Bernard came in, Cashae said, "See Jeremy?! This is how you supposed to do it." Shaun said, "Oh." Then he reached for something I had. I said, "Jeremy stop!" We all laughed. He was clowning and we all were playing. Alisha said, "Jeremy you so funny, we like you. We gotta keep you around." My cousins agreed and said, "Yeah." Bernard said, "Okay see, they call him Jeremy." My mama said, "Hmm mm."

Bernard said, "Watch this…" As he walked in the doorway, he had the phone pointed at us. We didn't look because we used to people watching us. Then Bernard said, "Aye yo Shaun!" In that moment, Shaun looked up quick and replied, "Yo, what's up??" Without looking I dropped my toys, my mouth dropped as I let out a silent breath and covered my eyes. The nannie was shocked.

Shaun didn't catch on until a few seconds after he saw me cover my eyes. He only looked at me with his eyes. My cousins and their friends looked confused and said, “Shaun?? Who’s Shaun?!” They kept playing though. My mama was able to see him answer and she also saw my response to it. From that she knew I was hiding something. She was beyond pissed.

In a calm voice she asked, “Bernard, can you please take everyone home?” He didn’t want anyone to know she was on the phone, so he said, “Alright ya’ll ready to pack up? We’re taking everybody home.” My mom said, “Please have Jamal take my nieces home too. I’ll be home in about 10 minutes.” He said, “All of Camille’s cousins, Jamal is taking ya’ll home.”

My cousins instantly looked at me confused. They would normally stay until their moms come get them. From that they knew I was in trouble. I still had my hand over my eyes. As they all got up to leave, I put both my hands on my eyes. Shaun didn't know what was going on with me. He tried to say bye. He had his hand on my shoulder and he leaned down over me. He whispered, "I feel like something's wrong. Camille I'm sorry for whatever I did."

Bernard said, "Come on Shaun." Shaun looked up at him and took a deep breath. Shaun quickly looked at me and said, "I'll see you later, okay?" I lowly said, "Bye Shaun." I only said it for him to hear. He looked at me shocked, he knew I knew not to say bye to him. He whispered, "Camille, it's never bye…it's see you later." I was shaking my head in a no motion as I repeated, "Bye Shaun."

He was left looking and feeling hurt. He couldn't understand why I was saying bye instead of see you later. But I did. I knew the security didn't do that for no reason. As they walked out of the room, the nannies handed out gift bags. The gift bags had a lot of good stuff in them. Our friends were shocked because the things in those bags were expensive. None of them knew why we had so much, they just knew we did.

After they left, I sat in my room and cried my eyes out. I knew what was coming. As they all pulled out the driveway, my mom pulled in. Bernard left as my mom pulled in, but Jamal was still sitting at the other end of the driveway. My cousins saw my mom when she got out the car. Carmen said, "Aw man, auntie look pissed." Alisha said, "I knew it. Camille in trouble." Cashae said,

"But what did she do?" Alicia said, "I have a feeling it has something to do with Jeremy."

Carmen had her hand under her chin as she calmly said, "You mean Shaun?" All my cousins eyes got big as they let out a deep breath. After my mom walked in the house, Jamal pulled off to take my cousins home. They drove separately from their friends, because my mama didn't want them to know where my cousins lived. I mean yeah, we lived next to each other, but they didn't need to know that.

Once my mom came in the house, she dismissed everyone (her staff) as she normally would when she's home. After they left, she threw her purse on the couch and looked up at my room with fire in her eyes. She charged up the stairs quietly. I didn't hear her. Then she opened my room door and scared the crap out of me! I jumped up facing her. I started to back up slowly while still looking at her. She did look pissed.

The scariest thing is when she appears calm about it. That's when I know she's pissed. She looked at me and said, "What the h*ll goin on with you??" I was terrified. She said, "You really had that boy in the house and sleeping over after I told you to break things off with him??" I lowly said, "You said we can invite a friend." She said, "So ya'll friends now, did you tell him what I said?"

I answered, "Yes." She said, "So are you still considered his girlfriend?" I paused for a second. Although I wanted to, I could not lie to her face. I said, "Yes." She yelled, "Why?!" I said, "I felt bad for him." My mama continued to yell, "I told you, you can't have a boyfriend! Yet you still date him behind my back?! Not only are you still dating him, you invite him over! You sneak him in the house and under a different name at that, he sleeps over and you lyin for him!! Why aren't you listening to me?!"

At that moment, in her mind she went back to when her mom was telling her these things. She saw me as herself and saw herself as her mom. In that moment, she finally understood how her mom felt and why her mom was telling her those things. She also knew why I wasn't listening and felt I thought like she did when she was a teen, "It wasn't that serious." She paused and was just sitting there thinking.

She scared me when she did that. I thought something was wrong with her. She was frustrated, she felt that I didn't understand the severity in it. As she came up out of her deep thinking, she took a deep breath as she looked around with her eyes. She put her finger up and said, "I know what I gotta do." She then walked out the room quick. I let out a breath of relief. I thought she was gonna beat my behind, but she didn't.

Not too long after, a nannie walked in my room. I was shocked because everybody was gone. The nannie said, "Your mom stepped out. She'll be back later tonight." My mama went to Cashae's house. She met up with my other aunties to tell them what had happened. They all were very testy around this time. They tried not to be around us much, because they would snap on us sometimes out the blue and they didn't like that.

We didn't understand why. We just thought they worked too much and needed a break. Once my mama told them what I did, they was mad for her. Latonya said, "Girl! I don't know, I probably would've beat Carmen a**." My mama said, "I wanted to tear Camille a** up! But I knew I would hurt her, so I had to leave. I don't understand why she actin out all of a sudden, or is it just me?"

Trinity said, "No, it's Camille. But it's not just her, I think Alisha got a lil so-called boyfriend too. Alicia not innocent either, she just quiet about hers." My mom was surprised to hear that. Latonya said, "Carmen got a lil friend too that's been getting her in trouble just like Camille." Beonca said, "Yep,

Cashae almost got suspended this week over some lil boy. It's like they goin boy crazy at the same time."

My mama shook her head in a no motion. She said, "I'm tired of it. I'm losing control of Camille at the age of 10, and I refuse to let it go any further." Trinity said, "What you gone do?" My mama said, "We been considerate of them, and did things according to how they feel and what they think would work best. Now it's to the point where, they got too comfortable. We made them feel like they have 100% say so over everything they do. That wasn't our intentions, they were our first born. We were kids still learning while we took care of them, but now they feel grown. They feel like they can do what they want despite what their parents tell them, and that ain't gone fly."

My aunties agreed. My mama continued, "They've been sweethearts all this time and now they showing us they're changing. We been through everything with them, we had them young. We felt bad for what they experienced growing up and we spoiled them. I think it's time we stop being the friend and start being the parent 100%. What we say goes, no matter what they think, say, or do. I'm about to get Camille a** back in line. I refuse to have a pregnant teen under my belt. This sh*t stops here!"

My aunties clapped in agreement. Although they were all pregnant teens, they did not want the same for their kids. Latonya said, "So what you have in mind?" My mom sternly looked at them and said, "I think it's time to make them a singing group." My aunties gasped as they looked at each other smiling. Beonca said, “Ooh, they gone be mad.”

My mama said, “I don’t care, because clearly they don’t care about what we say.” Trinity said, “I’m on board, what’s the plan?” My mama said, “We leave Chicago for good, we go back to Miami. They can start where we started, only they have all the resources to get where they need to be faster. We still won’t tell anybody they’re our kids, just to see how well they do on their own.” Beonca shook her head in a yes motion and said, “I like it.”

My mama said, “They’ll blow up so fast, they won’t have time to be running after these lil boys. They’ll be forced to be up under us, and we’ll be in control of their every move. We’ll manage them.” Latonya said, “D*mn! That’s a harsh a** punishment! But I'm there with you though. If we was already to this point in our career back then, I'm sure we wouldn't have come close to teen pregnancy."

My mama said, "Exactly! …and I'm willing to go that extra mile to protect Camille and my nieces from making the same dumb decisions we made. I gave Camille a choice and she chose to disobey me. So from this point on it's what I say, and she will fall in line. She have no other options." Beonca said, "I think it's a good idea and what better time than now? I mean we have to go back home anyway." They agreed.

Trinity said, "When you wana leave?" My mama said, "Let's put it this way…Camille's not steppin foot back in that school." My aunties were shocked but intrigued. At home I had been waiting for my mom to get back. I was really watching my back. I thought she would come back and then I would get a beatin. I know I didn't get beat a lot, but I just felt I would this time.

Before she got back, my nannie came in my room and told me it was time to get ready for bed. I took a shower and got ready for bed. I did everything I would have normally done the night before school. During this time, I thought about how I would have to face Shaun and explain to him why I responded to him the way I did. I had no idea how I would explain that to him. Although I told him how I would get in trouble for things that happened in school, I didn't tell him the severity in me getting in trouble because of him.

I guess it was because I knew he would want what's best for me. If he knew he was getting me in trouble, he probably would have backed off and I would have lost him. Although I was only 10 years old, I knew I didn't want to lose him. I still didn't quite understand what these feelings were I had for him, but I didn't want him to leave out of my life. At this point, I didn't even have to be his girlfriend. As long as he was my friend forever, I knew I would be okay.

After I took a shower, me and Crystal's dinner was ready. Once we were in the dining room, the nannie looked concerned or kind of sad as she put my water down next to my plate. I looked up at her and asked, "Where is my mom?" The nannie looked at me and answered, "She's running a little later than expected. She'll be here soon." The nannie walked away as me and Crystal finished our food.

After dinner, I was tired. I barely made it to my bed. I got to my bed just in time. As soon as I got to my bed, I fell on it. I was out like a light, I was in a deep sleep. I guess the playdate and the other activities that weekend had me worn out…or did they?

Chapter 4

Regulation

The next morning I woke up confused. As I opened my eyes, I immediately realized I wasn't in my room anymore. I thought I was dreaming! I stood up and started to hyperventilate as I started to freak out. This room looked a lot like my room at my grandma's house in Miami. But how did I get here?? I started to scream as I held both sides of my head.

Once I screamed, my room door flew open and in ran my grandma. She said, "Camille baby calm down!" But that freaked me out more. I jumped on the bed and screamed trying to run from her. I had my pillow shielding me. I yelled, “What is this?! How did I get here?! Am I dreaming?!” She calmly said, “No, it’s really Ma Ma Camille. Now come down from there.” Luckily my uncle was there. He ran in the room and said, “Cee Cee come down from there na.”

When I saw him, I slowly stepped down and put the pillow down. I was still breathing hard. By this time I was crying lightly and shaking a bit. I was scared and confused. I looked at both my grandma and my uncle back and forth. Then in a shaky voice, I said, “Are ya’ll real? Am I really here??” My grandma said, “Yes baby, we’re real. This is real life. You’re really here.”

I was still breathing kind of hard. I said, “Then where’s Mommie?” My grandma said,

"She'll be here soon." I looked around with my eyes in panic as I said, "That's what she said before I fell asleep." My grandma said, "Who?" I said, "The nannie!" At that point I started to scream again. I grabbed the pillow again, started to slap myself and started to yell, "Wake me up! Wake me up! I'm still sleeping!" In the mist of it I saw my grandma approaching me.

I was scared, I really thought I was dreaming. I yelled, "No don't touched me!" By that time she grabbed my arms to restrain me as she yelled, "Camille!" I stopped instantly and looked at her. Then I said, "You're real." She said, "Of course I am! What is wrong with you??" I covered my face taking a breath of relief. After they saw that I calmed down, they backed off a bit and stared at me.

I looked at Grandma Tam and said, “I’m sorry Ma Ma. I really don’t understand what’s happening.” My grandma said, “It’s okay baby. What’s the last thing you remember?” I said, “I was really tired. I just made it to my bed, and I fell on it. My other bed, everything went black…then I woke up here.” My grandma and my uncle looked confused. My grandma said, “That’s all?” I said, “Yes.”

Then she said, “But Camille, you were in a car, you got on a plane, you were in another car, and when you got here you were sleeping. Uncle Gary carried you upstairs and put you in this bed. You woke up hours later…you mean to tell me you went to sleep last night and didn’t wake up at all until a few minutes ago?” I was shocked as I said,

"Exactly! I didn't know that happened!" They both looked at me crazy.

Grandma Tam said, "That doesn't sound right. Why were you sleep so long? Who was the last person you saw?" I said, "The nannie." Grandma Tam said, "Did you notice anything out of the ordinary before you went to sleep?" I said, "Yes, at dinner. She put my water on the table, but she looked like she wanted to cry. It was almost like she didn't want to let the glass go."

Grandma Tam said, "How long after dinner did you feel tired?" I said, "I started to feel tired during dinner. But I barely finished my food before I ran upstairs to my bed." Grandma Tam said, "Why did you run?" I said, "Because something was wrong, I felt like I was gonna pass out. I guess I did.

I fell on my bed and then saw black. Now I'm here." My grandma and uncle looked at each other, they knew something happened.

Grandma Tam said, "Where was your mother?" I said, "I don't know. Before I drank the water, I asked the nannie where she was, and she said she would be there soon. I thought maybe it was the food because something tasted weird. But it didn't taste weird until after I drank the water." My grandma sternly said, "I need to speak with your mother." My grandma immediately called my mom.

When she asked her about it, I heard my grandma say, "What?? Toya but why?? …" Then she said, "Okay, I'll see you soon." When she got off the phone, she looked at me and said, "They gave you sleeping medicine." I was so confused and said, “Huh, why??” My grandma shook her head in a no motion and said, “Your mom asked the nannie to put the sleeping powder in your water. She wanted you to be sleep while she brought you here.”

I said, “But I would’ve came here with no problem.” My uncle said, “Not if you knew that we knew you was in trouble.” My mouth dropped a little. I gasped silently. He said, “Un huh…we heard you been givin yo mama a hard time lately.” I rested my chin on my fists as I looked sad. He continued, “You supposed to have a boyfriend she told you to break up with??” I covered my eyes with my right hand.

He said, “Don’t cover yo eyes now. Why you ain’t listenin to yo mama?” I looked up at him, my face was full of tears as I said, “I did. But…” He said, “If you listened there shouldn’t be no but’s! Now why you ain’t tell that boy you not his girlfriend no more??” I said, “I felt bad for him.” My uncle got mad, he said, “You felt bad for some boy and decided to listen to him over yo mama?! You know how much a boy can make you do just because you feel bad for him?!”

I was still looking sad. Uncle Gary continued, “Do you know that’s why you here?? Because you wouldn’t listen and leave that boy alone? Since you can’t listen yo mama sent you here, now you gone be with me!” I started to cry harder. I believed it, because my mama dropped me off to my grandma before and left me for months. My Uncle had his own house, but he just happened to be at my grandma’s house that day.

Then he looked at me and said, "Did you really invite that boy to yo house and had him spend the night?" I covered my face again. He said, "Naw don't get embarrassed now. Did you do that and tell everybody his name was something other than his real name?" My grandma looked at me shocked and said, "Camille!" She didn't hear that part of the story. I guess my mama didn't want her to know the severity in what happened.

My uncle said, "Camille, answer me. Is that true?" Through the tears I answered, "Yes." My grandma gasped so loud as she stared at me. My uncle said, "What?! You bold! When you started acting like this??" Then he reached his hand out and said, "Give me that phone." I looked at him and said, "He don't have my number." He said, "That don't matter. You don't wana listen to yo mama, you don't need the pleasure of havin this phone either."

I gave him my phone. I was so mad. My grandma said, "Camille hunney, you have to listen. You get just about everything you want, all you have to do is listen in order to keep it. You're getting older now, and your mom doesn't want you to make the same mistakes she made. She wants better for you." At that moment my mama walked in the room. She looked at everybody and then at me.

Then she asked, "Why she cryin?" They told her. My uncle gave my mom my phone. Then he said, "I told her she staying with me now." My mama smirked and said, "Really Gary?? No wonder she crying." They laughed a little bit. My mama took off her coat and said, “Camille, I need to talk to you.” She sat down. I looked at her. She tossed my phone to me. It landed in front of me.

Uncle Gary said, “No, don’t give it back to her until she listen!” My mama shook her head in a no motion and rolled her eyes jokingly. Come to find out Uncle Gary was playing this whole time. He took my phone to allow me to feel strict authority. It worked for the moment. As soon as he took my phone, I instantly started to think about ways I could listen in order to get it back.

After my mom tossed it to me, I didn’t touch it. I felt awkward because I knew my uncle took it. I didn’t know what to do. My mom looked at me and said, “I’m sure you’re wondering why you’re here. Since nothing else was working and you still did what you wanted to do, I decided it was best for us to move back home." I said, "Huh?!" She said, "I refuse for you to step foot back into that school, especially after doing what you did."

I looked off to the side for a second. She then said, "We're not going back to Chicago, we live here now." My mouth dropped. She said, "Yep. I know this takes you by surprise, but it took me by surprise when you decided not to tell that boy you're not his girlfriend." I was so mad, I couldn't even say anything. I just sat there looking upset. All I could think about was how Shaun must feel not seeing me.

I also thought of how he would think once he didn't see me again. Then my mom said, "Moving here is not the only thing." I looked up at her. She said, “You startin to show signs of defiance and I’m not gone deal with it. You will listen to me and do what I tell you to do. You and your cousins have been very bold lately…because of that, your aunties and I have decided that ya’ll will sing professionally.” I got so mad.

I folded my arms, took a deep breath, started crying and said, “But Mommie we don’t wana sing professionally!” She said, “And we didn’t want ya’ll to be hardheaded and defiant! But you were and now ya’ll gone sing professionally. We already have things set up in place for ya’ll. You have a week to get over it, because ya’ll start training next week.” I just sat there crying.

Then she said, “You may not understand now why we’re doing this, but one day you will.” I was so angry. I didn't know what took over me. But in that moment, I looked at her still crying and said, "If you do this, it's not gonna go away. It'll be a lifelong punishment. Please don't do this, I'll listen." She looked at me, shook her head in a no motion and said, "You had a few chances. You blew'em all. Now it's my turn to make sure you stay in line."

I didn't think it was possible, but I got even madder than I was. Before I knew it, I blurted out, "Why am I being punished for your mistakes?! Just because you had a baby at 15 doesn't mean I will!" Why did I do that? They all looked at me so shocked. My mama was really stunned. Although she knew I knew she had me at 15, I never mentioned it or brought attention to it. But because I knew this was why she was trying to stop me from dating and pulling me away from Shaun, and now forcing me to sing professionally, I shed light on it.

They were right I was beyond my years. They didn't have to tell me why all of this was happening, I could put two and two together. I was still working on my slick mouth. They all got mad at me. My uncle immediately yelled, "Who you talkin to like that?!" My grandma said, "Oh h*ll no!" My mama looked at her mom for a second and said, "See what I mean?"

My uncle said, "Camille you better calm all that down before you get yo behind beat!" My mama looked at him and said, "That's alright." She looked at me and said, "All of this is the reason why yo behind gone be there bright and early next week. I'ma make sure of that…and I want you to try me."

I squinted at her briefly. She then turned to my grandma who was sitting beside her, and said, “Ma, I’ma go before I get completely triggered.”

My grandma said, “Okay baby.” I had no idea where she was going. She started to grab her stuff. As she got up, she started to fan herself with her hand as she said, “Yeah I gotta get outta here…” She pointed at me and said, “Because I would hurt this lil girl.” She chuckled a little as she shook her head in a no motion and said, “Camille, you just don’t know.”

My grandma said, “I know, I know. Toya take it easy.” I was just sitting there still looking mad, but now I was kind of scared after she said that. As my mom got the rest of her stuff, she mumbled, “This girl really tried it. I don’t know who she think she talkin to…" My grandma said, "Toya don't talk yourself up now. Go ahead and cool off." My mom grabbed her keys and said, "I'm going."

Then she turned to me and with the same hand she was holding the keys with, she pointed to me and sternly said, "I'll deal with you later." I almost cried again. I was scared. Once she left, my grandma said, "Camille, why did you say that to your mom? I know you're upset but that's no reason to be disrespectful." She talked to me for a long time.

Eventually I felt bad about how I spoke to my mom and what I said to her. I cried because of how bad I felt. I wanted to apologize to her, but I didn't know how. I felt like I went too far this time.

After my grandma spoke to me, my uncle snatched my phone off my bed. He shook it back and forth as he stared at me. Before he walked out, he said, "When you act accordingly, you get this back." He was for real this time. I took a deep breath as they both walked out my room.

I had no phone, no company, and I was back in Miami for good. I had no idea what to do. I laid back and folded the pillow around both sides of my face. All I had was time to think. All of this happened so fast. How could my life change this fast over night?? I never knew a boy can cause this much trouble, it just wasn't making sense. The only person that seemed to know how I felt and could relate with daddy issues, was ripped away from me.

I started to feel myself close back up again. I didn't want to speak to anyone outside my family. I felt myself wanting to keep everything inside again and not tell anyone what I was feeling. I used to talk to my mom about everything, but this boy seemed to have drawn a wedge between us. So now I didn't have her to run to and talk to freely like I used to.

My world changed and I didn't know how to handle it. One thing I did want to do was fix it, but I didn't know how. I was left to just wait for my mom to get back and I didn't know when that was gonna be. My mama was gone all week! I didn't know where she went. I was left to deal with the discipline from my uncle and my grandma for what I did in Chicago, and for what I said to my mama.

Before this I had never been on punishment before. I still didn't realize I was on some type of punishment. I just knew my uncle took my phone and I couldn't use it. I didn't ask to go anywhere because I was still in my feelings about everything. So if I couldn't go anywhere, I wouldn't have known. The weekend crept up. By this time I was quiet. I knew the time was coming near for me to start this whole singing thing.

I didn't know what to expect and I wasn't ready. Once Monday came around, my mama called to make sure I was taken to where I was supposed to be. Me and my cousins was still not supposed to be seen with our parents. We all ended up at this building. We had our parents assistants with us. They helped with the business part of things. They also kept us safe and protected.

The people tried to carry on conversation with us, but we pretty much kept quiet. The people thought we were shy. The truth is none of us wanted to be there. We still spoke a little because we knew not to ruin our opportunity. Even though we didn't want it. We knew we would be in trouble when we got back home if we didn't get through it.

At the end, the guy in charge smiled and said, "One more thing…" We looked at him, then he said, "I want to hear them sing." We looked at each other as our mouths dropped a little. We didn't want to, but we knew we had to. About 5 seconds later, I looked at my cousins and lowly said, "Our song, ya'll ready?" I snapped my fingers as I counted, "One, two, three…" We all started to harmonize and sing the song we wrote.

The look on the people's faces was pure bliss. They sat there staring at us and enjoying our singing. This song was perfect because we all had a solo. They were able to hear us sing together and they were also able to hear us sing individually. As soon as we were done, we stopped singing and stared at the guy in charge. They all were smiling and looking like they were waiting for more.

After a few seconds, they gave us a standing ovation. It took us by surprise. That was the only time me and my cousins smiled while we were there. It was nice to see that other people enjoyed our singing. The guy in charged continued to clap as he shouted, "Bravo! That was terrific! They're ready!" Soon after, we left and went back home.

None of them knew we were the kids of our parents, they just knew they wanted us and NOW! They contacted our parents assistants who then contacted our parents. Before the end of the night our parents knew how well we did. My mom called my grandma that night. After they got off the phone with each other, my grandma said, "Camille?" I said, "Yes?" She said, "You girls did it, you pulled it off."

I said, "Huh?" I was confused. Then she said, "The executives loved you all. You and your cousins are going on tour." I can tell my grandma was excited, but she kept calm because she knew I didn't want to do any of this originally. I quickly said, "Tour?! But Ma Ma we just went to the place! I don't even know what happened!" Grandma Tam said, "I know baby, but don't worry. You girls are going to be on Alexi's tour."

My mouth dropped. I was so shocked. My grandma smiled as she shook her head in a yes motion. I finally said, "She have a tour?" Grandma Tam said, "Of course she does! Where do you think she's been all this time?" I said, "I knew she was performing, but I didn't know the tour was her tour. Does she know we're gonna be on her tour?" Grandma Tam said, "She will tonight. Ooh I just know she'll be so happy! My babies all performing together."

I didn't know how to feel. As I looked down with my eyes stretched wide, all I said was, "Whoa." Everything was happening so fast. I still didn't speak to my mama yet. Every day that passed by, I wanted to apologize to my mama even more. But she disappeared physically. She would only call. I didn't see Auntie Trice but one time and that's when I first came. Even then she stood right outside of the room door.

She had on a robe, her arms were crossed, she was squinting like she was tired, and she listened in when my grandma was talking to me about what I said to my mama. She even had input on it. She said, "Camille, I know you know better than that. You better mind yo manners." But after that she slowly walked to her room, and I haven't seen her since.

She left the house I think the next day and didn't come back yet. It was all just weird to me. When my mama told Alexi we were going to be on her tour, Alexi was so happy, she screamed! She couldn't wait to call me to congratulate me and talk about it. She ended up calling me later that night. After not being able to get through to me on my phone, she called my grandma phone.

When I got on the phone and said, "Hello?" Alexi screamed in excitement, and then she said, "Congratulations baby!! I heard you joining the tour!" I laughed a little bit and said, "Yes, thank you." She said, "You don't sound excited Cee Cee." I said, "I know I'm sorry. It's just something I didn't want to do. Not the tour, I'm happy it's your tour we're on. It's the singing all together, my mom is making me do this to punish me."

Alexi said, "Well see I wasn't gonna bring that up being that this is a happy moment. But since you brought it up…" She gave me a stern but fair talking to. She knew about everything that happened. I would not have guessed by the way she reacted towards the tour news. She talked to me for an hour. I cried at one point on the call. But by the time she was finished, I felt a little better.

I didn't feel completely better because I still hadn't apologized to my mama yet. I wanted to apologize to her face to face. We were supposed to start practice soon so that we can join the tour. Yes, we had the voices and the presence, but we never performed on stage and that big of a stage at that. We were about to take a huge step into something new and our very first audience was going to be thousands of people!

We were 10 years old, Carmen and Cashae were 9. I kept requesting to see my mom, but nothing was done. The week of practice came, and I still hadn't seen my mom. I didn't even speak to her over the phone. I figured she was that upset about what I said and how I said it. Or maybe it was me being distant and not realizing it. I think it was a bit of both. Another week had passed, and it was the day before the tour.

There was a lot going on as far as preparation. Quite a few people were at the house that day. I happen to look out the window, and saw my mama in the backseat of one of the SUV's we use when we're being discreet out in public. I gasped so quick and loud. My eyes were wide open. She had the window down and she was talking and laughing with Uncle Gary.

I immediately ran downstairs to go out there. No one told me she was there, and it looked like she was about to leave. Once the front door flew open, she looked at me with her eyes only. My uncle turned all the way around to look at me. I didn't stop, I kept running until I was standing in front of the car door directly in front of my mama. By the time I got to her I was out of breath.

They watched me as I caught my breath. Once I did, I blurted out, "Mommie!" She was still looking at me, then she said, "Why are you running all over the place? What I told you about doing that?" I was still breathing kind of hard as I said, "I'm sorry. I was trying to catch you." She said, "Oh my gosh." As she reached in her purse. She pulled out an inhaler.

She keeps one on her for me. I didn't know she kept it even when I wasn't with her. She gave it to me and said, "Here." I took it and used it. Then I gave it back and she put it back in her purse. After that, she asked Uncle Gary, "Gary, can you get her some water please?" He said, "Yeah." Then he took off running in the house. My mama looked at me and said, "Don't do that again." I responded, "Okay."

Then she said, "What's wrong?" I looked very remorseful. I was looking down playing with my hands. I was nervous. I opened my mouth as I looked up to my mama. Then I said, "I'm sorry." She looked confused and said, "What?" I said, "I'm sorry for what I said to you and for how I was acting." She showed compassion as she leaned her head to the side and softly said, "Oh."

I continued, “I’m sorry for disrespecting you and having a tone with you…and I’m sorry for sneaking Shaun in the house and telling everybody his name was Jeremy.” My mama looked curiously at me and said, “About that, why did you lie about his name?” I said, “His middle name is Jeremy, his first name is Shaun. But I still should’ve been honest and said it was Shaun. I’m sorry. I’m sorry for everything.” I had tears in my eyes. She knew it was a sincere apology. She was relieved that Jeremy was still his name, and I didn’t flat out make up a name for a boy I wanted to sneak into the house. She said, “Is that why you were looking for me?”

I shook my head in a yes motion because at this point, I couldn’t speak anymore. I didn’t even know she knew I was looking for her. No one told me that they told her I was looking for her. The tears started to fall from my eyes. Normally I know my mom would have gotten out of the car to embrace me. But she didn't. I thought maybe she was still upset with me. Then she said, "Aww okay, well I forgive you. I know you're frustrated, and things happen, but I'm happy you came to me to apologize." I cried harder at that point. I was happy she forgave me. When she saw me crying, she said, "Come here." I went closer to the car door.

As I did that, my uncle came back. He saw me walk up to the car. He instantly picked me up so that I was at the level my mom was at. The car was high. When he did that, my mama kissed my cheek. Then she gave me a hug through the window. After that he put me down and gave me my water. As I drank the water, my mama started to talk to me about the tour.

She was happy about it and not because it was punishment. She was happy to see her baby follow in her footsteps singing wise. She smiled and said, “So tomorrow’s the day! You ready?” My uncle thought I was gonna have a negative response. But I just made up with my mama, the last thing I wanted to do was respond negatively. To his surprise, I shook my head yes as I was still drinking my water.

He was shocked. My mama was surprised too, but she was better at not showing it. She wanted her reaction to seem as normal as possible. She smiled and said, “Yeah? How did you feel with practice and everything?” I answered, “It feels normal, like I’ve been doing it forever.” My mama was so proud. She said, “That’s my girl! It comes natural.” We both laughed a bit. She said, “Make sure you get to bed at an appropriate time Camille. I don't want you out there tired."

I said, "Okay." Then she said, "I gotta go. Gary bring her here again please." He picked me up again and brung me closer to her. She gave a me a kiss on the cheek again. I kissed her cheek back. Then she said, "I'll see you soon." I said, "Okay." She said, "Do good tomorrow, I love you." I said, "Okay, I love you too." She said, "Alright." I started to run back towards the house. As she yelled, "Cami…!" I stopped before she could get my full name out. I turned to her smiling.

Then I said, "Oh, I'm sorry." It was because I was running again. She had that problem out of me since I was little. I started to walk backwards towards the house as I waved at her saying, "See you later Mommie!" She waved back and said, "See you later!" Good thing I wasn't too close to the house, because people still didn't know she had kids. Like I said, there were a lot of people at the house that day.

They were further back from where we were though. When I got in the house, my mama left. I went back to my room feeling a lot better. That's all I wanted, was to right my wrongs with my mama. My uncle gave me my phone back, since I apologized and seemed to have learned my lesson.

As I calmly stared out the window with a closed mouth smile, for the first time ever I felt content and ready for the tour.

Chapter 5

Showtime

The next morning we woke up and everything was fast paced. This was something me and my cousins were not used to. We had someone moving us this way, while someone else was fixing us up that way. These people were multitasking, and they were fast. My cousins came over to my grandma's house.

Everyone thought it would be easier for us to all be together that day. We got our makeup done, wardrobe, and our hair done. They made sure we ate and was ready. All of this took hours. Once we were done, it was time to head out to the show.

The tour was in town that day, which a good thing. If we did a good job that day, we would be invited to perform more on that tour.

Even though we didn't want to sing professionally in the first place, we still wanted to do a good job. We knew we had thousands of strangers watching us. When we arrived at the show, we were taken to our dressing room. Just before we walked in there, we were immediately greeted by Alexi.

She happen to be headed to her dressing room when she saw us. She sped walked to us with her arms opened wide. She had a huge smile on her face as she yelled, "Heeeeey!!!" We all turned to her and smiled. We rushed her with hugs as we yelled, "Hiiiii!!" The people had no idea of our relation to each other. They just thought she was being welcoming to us because it was her tour, and they thought we were excited, and star struck.

She said, “I’m so happy ya’ll here!” We said, “Thank you!” She pointed to the dressing room and said, “This is ya’ll dressing room?” We said, “Yes.” She said, “Okay.” Then she walked to her dressing room which was right next door to ours. We went inside our dressing room. She didn’t want to say too much in front of the people, because she didn’t want to give our secret away.

Right before she was about to go on stage, there was a knock at our door. We said, “Come in.” She tip toed in smiling. We laughed as she closed the door softly behind her. She said, “Oh my gosh, I can’t believe my babies are on my tour! Ya’ll were just born yesterday!" Everyone laughed again. Alexi took a deep breath and asked, "So how ya'll feeling, ya'll ready?!" We smiled and said, "Yes."

She smiled and said, "Ya'll seem so calm!" We laughed again. I said, "We just still taking it all in." She said, "Okay, I get that. I had to sneak in here to talk to ya'll for real before the show start. I couldn't say much with everybody around me." She gave us a pep talk, a good one too. Right as she finished, there was a knock at the door.

Before we could say anything, the person said, "Alexi, are you in there??" She made a face like, dang I got caught! Then she answered, "Yeah!" The guy said, "It's showtime!" She said, "Okay!" She turned back to us and whispered, "Ya'll gone do great!" She hugged and kissed us all on the cheek. Then she said, “I’ll see ya’ll out there.”

Then she kind of ran out the room. The people called her name a couple more times while she was in there with us before she ran out. After seeing her and talking to her, we were more comfortable. The show started and she opened up the show with a bang! The crowd was excited and warmed up. Someone else performed after her. Then she came back out and performed again.

After that performance, she introduced us. She said, “We have a treat for ya’ll! This next group coming to the stage is gonna blow ya’ll minds! I heard them myself and I’m still shocked! Give it up for Angelic ya’ll!” The crowd started to scream, although they didn’t know us. But Alexi knew how to work a crowd. We didn't come on stage right away. Everything went black and there were a lot of sound effects. This was all planned. Alexi walked off stage and we took our place on stage standing next to each other.

We didn't even see each other, that's how dark the stage was. We figured Alexi went back to her dressing room for her next number. The sound effects stopped. Then there was a few loud song beats. They went something like, "Dunt…dunt…dunt…dunt." Every time the beat did that, random spot lights flashed around the stage. This was anticipation because no one could see anybody on stage.

They made sure the lights did not go on us. Then there was a 3 second pause. After that the song beat went, “Boom!” At that time the big light went on all of us. When the crowd saw us and saw how young we were, they instantly started to scream and go crazy. They thought it was so cute for kids to be on that tour performing. After a couple more seconds, the beat dropped.

We started to sing our song. Our parents loved our song so much, they let us sing that for our debut performance. After harmonizing at first, we started the solo parts of the songs, and also started the choreography we were taught during practice week. Our singing made the crowd hype, but when they saw our choreography with the singing, they were blown away!

They were screaming and everything. We were working that stage. You would think we did that all our lives, but this was our very first time. We ended it with a bang. As we posed, the music literally had a bang! The light flashed again and then went completely dark. The crowd was screaming, clapping, and cheering us on. When the lights came back on, we were off the stage.

As we ran past the workers, we saw our moms and Alexi. They were watching us from backstage the entire performance! We gasped and waved at them as we smiled and shouted, "Hi!!" They were clapping, smiling, and crying. They waved back to us. We couldn't stop because we couldn't let anybody know we knew each other. We ran all the way back to our dressing room.

When we got in there we sat down and stared at each other quietly. We were so shocked.

Our eyes were stretched wide. After about 5 seconds we all smiled and screamed. We couldn't believe that just happened. I said, "Oh my gosh! We did it! We really did it!" Carmen said, "Right?! I wasn't even nervous!" Alisha said, "That's because this is what we're meant to do!"

I said, "I have to admit, I had fun out there!" They all gasped. Then we laughed. Cashae said, "Camille, I'm surprised you did!" I said, "Yeah I didn't want to do this, probably the most out of all of us…but that wasn't so bad." Cashae said, "Yeah, I had fun too." My cousins agreed. Alexi had to go on again. After that performance, she came back to our room, and she was excited.

She said, "Ya'll did so good out there! We so proud of ya'll!" We said, "Thank you!" She was dressed in a different costume. We hugged her. Then I asked, “Mama, you going back out?” She looked down quickly glancing at her outfit and said, “Yeeeah, I’m about to do another number.” I said, “Oh, where’s Mommie? We didn’t know they were here.” Alexi said, “Oh yeah, they came to watch ya’ll perform. But they had to leave.”

My cousins said, “Oh dang.” Alexi said, “I gotta go back out there now.” Carmen said, “Auntie, what we supposed to do now?” Alexi said, “I think ya’ll about to get ready to go.” We said, “Oh.” She said, “They’re gonna let ya’ll know.” Then she hurried back to the stage. Five minutes passed by as we got our stuff together. Soon as we were ready to go, we stopped to the sound of the crowd being so loud. We looked at each other and laughed a little. Then Alicia said, “Dang, Auntie really know how to work a crowd don’t she?”

We all agreed and said, “Yeeeah.” As we approached the door of our dressing room to leave out, one of the executives burst in smiling. It was a lady this time. She scared us. We stopped in our tracks. She saw our faces and said, “I’m so sorry ladies, put your things down and come with me please. Quickly.” We were so confused. But we put our things down and followed after her.

We didn’t know where she was taking us. But once we got to end of the hall, she stopped walking and pointed. She said, “Go that way, just follow the hall.” The hall was dark, but we followed it. When we got to the other end there were some people there to guide us the rest of the way. As we followed them, we could hear the crowd even more. The more we walked the louder the crowd became.

We had no idea what was happening. We finally got to the end of that hallway and the people told us to walk out. As we made our way out of that hallway, I turned to my cousins and asked, "Are they saying, Angelic?" Carmen said, "Oh my gosh, I think they are." Finally there was an opening, and we were able to see some type of light. We walked out and unknowingly walked right back on stage.

We saw Alexi facing the crowd. We were shocked. We didn't know we went down the other entrance to the stage. When the crowd saw us, they started to cheer and scream again. That's when Alexi turned around and saw us. She smiled and said, "Come on ladies." We walked out looking confused, but we were smiling. Alexi hugged each of us as we came to her.

I had my arms out asking her what's going on. Then she moved the microphone from her mouth and said, "They requested for ya'll to perform again. They loved ya'll." Our mouths dropped as we gasped and held our faces. The crowd realized she must've told us and then they started to chant again, "Angelic, Angelic, Angelic!" The producers brought out microphones to us.

The crowd stopped chanting and started to cheer again. Alexi got back on the microphone and asked us, "So Angelic? Can ya'll help me close tonight?" The crowd started to go crazy again. We were honored she asked us. The crowd was excited for us. We answered, "Yes." She said, "Okay." The music started to play. She looked at us and said, "Ya'll know this one?" She had to play it off. She knew we knew all of her songs as well as all of our mamas songs.

We played along too and answered, "Yes." She started to sing. We joined in on the chorus. Then when the verse came, she random called our names. Whoever name she called is the person who sung that verse. The crowd loved it. But because me and Carmen didn't sing a solo in that song, when the song was over, she said, "Hold on, hold on, we gone play another track. Two of them didn't sing." The crowd laughed and so did we.

We thought we was gone be done. Then Alexi said, "Un huh, I noticed. Play the track let's go!" They started another song of hers. When the beat started, she said, “Camille take it away.” I started to sing the song. After my verse she called on Carmen to sing next. She killed that next verse. Alexi closed out the song after that. The crowd couldn’t believe we had voices like that. After finishing the song, we all hugged each other.

The crowd was cheering, we were laughing and smiling. We were so happy. Once the show was over, people wondered who we were. They were talking about it to other people. Of course people who did not attend that concert, didn’t know what people were talking about, but they were interested in finding out. Our family couldn’t stop telling us how good we were.

Someone put a small clip out that showed me and cousins on stage with Alexi as a song ended. They did it as a teaser. When people commented asking who we were, the person told them to go to the next concert and find out. That circulated so much and so fast, people who already purchased tickets for the next show were anxious to see us.

But the next show was that Monday. We performed on the tour Saturday. We did not attend the show that Monday. It was out of state and our parents were not prepared for it. After closing the show Monday, fans went to the internet. They were saying things like, "They didn't perform at our show," and "Aw man no fair we didn't see them." While others said, "Ya'll must be lyin, there was no kids performing at the show."

This caused so much controversy that the executives wanted us to join the tour again as soon as possible. Alexi toured a couple of states that week. But the next show was gonna be back in our state. A different city but back in our state. The executives and producers thought what better time than now. So they got us together and we rehearsed for two days. The show was that Friday.

The show started. The crowd was enjoying it. Some were anticipating seeing us. Others wondered if they would. As soon as they were not thinking about it anymore, Alexi said, "We have a treat for ya'll!" She introduced us the same way she did before, because of this the crowd started to scream loud. They couldn't believe it. When they saw us on stage, a lot of them said, "Oh crap, it's real! She really did have kids performing."

They took out their phones to record. They enjoyed our performance too. We didn't close the show with her that time. I guess they wanted to switch things up. After the show, those people couldn't wait to get online and boast. They were saying, "Ya'll just mad, those girls performed at our show too." That's when people really started to believe it.

Things went on like this for a couple of weeks. We would perform at some shows and not at others. People online were fighting back and forth over us performing at some shows and not at theirs. But there was enough people saying they saw us for them to know they were telling the truth. Some of those people put up a short clip of us singing too, just to prove it.

But they would tell people they have to go to the concert, and hope we show up to the one they're at. I think the producers and executives did this on purpose, because we had a fan base growing from all the controversy…and that fan base was growing fast! People wanted to know who we were, what our names were, and most of all they wanted to know our ages.

So many questions grew around our entire existence. People were trying to see how we looked from the snippets people were putting up of us at the concerts. They caught glimpses but they didn't know for sure. This went on for another month. We wasn't online ourselves because we were too young. But we were filled in on what was going and being said about our performances and us being on some shows and not on others.

It was funny, but we felt bad for the people who didn't see us that wanted to see us. When we mentioned that to our team, they replied, "In due time they'll know who you are, they all will, and they'll love it." We didn't know what they meant by that, but we just went along with it. It seemed like they were doing the same thing our parents were doing, hiding us.

We performed in two more shows that following week. We were supposed to perform in 3 shows that week. But after the second show something unexpected happened. We were in our dressing room all happy after we finished the show. I was tying my shoe and talking to my cousins. We all were laughing and playing. Out of nowhere one of our moms assistants bursts in our dressing room.

She was in a panic. She said, "Girls, get your things we have to go now!" We were scared. We followed her and heard her on the phone saying, "As soon as Alexi is off stage, get her there fast! I have the girls, so we all should meet up at the same time." We looked at each other worried and concerned. Wherever we were going, Alexi was going too.

They got us in a car and headed to wherever they were taking us. After Alexi closed her show, she ran backstage. Everybody was handing her, her stuff as she made her way through the hall. By the time she got to the door, all she did was jump in an SUV and the driver drove off. Alexi immediately called the assistant that was with us. The assistant had the phone on speaker.

Alexi said, “I’m not too far behind ya’ll. Don’t let them out the car until I get there.” The assistant said, “Okay.” We was really looking crazy. We finally pulled up to this place. It was big and looked like a house. We asked, “Where are we?” The assistant answered, “This is where your family members Latoya, Beonca, Trinity, and Latonya have been staying while you’ve been back in town.” We looked at each other and gasped.

We haven’t been seeing our moms since we got back. I didn’t know until that point that my cousins hadn’t seen their moms either. I mean I saw my mom in the driveway that day and again at the show, but they did not stay at our grandmas houses only we did. About 5 minutes later, Alexi pulled up. She got out the car almost immediately after the driver opened the door for her.

As she approached the car we was in, the assistant quickly said, “They requested to see you girls urgently. This is a family matter. Remember to remain calm no matter what.” We started to freak out. Carmen said, “What happened?! Something happened to them?!” The rest of us got scared as we whined and said, “Oh my gosh!” The assistant said, “Girls pull yourselves together. Everything is gonna be okay.” We straightened up and pretended nothing was wrong by the time Alexi got to the car.

When she did get to the car, the assistant opened the door. We got out. The assistant stayed in the car as she was instructed to. As we walked up to the house with Alexi, no one was around us. No security was required because we were safely inside a gated home property. So they all stayed closer by the gate securing us from there. I looked up at

Alexi, she seemed nervous. So I asked, "Mama? What's wrong?"

She glanced at me fast as she rubbed my back. She was still looking serious in the face. Then she said, "Nothing baby everything alright. I just need ya'll to be positive, okay?" We all stopped, gasped, and looked at her quick. She looked at us in a concerning manner. Carmen said, "Auntie, I'm scared." Cashae said, "Me too. If something happened to our mamas, please tell us before we go in there with them."

We were already in the house. She was referring to going in the individual rooms with them. Alexi said, "Listen, it's nothing to be afraid of. But please, I'm begging all of ya'll…" She closed her eyes when she said please. She opened her eyes again and continued, “Be on ya’ll best behavior. No temper tantrums, no negativity, no attitudes, ya’ll moms need all positivity right now. If you feel like you need to get something out, wait until we get back outside or at one of our houses.”

We were concerned but we understood. We said, “Yes ma’am.” She said, “Okay.” She then started to point out which rooms our moms were in. As she pointed to the room doors and said our names, we started to slowly walk to them. I was so scared to walk inside that room. We all were. I hesitated as I reached for the doorknob. I looked to the side at Alexi. She was standing at a distance from me, because she was watching us all go into the rooms.

She gave me a look that said, alright na, go in there and act right. I turned back to the door and slowly turned the knob. I took a deep breath and quickly walked right in. After I closed the door, I looked up and everything just stopped. I found myself staring silently at my mom, who was laying in the bed. She had her bottom half covered with the comforter. She was wearing a robe and holding a baby.

The baby was wrapped up in a blanket. I didn't know what was going on or how to feel. My mama looked up at me and smiled slightly with her mouth closed. I had to remember everything Alexi told me in that moment, because I was on the verge of losing my mind. My mama said, "Hey Camille." I said, "Hi Mommie." She looked down at the baby and then looked back at me. Then she calmly said, “Come here.”

I started to walk to her slowly. I kept looking back and forth from her to the baby. She laid the baby down on the other side of her. Once I reached her, she held out her arms for a hug. I embraced her and gave her a hug. She kissed my forehead and said, “I missed you.” I said, “I missed you too.” She said, “I heard ya’ll doing good for ya selves, performing, and getting fans. How do you like it?”

I smiled and said, “Yes. It’s surprisingly fun.” She said, “And you didn’t wana do it. I knew you could. My baby working stages. I’m proud of you.” I said, “Thank you Mommie.” She said, “You’re welcome.” I looked over at the baby and asked, “Who’s that?” My mama looked over to the baby, picked the baby up, looked back at me, and said, “Camille, I want you to meet your sister…Careecia.” I was freaked out a bit.

I took a quick deep breath. I was shook! This was a replay of when she introduced me to Crystal. I tried to keep my composure. My mama looked at me. I appeared to be in deep thought or in a daze. My mama said, “Camille? You okay?” I snapped back into reality. I looked at her and said, “Yes…” I pointed at the baby, smiled, put my left hand on my hip, and hyperactively asked, “Is this why you been trippin on me lately??”

My mama couldn’t contain herself, she lost it! She burst out laughing so hard and loud. That was her first time seeing the little sassy Camille in a long time. While she laughed, I chuckled a bit. Then I said, “Mommie, that’s not funny.” I pointed to the baby again, still smiling and said, “This is why you been so snappy lately? Like I know you had to be pregnant before we moved back, because you wouldn’t have had the baby yet.”

I was really in deep thought while she laughed her behind off. I continued, “I was scared of you because you used to snap out of nowhere! I didn’t know what to do sometimes…I should’ve known something was wrong when you said me and Crystal couldn’t have that ice cream you ordered, because it was bad for us…and then you ate it!” At this point, my mama was crying laughing. I was still thinking and said, “Mommie!”

She said, “Stop Camille please!” She was trying to stop laughing. I stopped talking. When she calmed down more, I asked, “Does Crystal know?” My mama shook her head in a no motion and said, “No, not yet. I wanted to tell you first.” I looked at her and said, “Mommie, you really got 3 kids…dannng.” She laughed again and said, “Camille I’ma beat yo a**. Wash your hands and come meet the baby.”

I went to the bathroom in her room and washed my hands. Afterwards I sat on the bed with her, and she handed me the baby. When I looked at Careecia, I smiled and lowly said, “Wow. She’s so pretty.” I looked at my mama and said, “Mommie, you had another me.” My mama looked at me, smiled, and said, “Camille, I love you with all of me. But one of you is more than enough.” I looked at her and laughed as I said, "Well, you should've stopped at Crystal. Now you got two of me."

My mama said, "Hmm. How you know she's like you?" I said, "I can tell." I pointed from me to the baby and back to me saying, "Sister intuition…plus she look like me." My mama said, "She look like me." I looked at my mom sarcastically talking with my hand. I smiled and slowly said, "I'm your twin." My mama looked at me and smiled. Then she said, "You really are my twin, in more ways than just looks."

I smiled again and said, "I know." She smiled and shook her head in a no motion fast. I gave Careecia so many kisses. I talked to her and sung to her. I told her I would protect her and that she was my baby. I told her I'm happy she's here.

My mama was so happy to see me taking it so well. She spoke to me more about our performances and things we had going on. She gave me an update on when she would be back home and when she would perform again.

My sister was a week old by the way. So you know what that means, my mama couldn't come out until after a month. We spent like an hour in those rooms. When it was time to go, my mama said, "Okay, you have to go now. You need to be home resting and preparing for the next show." I said, "Okay…is this why ya'll left the show that day ya'll watched us perform?"

She slowly shook her head in a yes motion. Then she said, "I heard ya'll had a standing ovation." I said, "Yes and we had to come back out and sing again. The crowd was calling our name." My mama smiled and said, "I'm so proud of ya'll." I said, "Thank you." We hugged and said our see you laters. As I was walking out, I turned back to my mama and said, "Oh yeah…congratulations."

My mama smiled so warmly and said, "Thank you baby." I smiled slightly and walked out the door closing it behind me. I was thinking deeply until I saw my cousins coming back in the hall where Alexi was. I got excited when I saw them. I ran to them. Cashae was looking shocked but happy. The rest of them just looked kind of shocked but they were quiet.

When I got to them, I sounded kind of hyped. I lowly said, "Oh my gosh!" At the same time we all said, "My mama had a baby!" Our mouths dropped as we looked at each other in suspense. I couldn't believe it! I said, "Wait, they all had babies?? Mama, did you know that??" Alexi calmly said, "Yes, but I had to respect their wishes and wait until they were ready to tell ya'll."

I said, "Wow." Carmen said, "So they had babies at the same time?" Alexi said, "No, some of the babies were born a couple weeks ago, some were born a few days ago, some a week ago. They're close in age, but none of them were born at the same time." At that moment I pointed to myself and said, "My sister was born a week ago." Cashae was shocked as she said, "You have a sister too?! My sister was born two weeks ago."

Carmen said, "Whaaat? I have a sister too! She was born a few days ago." Alisha said, "We have a sister too! She was born a week and a half ago." We all paused and then said, "All girls? Again?!" We were so shocked! Alexi said, "Shh, okay ya'll come on let's go." We walked outside with Alexi and got in the car. We ended up staying at Alexi's house that night.

My mama called her that night to check up on me. When they got on the phone, my mama asked, "How was Camille after ya'll left?" Alexi said, "Girl, when we got in that car she cried like a baby." My mama said, "I knew it!" She took a deep breath. Alexi said, "Yeeeah, I had to bring them home with me, because I honestly don't think any of them took the whole baby thing well." My mama said, "See, Camille was fine when she was in here. But I know my baby, I knew she would be bothered by it."

Alexi said, "Yeah, she just cried out of nowhere. She scared all of us. She had a loud outburst. I had to ask the driver to pull over and ask him to get out of the car so I can talk to her. I knew she was gone say some stuff. Once he did get out the car, Camille just spilled all of her emotions." My mama said, "She was holding it in." Alexi said, "Exactly, and you could see just how much she was holding it in. That's why I asked him to pull over. I knew she needed to get it out."

My mama asked, "What did she say?" Alexi said, "She was saying, it's never you and her anymore and now you have another baby. She also said she thought once Crystal got older like she is now, things would get easier as far as her spending more time with you. She said but instead you pushed her to the side and made her sing, so now all the time you have is gonna be spent with the baby and Crystal." My mama said, "D*mn."

Alexi said, "I think she's afraid of losing you like she lost Andre. You know how he did, pushed her aside so he could do what he wanted to do. But she would never dream of telling you that. She care too much about you and your feelings. Camille just want you to be happy Toya, even if it's at her expense." My mama was silently crying. Then she said, "And that's how I feel about her. She's the child, she shouldn't have to feel like she needs to compromise her happiness for me. I do that for her, and I'm happy to do it."

Alexi scratched the back of her head as she sarcastically said, "Yeah I know, ya'll act just alike." They both laughed. Alexi knew my mama well. She knew she was crying and wanted to lighten the mood. My mama said, "I know. I just told her she's my twin in more ways than just looks. I really gave birth to myself, inside and out!" They both laughed again.

Alexi said, "No you really did Toya!" My mama said, "Yeah. Ma was right, this is coming back on me. I'm left to figure out how to deal with not only my child as she gets older, but myself. She's me!" Alexi agreed as she said, "Yep." My mama said, "Wow. I have to get with her one on one, because I would never push her aside. More less push her aside in order for me to pay more attention to my other kids."

Alexi said, "Of course you wouldn't! You the person that would reschedule, cancel, and drop anything for yo babies. I know you!" My mama said, "Right! But now I need to make sure Camille knows that. She knew before, but with everything that happened with her friend and singing, Camille's been having mixed emotions. I understand, she don't know how to feel."

Alexi said, "Yeah, you right." My mama said, "This month can't go fast enough." Alexi said, "Yeah, I figured she probably needed some tlc, that motherly love. Nobody can compare to you for her, but since you can't come out right now, you know I had to step in. In case she needed a cuddle." My mom was a bit relieved as she said, "Thank you Alexi. I'm so happy we have you."

Alexi said, "You know I got you." Just then I walked into Alexi's room and said, "Mama?" I was rubbing my eyes, you can tell I had been crying. She immediately said, “Uh! See? Here she go. Hey baby, what’s wrong?” I was standing at the door. Alexi reached out her arm and said, “Come here.” I walked to her and climbed in the bed on the side of her.

I rested my head on her shoulder as she wrapped her arms around me. I wrapped my arms around her too. I just sat there calmly. She kissed my forehead. I smiled slightly. My mama said, “That’s Camille?” Alexi said, “Yeah, she just came in. She just needed a hug.” I sniffed when she said that. Alexi looked down at my face and saw that I was still crying.

She said, “Camille, Mommie’s on the phone.” Through the tears I said, “Hi, Mommie.”

My body was jumping and everything as I was crying. My mom heard me and said, "Let me speak to her." Alexi passed me the phone. I took it right away and said, "Hello?" My voice was cracking. My mama said, "Camille, I don't want you to feel how you been feeling."

I started to cry a little harder. She said, "Mommie didn't push you to the side for anybody or anything. I wanted to tell you about the baby before she got here, but I didn't want you worried about another thing. I know I haven't been sleeping at Ma Ma's house since we've been back, but I haven't left you." I said, "Okay." I was still crying pretty hard.

Alexi was rubbing my arm the whole time to comfort me more. My mama continued, "When I leave here, we'll spend a lot of time together just me and you. I've been wanting to do that for a long time and I'm sorry we haven't for a long time." I said, "Okay." She said, "Okay, I'll see you soon. I love you." I said, "Okay, I love you too." She said, "Okay, give the phone back to Alexi."

I did and wrapped my arm across Alexi's stomach again. Alexi finished talking to my mama. After they were done, Alexi just cuddled with me until I fell asleep. I was happy to have her there as a mother figure. I don't know what I would've done if she wasn't present in my life.

Chapter 6

Reconnected

We missed the next few shows. Me and my cousins needed some time to deal with our feelings. We had a lot to digest after finding out we all had a new baby sister. We could only miss a few shows. After the third show we missed, the executives, producers, and fans basically demanded us to come back.

We gave the tour mystery, because of the speculations of our appearances tickets sales were through the roof! Alexi's tour shows started to sell out everywhere. Fans didn't care if they bought a ticket on a night we didn't make an appearance. It was the thrill of whether or not they would catch us on the tour. If they did catch us, they were extremely happy. Some people even purchased a second ticket if they didn't see us at the first show they paid for. It became a "thing" to spot us on the tour. Everyone on the tour and everyone working on the tour loved it.

We started to appear at more shows, so more people was now able to say we really were performing on the tour. Some of the shows were out of town. That was difficult for our moms, but they couldn't see us anyway. They all were recovering from giving birth. Our grandmas tried so hard to come with us when we had shows out of town. But because the world knew whose parents they were, we couldn't be seen with them…not yet.

During the times we had shows out of town, our moms would send family members no one knew were related to watch us and keep us safe. Of course we had Alexi looking out for us too, but she had to focus on her stuff, so we needed more people to help. Going to shows out of town aloud me and my cousins to experience independence in the real world.

We were pretty much independent on our own growing up, but this really showed us we can make it in the world without holding our mothers hands. We started to really feel like we were being pushed to grow up faster. We had responsibilities and huge obligations. I was forced to take on a lot of responsibility growing up, given the way I was treated by my father and having two teen parents.

But having an obligation to so many people, strangers, was absurd.

At ten years old, I had so much to think about and so much pressure on my shoulders. I refused to tell anyone how I was feeling, I just needed to find a way to make these feelings go away. Me and cousins continued to do the shows, no matter if they were in town or out of town. We were all over. We made a name for ourselves, and everyone had nothing but positive things to say about us.

Soon the tour came to an end. Alexi had been on tour for about a year. We came in towards the end of that tour year. Once the end of the tour came, people started to ask about me and my cousins more. When the tour ended it was like we disappeared, but we didn't. This made the people want us more, it was all a part of the executives and producers plan. Alexi did so well on her own, that people started to ask when she would have another tour.

She soon had interviews regarding the tour she just finished. When me and my cousins did the tour, we knew we had to perform but not once did we think that we would get paid. We never even thought about payment, we just knew we had to sing as punishment. But before Alexi went to an interview on a Friday evening, she stopped by my grandma's house.

My cousins, my mom, and my aunties all happen to be there. We were happy to see her. We haven't seen her since the last show we did a couple of weeks back. We all greeted her with hugs. She hugged us back as she said, “Hiiiii! I missed ya’ll!” We said, “We missed you too!” She sat down and so did we. She was so happy that day. She smiled as she congratulated us on our performances.

She clasped her hands together once as she chuckled and said, “Ya’ll did so well! I’m so proud of ya’ll! Ya’ll rocked the stage!” We were all smiles as we bashfully said, “Thank you.” She then said, “I have an interview I need to be at in a couple of hours, so I can’t stay too long. But I came here to give you girls your first checks!” Me and my cousins looked at each other confused and said, “Checks?!”

Our mamas started laughing. Alexi looked at us sarcastically and shocked as she said, “Ya’ll didn't think ya'll was working for free did ya'll?!" We were still looking confused. Carmen smiled and said, "Work?? We were just singing." Alexi shook her head in a yes motion and spoke with her hand as she said, "Yeah! That was working." I looked off to the side as I said, "Oh!"

Our parents started laughing again. Cashae smiled still looking confused as she said, "We only sung because it was punishment…we get paid for punishment??" Beonca said, "No, ya'll sing because of a punishment. Ya'll just happen to be paid because ya'll not working for free." I looked at my cousins as I pointed to our moms and sarcastically said, "So they made us get jobs!" Everybody in the room started laughing.

Our moms laughed the hardest. Alexi said, "I have the checks here." She handed them to each of us and said, "Congratulations!" We said, "Thank you." As she handed them to us. Then we sat there staring at the envelopes. My mama smiled and sarcastically said, "Ya'll gone open'em??" We said, "Oh!" We all laughed again. Our mamas waited. As we ripped open the checks, we had no idea what to expect.

I mean we didn't expect anything to begin with. After we ripped off the top of the envelope we paused. We looked at each other. I smiled and said, "Same time?" My cousin smiled and they all answered, "Yeah." Everyone in the room laughed again. We gripped the paper inside the envelope. Then I counted, "One, two, three, look!" We all pulled the paper out of the envelope and looked at the checks.

Not even our mamas knew how much we were getting paid. We gasped, our mouths were wide open, and our eyes were stretched so wide. It made our moms wonder how much they were. We then started to look over each other's shoulders at each other's checks. They were all the same. Latonya said, "What are ya'll doin?? What is it?!" Everybody laughed again.

We looked back at our own checks again. I said, "They all say five million, eight hundred ninety-five thousand, six hundred dollars…each." Our moms gave us an impressed look. Alexi chuckled a bit. We were in shock! I said, "Mommie, is that right?" She started to run through her thoughts as she looked like she was thinking and said, "Let's see, ya'll joined the tour the last couple months. Ya'll did 24 shows and mostly all of them sold out…yep! That's about right."

We couldn't believe it was that easy for us to make that kind of money. Our mouths were wide open. I said, "Mommie!" Then I covered my eyes as I collected myself. I uncovered my eyes and looked at my cousins with my hands on my chest, as I loudly whispered, "We're millionaires!" The adults laughed more because we were already millionaires because of them. But they knew where we were coming from.

We were proud of ourselves. We were no longer millionaires solely because of our parents, but we were now millionaires because of ourselves.

I told my cousins, “We’re millionaires at the age of ten!” I pointed to Carmen and Cashae and said, “Well nine for ya’ll.” We all laughed again. We were super stoked about our accomplishment.

I looked up at Alexi and crossed my arms still looking confused. I said, “Mama! You must make a lot of money on these tours. We got all this money for just the two months we was there. You been on tour for a whole year!” She chuckled as she shook her head in a yes motion. I looked at my mama and said, “Mommie, this what ya’ll been doing all our lives?!” I pointed to her and my aunties when I said that.

They laughed as she shook her head in a yes motion and answered, “Yes.” I looked so shocked as I said, “Whoa, and it’s been like ten years!” She said, “Yep.” I shook my head in a no motion as I looked back down and said, “Oh wow, then I know ya’ll packin.” They all laughed again. Soon Alexi had to leave for her interview. We all said our goodbyes and she left.

We gave our checks to our moms, they were going to deposit them into our accounts. We still couldn’t believe we made that kind of money! The only other people who knew were our grandmas. That was because our moms told them afterwards. They were so proud of us. Since people started to get better glimpses of us, we couldn’t go to the places we normally went to when we were back home in Miami.

We had to start traveling discreetly like our moms, but just not as heavy yet. When Alexi went to the interview, they asked her about the tour. They had a really good discussion about it. Then the host said, “I know you know it’s comin! Who is this girl group, and when I say girl group, I really mean little girl group, that fans have been raving about on your tour?!”

Alexi laughed and then calmly answered, “Aw man! The speculations were wild! But yes, there really was a girl group on my tour. I’m sorry for the fans that did not see them during the time of the shows they purchased. The girl group everyone has been talking about is a singing group who goes by the name of Angelic. They joined the last couple of months of the tour.”

The host said, “Nice! How did they come about joining your tour?” Alexi smiled as she said,

"Um, you know it was a shock to me. I had no clue anyone else was going to join the tour. But their team reached out to my team. By the time I found out, they were already in route." They both laughed. Alexi continued, "Like they were already preparing to perform."

The host said, "Okay, okay, well I heard they rocked the stages! Everybody loved them. The people want more. Can you tell us when we can hear from them again?" Alexi put her hand on her chest as she said, "Oh! I don't know. Their management team is different from mine. You would have to reach out to their managers to find out."

The host then asked, "How was it working with them? Did you all get along well? I know their kids, but it was still business. How is it working with kids?" Alexi said, "Yeah, it was nice. I can say they're very mature and handle business flawlessly. They were a pleasure to work with and we had some fun times. I do hope we can work together again."

The host was smiling. Then he said, "Nice! How old are they? What are their names??" Alexi laughed and said, "Look, I'ma leave that for them to answer when you get a hold of their management team. It's not my business to tell." The host laughed too and said, "Okay I understand. We definitely will be on the search for Angelic." Once she finished the interview, she was so happy. She went home to get some rest.

We listened in on her interview. We loved it and thought it was hilarious, how the host kept trying to get information about us out of Alexi. The way she kept rejecting it was even funnier. Our moms were our managers, the people just didn't know it. Our moms had people to speak for them over the phone and during in person interviews.

They were still trying to keep us a secret, but this time it was to see how well we would do on our own, with our career. So far, we were off to a great start! Those producers and executives did not manage us. Our moms sent us there because it would help us to have more people listen to us. Those people they sent us to before we joined the tour, are some of the most well known in the industry. They get information out fast about talent.

This actually helped us in the upcoming weeks. They sent out so many things regarding us to so many places. Just when we thought things died down for us, they started to pick up like crazy. Our moms phones were ringing off the hook. People were trying to interview us, book us for shows, and private events, we got some tv interview offers, and photoshoots.

Our moms managed it all very well. They looked at everything and chose wisely. They wanted us safe, and they did not want us to be overwhelmed. We didn't even know about half the offers we received. Our moms only presented us with the offers they decided to go through with. During these times in between, my mama spent more time with me. We had some mother daughter dates and caught up on a lot of things.

We both needed those bonding moments. I no longer felt that she would give all her love and attention to my sisters anymore. She showed me that she always have time and love for me too. Now I was able to focus on everything else we had coming our way. After another couple of weeks, our moms finally allowed us to do a radio interview.

Before the interview, we were coached thoroughly. By the time the interview came, we knew what to say, what not to say, and how to say it. We had to get used to not referring to Alexi as auntie or mama in my case, when speaking with interviewers or people in general. We were taught not bring up our parents unless we are asked about them. Even then, we were to keep it short and change the subject.

We ended up going to the same radio host as Alexi did. He actually went through with his plan and got us to come on his radio show. My mama had one of their agents come with us to the interview. When we walked in, the host was so happy. He said, "Whaaaat?! Ya'll won't believe who just walked in the building! Ya'll favorite radio host got what ya'll demanded! Stay tuned to find out who our special guests are!"

He cut to a commercial break to greet us. The agent went over what was appropriate for him to discuss with us and what was not. When the commercial break was over, the host came back on and said, "We got ya'll girls in the building! Everybody requested them and now they are here! Ladies and gentlemen welcome the new singing group sensation, Angelic!" We laughed and said, "Thank you."

The listeners were so shocked. They couldn't believe he found us and got us on his show. The people who never saw us now believed we performed on Alexi's tour. The host was so happy to have us. He said, "So, we have the notorious Angelic in the building!" We smiled as we said, "Hi!" He told us, "It was so hard for me to get you ladies here, but the process was worth it. I'm so happy to have you."

We all said, "Thank you for having us." He chuckled and said, "Wow ya'll are so polite. I can tell ya'll parents are doing a great job raising you young ladies." We said, "Yes thank you." Then he said, "Speaking of young, we have to ask. Everyone is dying to know, what are your ages?" We laughed. He continued, "Can ya'll tell everybody ya'll names and ages?"

Since Alisha was sitting on one end, she started first. She said, "My name's Alisha and I'm ten years old." Cashae said, "My name is Cashae I'm nine years old." The radio host was shocked! He said, "What?!" We chuckled a little but kept going. Alicia said, "My name is Alicia I'm ten years old." Carmen said, "My name is Carmen I'm 9 years old." I went last, I said, "My name's Camille I'm ten years old."

We went from right to left. I was sitting next to the agent. Alisha was sitting closer towards the door. The radio host said, "Wow! You girls started early!" We laughed and said, "Yes." Then he said,

“Wait! Alisha and Alicia, are you twins??” They laughed and said, “Yes.” He said, “I knew it! You’re identical!” Then he asked, “Is this your first time doing an interview?”

We all said, “Yes.” The host got so happy, he shouted, “Yes! You heard it here everybody, Angelic’s first interview is with none other than your favorite radio host!” We giggled. He asked, “What is the relation between you girls? Are you friends?” We all answered, “Cousins.” He was shocked. He said, “Really?! Nice! So the fans want to know if we can expect to see you again soon.”

Alisha answered, “We have a few things in the works. Some things we cannot speak on yet, but everyone will know really soon. So just keep an eye out.” The host smiled and said, “Okay, okay!” We got through the entire interview and did great. When the host was closing out, he looked at us curiously while he pointed and said, "This entire interview, I knew you girls reminded me of someone! I couldn't put my finger on it, but now I got it…"

We looked at him waiting. The entire time we was in our heads like, oh gosh don't say our moms. Then he smiled and said, "Are ya'll familiar with the group Dynasty Chosen??" We threw our hands up, dropped them, and chuckled as we looked at each other. The host laughed and said, "What?" We said, "Everybody tells us that!" He laughed and said, "It's true, you girls look just like them! Like I can tell each of you who you look like."

We just looked at him while smiling with our mouths closed. Then he said, “Alright…” He pointed at each of us as he said, “Camille, you look like Latoya. Carmen, you look like Latonya. Cashae, you look like Beonca…Alisha and Alicia, this is crazy. Ya’ll know who ya’ll look like?? …Trinity!” We all laughed. The host was looking kind of spooked. He said, “No really! You girls can go for their kids! I mean we all know they don’t have kids. But if they did, I would expect for them to look just like you all!”

I said, “I guess everybody has a twin.” The host said, “Yeah! Have you girls ever worked with them before?” We all said, “No.” He said, “You should! That would be epic!” We chuckled. Then he closed out the interview. We survived our first interview, and it was live! The people who was waiting were happy to hear from us. As for everyone else, we gained more fans and curious people after that interview.

Everyone just wanted to know more. During that week, there was an announcement stating that we would be performing locally. This was huge for us. Although our first performance was during a huge successful tour, the place and event we were performing at locally, was the same place our moms and Alexi performed at when they started out.

We were happy to do it. Before we headed to the concert, our moms wished us well. They cried. They said we were babies when they performed there, and now we were performing there. They really wanted to go but wanted to keep a low profile. Ironically, they were watching us on video call, just as we had watched them on video call perform years back at the same venue. Life has its way of repeating itself.

They were so proud of us. The crowd really loved us too. They started chanting our name again at the end of our performance. The fans made that the thing since seeing us on the tour. This time we held our microphones up in the air. We moved them back and forth going to the rhythm of them chanting. After like the 6th chant, we got back on the microphone and said, "Thank you!" We got off stage, then the next performer came on.

I guess they felt if they chant our names after every performance, we would go back out and perform again. But that only worked on tour and not even every time lol. We were already preparing to leave as soon as we got off stage. We had some people to talk to just like our moms did when they performed. The only difference is we didn't need any agents or management. We already had that. Of anything it was to get more exposure.

We were getting used to speaking to people business wise. You wouldn't think we were shy, but we were. After we spoke to a number of people, we were escorted to our ride, and we headed home. Our moms hugged and kissed us. They told us how proud they were of us. Then they told us we had a photoshoot that night. We didn't know it yet, but we had a busy week ahead of us.

Our parents had the wardrobe, makeup, and hairstylists come to our house to get us ready. They had us looking really cute. Then we went to the photoshoot. Our moms were watching from video calls again. They wanted to make sure everything was done exactly how they wanted it to be done. But they didn't want anyone to see us all together. Even when the stylists came to the house, our moms were upstairs in the room.

At the photoshoot, we took individual pictures, groups pictures, personality pictures, and fun pictures. We had so many wardrobe changes. The stylists traveled with us because we needed them. Our hairstyles were changed a few times, so was our makeup. They did this in order to get weeks worth of photos instead of one day's worth. We had a very late night, but it worked out though.

Our pictures came out so well. We really looked like stars. When we got home, we got ready for bed and knocked out. Meanwhile our moms were looking over our photos. They were sent to them after the photoshoot. Our moms had to approve the photos. If any of them needed to be corrected, our moms told the editor, and they corrected them.

By the time we woke up, the photos were all finished. We didn't see them, because we had to go to an early rehearsal for our upcoming shows. After rehearsals, we headed to the studio to record more songs. We had a week of rehearsals, recordings, and we had a video shoot. We shot a video for the song we made. The same song we performed first for everybody.

During that week, it was also announced that we would be having a meet and greet that upcoming week. The fans were so happy to know this. They were excited to have a chance to see us up close and personal. The meet and greet was set up for the next Friday. During that week we had more performances leading up to the meet and greet. Our video was released early that week as well.

This made the fans want to meet us even more. They were able to see us up close and in detail from watching the video. The video showed a close up of each of us with our names across the bottom of the screen, just before the song started. It was the opening of the video. This allowed fans to put a face to our names. A lot of them didn't know who was who this whole time. But thanks to the video, they knew now.

We performed four times that week. The ratings for our video were through the roof, because like I said before, fans wanted to know more about us. Everyone including ourselves, couldn't believe how well we were doing, and we just started. The night before the meet and greet, our moms prepped us. They told us what to do, what not to do, and to have fun. They also told us we would be able to relax that weekend.

We were happy about that. The next day we went down to where the meet and greet was being held. We took our seats and soon the doors opened. There were so many people lined up to meet us. When they saw us, they were all smiles. Some of them were nervous, but we made them more comfortable. We handed out pictures of ourselves that were already signed.

We also gave hugs and took pictures with them. The people who came to see us honestly had a great time. Also, this was the first time me and my cousins saw some of our pictures from the photoshoot. Our moms had some life size cut outs made of us. They also had our pictures really big around the room. They had the place decorated really nicely.

We were there for hours. We had to take a bathroom break and was right back to it. There were so many people that showed up, the security had to close the gate at a certain time in order for us to get out of there at an appropriate time. Towards the end, I asked, "How many more people are out there?" The security said, "About ten, but we about to shut it down." I said, "No. It's only ten. I'm sure they waited all day. We can do ten more people, we're just going home to relax afterwards."

My cousins agreed and said, "Yeah let them in. We can do it." So security started to let them in. We greeted them just as we greeted the first people that came in. We didn't want them to feel bad. They were actually happy because they knew we told security to let them through. The security told them we said to let them in after they stopped them from coming in. When the last batch of people came in, I was looking down at something on the table. One of them walked in front of me and said, "What's up Camille?"

I looked up at them and then lowly gasped. My mouth dropped. Then the person said, "How you been?" I couldn't believe my eyes. It was

Shaun! But what was he doing here in Miami?? Last time I saw him, we was in Chicago. I was excited as I smiled and whispered, "What are you doin here?!" My cousins looked over to me from the side of their eyes. They kept doing what they were doing with the fans in front of them.

I handed Shaun a picture as we did everyone else. He said, "Thank you. I have something for you too." He handed me a brown envelope. I took it and said, "Thank you." He then asked, "Is it okay if we all take a group picture?" I said, "Yeah. Just let us get the other people out the way and we'll do it. Do you mind waiting?" He said, "No." I said, "Okay, stand over here." I had him to stand next to the table where I was sitting.

Other people wondered why he was standing there but didn't ask. After we got the last person out, it was just Shaun in there. I turned to my cousins and said, "Can we get a group picture with him? He waited to take one." My cousins said, "Okay, yeah." They got up immediately to take the picture. We had Shaun in the middle of all of us in the picture.

One of the assistants took the picture. The picture came out really nice. We took one picture normal and the other picture we took clowning around. The assistants and security thought it was because he was the last fan there, so we gave him something extra. But it was because we knew who he was and was comfortable with him. After the pictures, he started to hug all of us separately.

He hugged me last purposely. He whispered in my ear, “My number is in the envelope.” I chuckled a bit and said, “Okay.” After that we stopped hugging. He turned to everyone and thanked us for doing what we did for him. Then he left. Me and my cousins headed home after that. During the ride home, my cousins were all staring at me smirking.

I can tell they had a lot to say, but they couldn’t say it around the people in the car. As Carmen was getting dropped off, she looked at me as she got out the car and said, “We gone be at yo house tomorrow, Camille.” I laughed which made her laugh. Then she said, “You know why.” Then she walked towards her house door. By the time I got home, I was ready to lay down and relax.

We had a long week. I took a shower, said hello to my mom, then I laid down in my bed to relax. Just as I was letting out a breath of relief, I remembered that I had that envelope from Shaun. Of course I hid it before I came in the house, because I didn't want my mom to see it. I was nervous to open it, I didn't know what else was in it. I sat there thinking for a few minutes. It has been a while and I did miss him when I left.

I've been so focused on singing, performing, and other things my mama had been occupying me with, that I didn't really give it much thought after a while. But seeing him again brought back so many memories. Memories that I missed. I couldn't help but think that him finding me again was no coincidence. He traveled a long way to be there, but why was he really in Miami? Was it for me? Or was it for something else and he just happen to stop by our meet and greet? Shaun was definitely a mystery in a lot of ways. But he seemed to be as open and honest with me as he could be. Whatever the reason was, I just had to find out. I opened the envelope. Inside was a card. I opened the card, it read:

Camille,

I missed you so much. I've been sad since you disappeared. I didn't know what to do anymore. The one thing that made me happy was gone. I closed up and nothing was the same. I stopped by your house and saw that it was sold. My heart ached feeling I would never see you again. I feel bad for getting you in trouble, I just feel like I did. But now I found you again. I hope you forgive me and can still be my girlfriend. I'll never lose you again. Call me.

Forever Yours,

Shaun

After seeing that card, my mouth dropped. I couldn't believe he still felt the same way he did when I was there. I was happy he found me again. Although I wasn't allowed to date, I was happy he still wanted me to be his girlfriend. I was scared to call him, because I didn't want my mom to see it in my call history. But I just had to speak to him. I missed him and I had so many questions.

There was a piece of paper in the envelope with his number on it. I looked at it, took a deep breath, and called his number. He picked up and said, “Hello?” I said, “Hello?” He smiled and calmly said, “What’s up Camille?”

Chapter 7

Entangled

After hearing Shaun's voice, especially after he knew exactly who I was, made me blush. I was so happy he didn't forget about me. I was more interested in knowing how he found me again. Also, I called him from my house phone. I was scared to call him from my cell phone, because my mom constantly checks my phone and call log.

After Shaun said, "What's up Camille?" I smiled and said, "Hey Shaun, how'd you know it was me?" He smiled and said, "I had a feeling you would call." We both laughed a little. He said, "I'm so happy I found you again." I said, "Yeah about that, how did you do that?" He said, "Did you forget I told you I be in Miami?"

I said, "No, but I thought you were just saying that. I didn't think you were really in Miami often." He said, "Yeah, I've been working on a lot of stuff. Ironically, it caused me to move to Miami for a while." I gasped. He said, "After you left, I had no idea where you went. I was sad. When I had to leave Chicago, I thought you would come back, and I'll never see you again."

I was quietly listening. Then he said, "When I came down here, I was watching some videos online. Everybody was talking about a new singing group. I'm into music so I wanted to see what this new singing group was about…then I saw you! I was so shocked. I thought I was going crazy. I'm like that's Camille! So that's where she went! I had to find you. So I started to follow the updates on ya'll. Then I saw ya'll was having a meet and greet, I couldn't miss that. I didn't know you sing."

I giggled and said, "Yeah." He said, "I was gonna go to one of ya'll concerts, but I needed to get up close and personal to you while I could…is that why you was so secretive?? You was famous all this time??" I laughed and said, "No, this was something we just started to do. When we left Chicago, it wasn't just to sing. Me and my cousins were in trouble, so our moms took us back to Miami, to our grandmas houses. Then we were forced to sing."

Shaun was shocked. He said, "Forced to sing?" I said, "Yeah, we didn't want this…it's our punishment." Shaun grew more and more concerned as I revealed more things about us. He said, "Punishment?? Camille, ya'll were in that much trouble?? Camille, who are ya'll parents?? How can ya'll up and move that fast and get another house just like that??"

I paused because I heard a noise. Shaun said, "Camille?" I said, "Huh?" He asked, "Why are ya'll in trouble?" I said, "Because our moms don't want us to keep certain company." He said, "Camille?" I said, "Yes?" He asked, "Are you in trouble because of me?" There was a pause. Then I said, "I think my mom's coming, I gotta go." Shaun said, "Real quick, are you in trouble because of me?" I said, "Yes, but don't worry about it, it's okay. I have to go."

He said, “Okay.” I said, “Shaun, this is my house phone. Please don’t call it back. I’ll call you again as soon as I can.” He said, “Okay, I look forward to it.” I said, “Good, goodnight.” He said, “Goodnight.” I hung up fast and pretended to be sleep. I did it just in time too. My mama came in my room fast looking confused. She thought she heard someone talking.

When she saw that I was “sleep”, she looked around the room with her eyes, turning her head from one side to the other. She looked at me as she squinted her eyes and slowly closed the door. I opened my eyes and let out a breath of relief. I almost got caught! I was scared as heck! Shaun laid down after we hung up. He was on his back with his hands behind his head. He felt a few different emotions, but overall he was happy.

He had a lot of questions. He didn't want me to be in trouble, but he didn't want to let me go. I was special to him, and he loved how I made him feel. He laid there for a minute thinking about me and thinking about the next time I call him. He smiled to himself with his mouth closed. Soon after he went to sleep happy knowing that we successfully reconnected.

The next day my cousins came over, just like they said they would. Once we were in my room together all my cousins looked at me with a smirk on their faces. Then Carmen said, "Spill." I smiled a little bit and said, "What?" I was acting like I had no idea what she was talking about. But it didn't work. Not with my cousins. Alisha said, "Don't play stupid. What's up with you and Shaun?"

I blushed. All my cousins said, “Ooooh, she blushin!” I said, “Stop…what about us?” Cashae said, “We saw how both of ya’ll was looking when he came up to you.” I smiled as I said, “Yeah, so? He was saying hi.” Alicia said, “That look like more than just a hi.” Carmen said, “Yeah, what was in that envelope?” I said, “You saw the envelope?!” She said, “Duh! We all saw it!”

I laughed as I shyly covered my mouth. I got up and got the note from its hiding place. I handed it to Carmen. They all rushed to her and read it together. Then they started to say things like, “Awww”, and “Whaaat??” Cashae said, “Camille, what you gone do?” I took a deep breath and smiled as I thought about him. Then I said, “I don’t know. I really like him…but my mom.”

Carmen said, “Well shoot, he came after you girl. You left the state and he still found you in another state.” I said, “That’s because he be down here sometimes, and he said he working on some stuff.” My cousins gave me a look like I was the most naïve person in the world at that point. I looked back at them confused.

Carmen said, “Camille, I know he 10 and all, but what child is gone end up in the same state as the person he misses. Then “randomly” show up to her meet and greet after she disappeared, and wait for hours and hours to hand you an envelope just to tell you he misses you and to call him?” My mouth dropped. Carmen said, “Oh okay!” Alisha said, “Camille, do you understand how much this boy like you?”

I said, “I mean yeah, he tells me.” She said, “No, but do you understand he’s for real?” I was getting slightly frustrated and started to talk with my hands. I said, “Yeah, I think so. But where you goin with this Lisha??” Alisha then said, “He asked you to be his girlfriend and you said yes.” I said, “Yes.” She then said, “He wasn’t playing.” I said, “I know he wasn’t.”

Alisha said, “I think he’s gonna be around long term." I got scared and said, “What you mean?” She said, “I MEAN, you better figure out what you gone do, because you already trippin bout yo mama. This boy plan to stay around for as long as you allow him to.” Carmen said, “Yep. I feel like he would be around long term too.” I said, “Why you feel like that?”

Carmen answered, “Because he followed you, Camille! I don’t care what excuse he gave you, that boy found out where you was and followed you. He probably don’t want you to think he crazy, but this is no coincidence.” I said, “Oh my gosh, I felt the same way. About this not being a coincidence, but I can’t put my finger on it.” I told them the reason he gave me for seeing me in Miami.

They did not believe it one bit. They believed that he was following our updates online after he realized it was us, then decided to travel to Miami just to see me. Carmen said, “I’m not mad at it Camille. I just think because of that, he’ll be around for a while…Heck! We had boyfriends too or whatever you wana call’em. You think they gone come looking for us??”

I said, "But they're kids." My cousins all said, "Shaun is too!" I said, "I know but like I said, he be down here too. Maybe the boyfriends ya'll had can't do anything about that. They probably never been down here." They all said, "Hmm." Then Cashae said, "Well, our mamas took us away from them. We never gone see them again." Carmen said, "We just gone find new ones."

I looked at Carmen shocked. My mouth dropped as I said, "Ya'll not new to this are ya'll??" They smirked at me again. Then I said, "Am I the last one to come in contact with a boy?? My gosh." Alicia said, "Well now you the only one with a boyfriend. So what you gone do?" I let out a deep breath. Then I said, "I don't wana go against my mom, but I don't wana let him go…I think I'll keep him around while I figure this out."

Alisha smiled and said, “Well, your secret’s safe with us.” They all agreed. I smiled and said, “Thanks.” In that moment, we all realized we can talk to each other about everything, and trust that it would never get out. We talked about things before but never about boys. Heck, I didn’t even know they all had experienced dating before I did.

It was nice to know that my closed box of no one to talk to, opened up to 4 people. I was able to talk to my mom about absolutely everything for as long as I can remember. But about Shaun, I knew I could not bring him up to her. After the trouble I got in because of him, I needed to keep things under wrap and pretend I left it all back in Chicago. My cousins ended up staying the night at my house.

Lashae came over that night too. We wasn't sure if we were able to talk in front of her about the boys we've encountered. That is until she started to spill about her experience. When she came in, she seemed kind of irritated. She had us confused, I was reading her body language and it wasn't changing. I finally opened my mouth and asked her, "Shae what's wrong?"

She wasted no time. She took a deep breath and said, "I got in trouble because my parents found out I have a boyfriend." We all gasped. She said, "Yeah, like what's the big deal? We only see each other at school." The rest of us held our chest and said, "We thought we was the only one!" Lashae said, "What?" I said, "Girl, we got in trouble for having boyfriends back in Chicago. They moved us all the way back home to get us away from them."

Lashae said, "Wow!" Alicia said, "It worked too, except for Camille. Her boyfriend followed her down here." Lashae gasped as she looked at me smiling. She said, "For real?!" I smiled and said, "Yeah, he did. But my mama don't know." Lashae said, "Oh girl, she can't know! None of them can, we'll get in so much trouble."

Alisha said, "You still have your boyfriend Shae?" She said, "I don't know after this weekend. My parents goin above and beyond. They supposed to go out to the school and change my class and everything." We said, "Ooh!" She said, "Right! That's embarrassing." Cashae said, "Well Camille, looks like you gone still be the only one with a boyfriend for now."

Lashae told me, “Just don’t do anything obvious or permanent that would be too big to hide, then you won’t get caught.” I said, “What did you do?” She looked at me for a second and then rolled her eyes as she looked towards the other side of the room. Then she said, “I called him.” I got scared as I responded, “Huh?!”

She repeated herself, “I called him. My mom checks my phone randomly every week. She saw a number I spend a lot of time on the phone with, and when she called it, he answered.” We said, “What he said?” She quickly said, “Hey bae.” Then she covered her eyes and put her head down. We all burst out laughing so hard and loud. I said, “Oh my gosh, I can’t imagine if that happened to my mom.”

Cashae asked, “Camille, what phone you used to call Shaun?” I said, “The house phone, and I didn’t stay on too long.” Lashae said, “Be careful with that too Camille. If she suspect you doing something and she don’t find anything in your phone, she just might check the house phone. That happened to me too, that’s why I used my cell phone. I knew I was gonna get caught one day, so I just used my cell phone until I did.”

I was confused and nervous as I said, “Wait, your mom checked the house phone records?” Lashae shook her head in a yes motion slowly. I whispered, “Oh my gosh.” I started to get scared and hyperventilate. Alisha immediately said, “Camille, it’s fine. It was only one time.” Lashae looked concerned as she asked, “What’s wrong?” Cashae answered, “Oh, she’s just nervous because she called her boyfriend from her house phone last night."

Lashae said, "Oh, well Camille I did it a lot before I got caught." She was attempting to calm me down, but I was too far gone. They knew what that meant. They were running around trying to find my pump and my asthma machine. I was really trippin. I was scared for my mom to find out what I did. By the time my cousins found my pump, I tried it, and it didn't help.

They freaked out. Alisha grabbed my machine and yelled, "Go get her mama!" While Carmen and Cashae ran to get my mama, Alisha, Lashae and Alicia were working fast to get my machine together. They were putting the medicine in it and getting it plugged in. Alisha was just putting the facemask around my head as my mom ran in the room.

Cashae and Carmen was right behind her. I was still hyperventilating. My mom sat in front of me trying to calm me down. At this point I was scared because my breathing was off. I started to calm down, but I was wheezing. My mom got on the phone with the doctor and was telling him what was happening. My mom didn't want me to go to the hospital because people would recognize us both.

So the doctor had to make a house call. My mom helped me downstairs. My cousins stayed in my room. My mama came back up before the doctor got there and asked my cousins, "What happened to her?" My cousins looked at each other worried. Then they told my mama, “We don’t know.” Lashae said, “We were talking, and she just started to panic.”

Latoya said, “Panic? About what??” My cousins were scared, but Carmen thought on her toes. She burst out with, “All we heard her say was oh my gosh, then she started to breathe funny.” Cashae said, “We tried to calm her down, but nothing helped. Not even her pump.” My mama picked up my pump and said, “So she used this??” My cousins answered, “Yes.”

That made my mom worry a little more. She knew I needed medical attention because if my pump didn’t work, that means it went too far. She looked at my cousins and said, “Go down there and keep ya’ll cousin company.” They all ran out the room and downstairs to where I was. The doctor finally came. My mom explained everything she knew to him over the phone. She stayed upstairs while he was there. He knew exactly what to do.

The doctor treated me in my living room. My cousins sat with me the entire time. It didn't take long for him to stabilize my breathing. I was so grateful. Once he was done, he left. I laid there for about an hour, my cousins were in there with me while I laid there. After an hour, my mama came from upstairs. As she walked slowly down the stairs, she looked at us as if she was looking through us.

Once she got down by us, she calmly asked, "Camille, how you feelin?" I softly answered, "Better. I can breathe again." She said, "Good."

Then she asked my cousins, "Everybody alright?" They all nervously answered, "Yeees." My mom then calmly said, "Okay. Well, it's been enough activity for one night. Ya'll go upstairs and go to bed." We said, "Okay."

We all got up and slowly walked past my mama. She stood there and was in a daze after we passed by her. Once we got upstairs, we laid down. Right before Carmen fell asleep, she lifted her head and whispered, "Camille, is your mom okay? She looked like she wanted to cry…either that or she was pissed off." I whispered back, "I don't know. I didn't notice."

Carmen then whispered, "Camille, don't let Shaun distract you this much. You always know how your mom is feeling just by looking at her. Pay attention, if you gone do this be safe about it. Pay attention to yo mama. Don't get caught off guard." I was slightly confused as to why she said that, but I said, "Okay." Then she turned her head the other way and went to sleep.

I had a lot to think about, but I went to sleep not too long after she did. Carmen was the last one out of my cousins to fall asleep. The next day when we did wake up, we all woke up in silence. It was weird, but we had to admit the night before was a bit rough. My cousins stayed at my house all day. It wasn't until around 8 o'clock that night that they went home.

I was at the door as they left out to go get in the cars with their moms. After they got in the cars, I closed the door. I turned around just to see my mom staring at me a few feet away. She looked kind of pissed off. It made me stop in my tracks. I stared back at her. Then she lifted her right hand up from behind her back.

She was holding an envelope, but not just any envelope. She was holding the envelope Shaun gave me at the meet and greet! When I noticed that, I lightly gasped and my mouth dropped a bit. In a serious tone, she then asked, "Where did you get this?" I paused for a couple seconds and then I replied, "He gave it to me at the meet and greet."

My mom couldn't believe it. The expression on her face was surprised and pissed off at the same time. She said, "I found this in your room, under yo bed right after the doctor left." At that point, I realized exactly what Carmen meant when she said pay attention to my mama. I didn't know what to do at this point, I felt like things had already gone too far.

So I sat there feeling terrified as I waited for whatever would take place next. She finally said, "What is he doin at ya'll meet and greet?? We left him back in Chicago…is he following you?!" I got scared and instantly answered, "No, he said he had a lot of stuff to do. The stuff he had to do caused him to…" I paused for a second. Then I said, "To be down here."

I did NOT want to tell her he moved to Miami. I was too afraid that she might be mad enough to move us back to Chicago. I didn't like Chicago. I knew a lot more people and had a lot more freedom in Miami. My mom still got mad.

She said, "How do you know that? That wasn't in this note. Have you been in contact with him?!"

I didn't have to say anything, the look on my face gave me away. Even with the guilt all over my face, I still said, "Only once." She said, "How?!" I said, "Over the phone." She said, "Camille!" I jumped a little. She was so shocked that I did something like that. But it scared her even more that I did it and she didn't know about it.

She then said, "Where is the number he gave you? Because it's not in here." I started to walk to my room. My mom looked at me upset and confused. She followed me to my room. When I got in there, I grabbed one of my bags I normally carry around with me. I opened it and pulled the piece of paper with the number on it out of a small pocket inside my bag.

My mama looked at me surprised. I turned to her and handed her the number. She took it and looked at it. She looked back at me and said, “Give me yo phone.” I grabbed my phone and gave it to her. I was disappointed. I never got my phone taken before. She then gave me another lecture on why she don’t want me and Shaun in contact with each other.

After that, she left out my room. Since I didn’t have my phone, all I could do was sit there and think about it all. I really felt stuck between a rock and a hard place. I loved and respected my mama, I never would think of going against her. But I felt that she didn’t understand. I felt like she was coming down too hard on me. She had her reasons, but it didn't seem necessary.

I mean come on, Shaun was sweet, polite, innocent, and he was very good at always being there for me. He was a good friend, and I didn't want to lose that. It seemed unfair for me to disappear out of his life when all he wanted was for me to be around. It wasn't that serious to me. I didn't understand why she made it a big deal.

After an hour, my mama came back in my room. She said, "This number is nowhere in your phone or on your phone records." I was shocked as I stood there looking at her with my mouth wide open. She said, "Yes, I did check your phone records. What you think this is?? How did you call him if you didn't use your phone??" I looked kind of sad. I didn't want to reveal the whole house phone plan. I planned to maybe use it again down the line!

My mama saw my facial expression and said, "Tell me…NOW!" I let out a quick deep breath and said, "I used the house phone." Her eyes got big as she yelled, "You what?! Camille, why would you use the house phone?! Now he has this number!" I said, "He's not gonna call it. I told him not to." My mama paused to look at me. She looked at me sarcastically and shocked.

She had one hand on her hip. She then said, "I don't know whether to be more mad because you gave him the house number, or the fact that you told him not to call back because you being sneaky!" I was looking down as my eyes looked from left to right nervously. She continued to say, "Camille, what the h*ll is wrong with you?! You don't do this! Where is my innocent baby?!"

I was quietly listening. Then she grabbed both sides of her head as she took a deep breath and said, "Camille, you stressin me out with this sh*t and now you startin to be sneaky. This don't work for me and if you don't cut it out, you'll shortly find out it's not gone work for you either." I looked at her with my eyes only when she said that.

I wasn't sure what she meant by that, but it seemed like a pretty scary threat of some sort. Whatever it was, I didn't want to find out. Without saying another word, my mama looked at me for a second and then walked out. I didn't know what was happening. I just knew I was more scared than what I seemed to be. I was on edge the entire time she was gone.

She finally came back in the room about 20 minutes later. She stared at me for a few seconds attempting to collect herself. She had her arms folded and she looked very upset. Then she said, "I saw the number in the house phone records. I can't believe you called that boy, even after I told you not…" She stopped talking and took a deep breath as she looked up shaking her head.

She looked back at me and said, "And then it was late…" She bald up her fist, rolled her eyes, unbald her fist, hit her thigh, looked back at me and said, "Why would you be on the phone with a boy that late??" She looked up again and bald that fist back up. She started to talk with that hand as she moved it up and down. She said, "And you snuck behind my…"

She took another deep breath, unbald her fist, looked at me sternly and said, "Camille, you are not allowed to be a girlfriend, talk, speak, date, or keep up with this boy! You already sneakin and getting in trouble for this boy and you just met him! I could not imagine if he stayed around. This stops today! Let me find out you still have ties with this boy and bein sneaky after this, I'ma wear yo a** out! You understand me?!"

I answered, "Yes ma'am." I knew my mom was mad, but I had no idea she was this mad. I admit, I was scared. I didn't know what the future would hold. Since Shaun lives in Miami now, I knew it wouldn't be long before we both crossed paths again. I also knew if he didn't hear from me soon, he would start to follow our updates again to catch me in person.

Something had to be done, but what? I side eyed my mom as I watched her leave my room in route to hers. I reached my hand down in my back pocket. I kept my eyes on the hallway to be sure she didn't circle back around. Once I heard her room door close, I stopped looking at the hallway. I looked down at my hand as I took it out of my pocket, pulling out a new piece of paper with Shaun's number written on it.

Chapter 8

Clever

After the night I had, I knew I had to be very careful with my situation. Once the week started, it was back to work for us. We were all in homeschool for the time being. We would do our schooling around our work. Most of the time we would be able to do a lot of our schooling, if not all of it, in the morning time before we had any work.

But other times we would be interrupted and have to finish our work later in the day. Like we would start our work and about 30 minutes in we would have a photoshoot. Sometimes we would have an interview for a magazine or a meeting about an appearance. I hated those days when I had to finish my schooling late at night. I wanted to get it over with during the morning.

Either way it went, our parents succeeded majorly this time with occupying our time. Me and my cousins had a lot of fun times with this whole singing thing. But it did not change the fact that we ultimately did not want to do it. We just wanted to be free and do things other kids were able to do. But we never could because of who our parents were.

We really couldn't do it now, being that we were forced into fame. Some time went on. We booked shows, tons of photoshoots, we wrote and sung more songs, we also shot a lot more music videos for our songs. Our moms wrote some songs for us too. We were able to complete our first album which contained mostly songs me and cousins wrote.

Our parents told us we were really good at writing songs just like they were. So they allowed us to write our songs and go over the songs with them, and together we determined if the songs would make the cut for the album. We released a few music videos during this time and a few more songs.

We gained a lot more fans. During these times we were not allowed to do any interviews. Our moms knew the interviewers would try to pressure us into telling them who our parents were. They just didn't see any point of that, so they stayed clear of it. Other than that, we were everywhere!

We even appeared on some popular tv shows as ourselves.

The tv shows where the characters would be so happy that they got us to come to their house, or to their party, and are happy because the people who bullied them got to see that the person knew us and was our friend. Most shows were like that. We had fun doing appearances on tv shows. It got us a lot more publicity, they turned us into actors.

So now people would refer to us as singers/songwriters/actresses. We didn't even ask for that, when people would ask us what we were we would say singers. It's safe to say we blew up and we blew up fast! People loved us and everything we did. They started to ask when we would have our own tour. It all happened so fast.

One day we're somewhat normal and no one knows us, and now BAM! Everyone knows us and wants to meet us.

We weren't quite ready to host our own tour, but we went to the top of the ladder almost instantly and it wasn't because of our parents. Well, it was because they made us do it and they're our managers, but it wasn't because of their fame. Our moms saw that we were able to rise to the top on our own. They were proud and impressed.

Since we were doing so well without the world knowing they were our moms, our moms were not as concerned if people found out we were their kids. It wasn't something that any of us would blurt out, but if the truth was revealed no one would be upset. This helped us all to calm down a lot. For once in our life we didn't feel like we had to walk on eggshells around our parents careers.

Although we couldn't do interviews for the time being, our parents still did them. One in particular sparked a lot of people's interest. The interviewer asked questions about them and upcoming projects per usual. Everything was going well, but then the interviewer threw a curve ball at them at the end of the interview.

Kind of like how they did us on our first interview. But this interviewer asked, "So what do ya'll think of Angelic?" Our moms were shocked, but they knew how to play it. They acted as if the subject didn't startle them. In reality, they all paused for a split second and looked at each other quickly. My mom had her hand on the side of her neck as she drug her hand downward with a bit of pressure.

She looked over at her sisters as she did this. Latonya said, “They’re really talented.” They all agreed by saying, “Yeeah.” My mom smiled and said, “They’re so cute.” They all agreed again saying, “Yeah, they’re cute.” Then the host said, “Have you ever worked with them?” They didn’t want to say much so they answered, “No.” The host said, “So do you plan to work with them?”

Our moms looked confused. Beonca said, “What do you mean? We’re all singers but they’re kids. Our music is a bit different from theirs.” They all laughed. Then the host said, “Right, right. But I mean like do a show together. Like they were on Alexi’s tour, we know you’re familiar with her.

They appeared in other shows with other adult artists. They did their thing, and the adults did theirs."

My mama said, "Oh okay, I mean there hasn't been any talk about that. So we wouldn't know the answer to that." The host said, "Man! That would be epic! Dynasty Chosen and Angelic in the same show or on the same tour! It's crazy Alexi had the pleasure of having them on her tour, but you ladies have never crossed paths?? They're your freakin twins!"

The host was all smiles, she was excited. Our mamas said, "What?!" The host said, "You have mini's running around with your faces and you haven't come in contact??" The host laughed again and said, "That's crazy! The girls of Angelic look just like you all and the twins looks just like Trinity. Do you not see it??"

Our moms played it off and laughed a bit. Then my mom rubbed her hands together as she leaned inward toward her sisters. Then she said, "We hear it all the time, but we haven't analyzed it. I mean they say everyone has a twin. Maybe they are our twins in kid form." They all laughed again. Soon the interview ended.

They were so happy to leave that interview. During all this time of course my best friend Que caught wind of us. She was in complete shock when she first saw us on tv. She had no warning, she just happened to be watching tv and saw us singing. She stood there with her mouth wide open for about 5 minutes straight. Her mom was concerned. The last time Que saw me was the Summer before, just before we went back to Chicago.

We were 9 years old then. She had no idea where I went. All she knew was that I did not show up to dance class for the summer session that year. Well I guess now she knew why. She felt a few different ways. We always exchanged birthday gifts during the summer dance session. I had a feeling she brought a gift for me, but me not showing up probably crushed her.

Her mama waited until the show cut to a commercial to ask Que, "Shaquavia, are you okay?" Que whispered, "So that's what happened. Camille, why didn't you tell me?" This whole time Que was facing the tv. Her back was turned to her mom. Her mom said, "What'd you say?" Que turned to her mom quickly with a face full of tears. Her mom looked at her in concern for a few seconds.

Then Que covered her eyes and ran away crying out loud. Her mom took a deep breath and batted her eyes a bit as she got up fast to go after her. She found Que in her room crying in her pillow. Her mom said, "I'm sorry baby, everything will be okay." Que turned to her mom and said, "The last time I saw her she said she'll see me next summer. I went to dance class, and she wasn't there."

Her mom said, "Aw baby, I'm sure it wasn't in Camille's hands. She's a kid just like you, she has to do what her parents say." Que said, "Then why wouldn't she tell me?" Her mom said, "Maybe she didn't know." Que thought for a second and then said, “And now my birthday is almost here. She never could make it to my parties. All we had was the Summer and now I can’t look forward to that either.”

Her mom felt bad and said, “I’m sorry baby. We’ll make sure you enjoy your birthday.” Que said, “Now she’s famous! I’ll probably never see her again.” Her mom said, “Don’t say that.” Que said, “Seriously. I think Camille has forgotten about me.” Her mom said, “Que…” Que cut her off and said, “No, it’s okay. The best thing would be for me to move on….” She took a deep breath and said, “And forget this ever happened, all of it.”

She shook her in a no motion as she said that last sentence. Her mom didn’t know what to do or how to response. Que got up to walk to a different part of the house. When she got up, she said, "I'm fine Ma. Really, I am." Then she left out the room. Her mom just sat there taking another deep breath. Que didn't mention a thing about it after that day.

But her mom did notice how Que would sit in front of the tv for hours on end. She would be multi-tasking as she watched the tv. Like she would be playing with her toys without looking at her toys, because her eyes were glued to the tv. This wasn't the most concerning part. The things she would watch is what made her mom's concerns grow.

Que would watch a channel that we would pop up on. Whether we were singing, acting, or being interviewed at a show. She would watch our videos all the way through with what seemed like no emotion at all. But she seemed invested as she watched us. Her mom noticed that she would only be stuck on the tv whenever she saw me and my cousins on it.

Once the show, interview, or videos were over, Que would start doing what she was doing before we came on the tv like nothing happened. Her mom asked her once, “Que, you okay?” Que looked at her confused, smiled, and said, “Yes, I’m fine, why you asked me that??” Since Que’s response was so nonchalant, her mom decided to not ask her about it anymore.

Que acted this way for the longest. During these times we were still performing and doing everything we normally would for work. On the day of Que’s birthday which was also her birthday party, she had a bunch of weird requests. For example, Que would not let anyone turn the tv off or change the channel. No one knew what she was watching, because different shows that had nothing to do with each other were playing one after another.

The reason it was known that she didn't want the tv off, was because when her mom tried to turn it off during the party Que yelled, "No Mommie please don't!" Her mom looked at her for a few seconds and so did her party guests. That's when her mom realized she was heavily affected by this whole situation. Her mom wanted to console her.

But Que wouldn't allow herself to be consoled by anyone since I missed summer dance class, and since she found out I was famous. During a portion of her party when everyone was playing games, they noticed Que was missing. The party went to go find her. When they did, she was in the living room watching tv. I mean she was glued to it. They noticed she was watching an interview we did.

Her mom was the only one that knew what was going on. She took a deep breath as she picked up the remote. She pointed it at the tv and said, “Que, no this is…we can’t do this.” Que gasped as she stood up fast and said, “Mommie no please!” Que was reaching for the remote as she whined. Her mom turned the tv off and Que started to cry instantly.

Her mom immediately hugged her and held her tightly. Some of her guests said, “What’s wrong with Que??” Her mom said, “She’ll be okay. It’s time to play games and Que wants to watch tv." One girl said, "It's okay, we love Angelic! We can sit and watch it with her. We don't have to play games. She's the birthday girl!" The other guests agreed and said, "Yeah!"

The same girl then said, "She deserves everything she wants, and we'll give that to her." Que looked at the girl and said, "I wish you could." Then she looked up at her mom still crying and said, "This is the only way I can see her now, so I wana watch. I miss her Mommie. I want my best friend!" The guests looked confused.

Another girl asked, "What is she talkin about??" Que said, "My best friend! Camille is my best friend, and now I can only see her on tv. I miss her!" The girl looked around sarcastically and shocked as she took a deep breath. None of them knew what to think. Then the girl pointed at Que and said, "So, you're saying that Camille from Angelic is your best friend??"

She pointed to the tv when she said my name and then she pointed back at Que. Que looked at her and said, "Yes!" It was quiet for a second, then some of the guests burst out laughing. Que looked at them so confused and said, "You don't have to believe me! She is my best friend, and I rather her be here than having fake people like ya'll here to celebrate my birthday!"

Everyone in that room gasped so loud including her mom. But Que was only talking to the people that laughed at her, not all of them laughed. It was more that didn't laugh than there were that laughed. So they didn't take offense to it. The girls that laughed did as they should have. Que stormed off to the next room right after that.

Her mom told the girls, "Que is having a hard time today. Let's please try and make her day better, okay?" They all shook their heads yes in agreement. Que's mom went after her. After talking to Que for about 5 minutes, her mom was able to convince her to come out and at least watch the other guests play games.

Soon Que got up and started to play some games herself. Her mom was happy to see her smiling and having fun again. Sometime after, it was time for presents. You can tell Que still had a lot on her mind, but she was trying to enjoy herself. She had such a humble smile on her face. Que thanked everyone for the gifts. After the last gift, her auntie said, "Okay time to sing happy birthday."

Right after she said that Que's mom said, "Wait! There's one more gift." Que was surprised and so were her guests. Que looked at her mom and then looked around wondering where her gift was. Then her mom pointed towards a door and said, "Ask her Auntie to bring her gift please?" When she said that, Que looked back at her cake as she patiently waited.

The door opened and everyone gasped and said, "Oh my gosh!" Some of the girls let out a quick scream before covering their mouths. Que's back was turned towards that door. She figured she must've got a good present. Her mom said, "Que, happy birthday baby!" Then she held up her hand in the direction of the door. Que turned around. Her eyes got so big, she gasped, and immediately got up.

She covered her mouth and her eyes filled up with tears. She yelled, "Camille!" I smiled and covered my mouth with teary eyes. We were a distance away from each other. We both took off running towards each other until we hugged each other. Que was crying so hard, she made me cry. I wasn't crying as hard, but I was so happy to see her again.

Everyone said, "Awwwww." There were so many flashes from people's cameras. When Que loosened up her hug, she looked at me and said, "You came, you made it to one of my parties." She covered her mouth and started crying again. I hugged her more and said, “Yes, I’m here. I’m so happy I was able to come.” Then her mom came up and said, “Camille, thank you so much for coming.”

I looked at her as she hugged me. Then I said, “Thank you for inviting me.” Que gasped and said, “Mommie, how did you invite her??” Her mom said, “I still had the number for her assistant. I saw how sad you were, and I wanted ya’ll to reunite. So I called and explained the situation. It was no surprise at all that Camille was just as happy to have found you again.”

Que looked at me and said, “You spoke to my mom??” I smiled and said, “No, she spoke to our assistant, and the assistant spoke to my mom, and my mom spoke to me.” We all laughed. I said, “Normally this type of stuff is impossible, but when my mom heard it was for you, she made it happen." Que smiled and said, "Wow! I haven't met your mom yet, but she is amazing!"

I grabbed her hand and said, "Don't worry, you will soon." Que said, "Can you please tell her thank you?" I smiled and said, "I will." At that time Que started to hug my cousins and saying hi to them. Then her mom said, "You girls ready for the party??" We smiled and said, "Yes." She said, "Come on." We followed her to the guests.

We had security and a few assistants with us in order for us to be at the party. Once we got to the people at the party, they were all smiling. Que's mom introduced us to them. When we said hi to them they went crazy. Que asked me to sit next to her in front of her cake. She said it was time to sing happy birthday. I said, “Wait, we have gifts for you too.” Que’s mouth dropped.

Everyone else was surprised as well. At that time, the assistants pulled out the gifts we each had for Que and handed them to us. Que was so surprised to get a gift from each of us. She jumped up and hugged every one of us. Her guests laughed. Then she sat down with the biggest smile on her face and started to opened them.

She opened gifts from my cousins first. Every time she opened a gift her and everyone else gasped. When we shop, we just shop and get what we want. We don’t pay much attention to the price. So all of our gifts were really expensive gifts. But we didn’t look at it that way. It was normal to us, it always has been. But Que, her mom, and her guests were blown away.

Once she opened my gift, I told her to unzip this small part on it. When she did, she covered her mouth, gasped, and immediately hugged me. She cried a bit too. She looked back down at it and said, "This is the best gift I've gotten today." It was a piece of paper with my number on it that said, we will always be connected now. She was so happy that I wasn't going to lose contact with her anymore.

She turned to her mom and said, "Mommie this is the best birthday ever, thank you." Her mom said, "Aww baby, you're welcome." She looked at me and said, "Camille, can I trouble you all to give Que a special happy birthday…she had a rough day." I looked at Que sympathetically. Then I stood up and said, "I must say Que, I am honored to be here with you on your birthday." I turned to the crowd and continued, "No one here knows but, Que and I have been best friends since the age of 7. We met during our summer dance classes…"

Everyone was listening. The girls that laughed at her were still throwing shade with their facials, because they were mad she was telling the truth. The girl who asked her about it was the biggest Angelic fan there. Then I continued, "Every year we would see each other and we would exchange gifts. That was the only time we were able to see each other, because during the year I lived out of state…"

I slightly turned towards Que and said, "Unfortunately, this Summer I wasn't able to attend dance classes due to the things that made me who I am now." Everyone chuckled including us. Then I said, "And Que for that I'm sorry. I thought about you every day and I am honored to be here at your party celebrating with you. I love you." She smiled and said, "I love you too."

At that moment I started to sing happy birthday to her, and my cousins joined in shortly after. Que cried and smiled. She had her mouth covered by her hand the whole time. Everyone was recording us. At the end, everyone clapped. Que got up and we all group hugged her. Everyone got a lot of good pictures of us that day. After we sung, everyone sung happy birthday to her the regular way and so did we.

After everyone sung happy birthday, we took some time to take pictures with all the guests. Then we started to play games and do things with Que and her guests. They were all so happy, they couldn't believe they were at a party with Angelic and playing games with them. We had a lot of fun too. We never got a chance to go to a birthday party outside our family, so we were just as happy as they were.

We were glad we were allowed to stay until the end of the party. We had brief moments where it would just be us and Que doing something together. Her guests were watching us during these times. Like at one point we were sitting on the couch, and I had Que's phone. My cousins and Que were all looking at what I was doing on her phone, which was calling myself.

I did that so I can have her number in my phone. The girls didn't know what we were doing. Shortly after, Que's mom had everybody take a picture together. After the picture was taken everybody was walking away. Then Que's mom stopped me and my cousins and said, "Camille, we wana get you girls with Que."

We said, "Okay." So we stayed there. Some of the other girls were not thrilled. When I say some of them, I mean the same girls that laughed at Que. After we were done with the pictures, I told Que I had to use the bathroom. So I left my cousins there with Que. I had to pass by the group of girls on my way to the bathroom.

I wasn't paying attention to them. They were smiling as I passed by them. There were more people walking back and forth in that area at that time too. I wasn't that close to them, but I guess I was close enough. They looked star struck. Right after I passed by them, I heard them whispering. I didn't stay in the bathroom for too long.

I came out with the intention of rushing back to my cousins and Que. But I was stopped in my tracks by the laughter and gossip I heard from the same group of girls. When I first came out, I heard them laughing hard and still whispering. They couldn't see me because I was standing on the wall in the hallway, they were beyond the wall near the dining room.

I walked closer to the end of the hallway, and I just stood there to listen. I had no idea what was going on. Que never told me what they said to her. The main girl who said something to Que earlier that day, was the one talking at that moment. She laughed at first and said, "I think this is all an act. You can pay celebrities for appearances like this. I think they paid Angelic to come out here."

I was shocked. But not as shocked as I was when she said, "They must've paid Camille a pretty penny to act like she her best friend. You know they act too." Her friends uneasily agreed. They wanted to agree with her because they were followers. But then again, they knew they didn't agree because they liked us. Then she continued to say, "Her acting distant today and making up stories about Camille, pretending to be sad. I think it was all set up, because she knew they paid Camille to come here today."

I was shocked at what I was hearing. Then she said, "And her mama acting like Camille being here was a surprise. Saving it for last and everything. They knew what was gone happen. They lyin to us. They probably gave Camille a script to follow to act like they know each other. They made her give a speech and everything saying that's her best friend."

Now that pissed me off. Right after that, I hurried and walked back past them. I didn't look at them. I looked normal as if nothing happened. We've been trained all our lives to act like everything was okay in the public's eye. When I got by my cousins, I didn't stop walking. I grabbed Carmen's arm and told them, "Come here real quick ya'll. Que you too."

They followed me immediately without question. I led them to the backyard and of course security followed us. The girls saw when I grabbed Carmen and they saw when they all followed me. But they didn't see when I told them to come here. We asked security to give us a minute. So they stood by the back door while we all talked in the middle of the backyard.

Once we were at a good distance away from security, Alisha said, "What's up Camille?" I said, "Que, what type of people you invited to yo party??" Que looked confused, but my cousins knew something wasn't right. My cousins immediately said, "What happened??" I told them everything I heard. I was also able to tell them who said what and how they reacted to what was being said.

My cousins let out a deep breath. Que was shocked as she softly said, “What??” I said, “Yeah. They pissed me off. Normally I would say something, but I can’t because of who I am. I would be in so much trouble with my mama if I did. Those are not your friends.” Que couldn’t believe they said all that. Her feelings were hurt, which upset me more.

Then she got mad as she thought about it more. She said, “I’ma say something right now!” We all said, “No!” Then we tried to calm her down by saying, “Shh.” But that all startled security. Security said, “Ya’ll ladies alright??” We turned to them and said, “Yes, we’re fine.” They thought we were getting into it with Que or something. She calmed down after witnessing how quick security jumped to our defense.

Then she took a deep breath and said, "Then what do I do? They started with me earlier…" She then explained to us what happened earlier and what they did. I was devastated. I said, "That's why you had a hard time! I'm so sorry Que. Me not showing up to dance this Summer was completely out of my control."

Que said, "I know. It's okay. What's not okay is keeping these so-called friends around me." I said, "Yes, something has to be done and something will be done…do you have any of the pictures we all used to take in dance class?" Que said, "Yeah, I have all of'em." I said, "Good! Go get'em and we'll be in there in a minute." She said, "Okay." Then she took off running.

After she went in the house, my cousins looked at me and they all looked pissed. I said, "I know, I know." Cashae said, "What that girl said about you? About us??" Alicia said, "For real." Carmen said, "We never fought anybody before, but for obvious reasons I have a lot of tension to release, and this seems like the perfect time to release it."

I corrected her by saying, "Perfect situation, wrong timing. Calm yo nerves." She sucked her teeth, let out a deep breath, and rolled her eyes, as she looked the other way with her arms crossed. At that time I pulled out my phone. My cousins, including Carmen, looked at me. Carmen did a double take and said, "What are you doing?" As I put the phone to my ear, I put the palm of my hand up and said, "Wait a minute, you'll see."

My cousins got quiet. Then they heard me say, "Mommie?" They all looked at me crazy. They had no idea why I was calling my mama. Back in the house, Que was going through her things as fast as she could. She found all the pictures we would randomly take during our summer dance classes. She still wasn't sure why I told her to get them.

Once she had all of them, she hid them under her clothes and headed back out of her room. As she walked out of her room, we were just walking back in the house. She was relieved to see us coming back in. We were just as relieved to see her. As she started to run to us, the same girl said, "Oh my gosh, why don't she leave them alone? She don't think she gettin on they nerves?? She paid them, they did they job."

Her friends started to laugh again. Que paused for a second and took a deep breath while she rolled her eyes. They couldn't tell she heard them because her back was turned to them. It just seemed like she stopped because someone was walking past her. But we saw her face. We didn't know what happened, but we knew something did.

After pausing she rushed to us. As she got to me, she handed me the pictures. Carmen looked at her and said, "What's wrong? They said something to you again?" Que said, "Yeah." Then she whispered to us what she heard the girl say. That bothered us, but we had to have a poker face on. We all looked down at the pictures and took a deep breath instead.

As we did that, Cashae said, "She gone get smacked, she look like she bout my age." Que shook her head in a yes motion and said, "She is." We had to say all this with a straight face. It's so hard to be that mad with a straight face, but we were taught to do that. We were always able to express our anger and emotions once we got out of the public's eye. We couldn't wait to get home to do just that.

Not too long after, Que's mom was curious as to what we were looking at. So she came over to us and asked. Then she saw the pictures and loudly said, "AWWW! NOW THAT'S CUTE!" Everybody started to pay attention. Then she smiled and asked, "YA'LL KEPT THESE ALL THESE YEARS??" We all smiled. Me and Que shook our heads yes. Que answered, "Yes."

It wasn't long before everybody wanted to know what we were looking at. When that girl heard Que's mom say ya'll kept these for this long, she made another comment. She said, "Oh great, another act to make us believe she really know them. They need to give it up, it's obvious they booked them." Her friends laughed again. Only this time one of Que's real friends walked up and heard her. She looked at them confused but with a slight grin.

Then she said, "Do ya'll know how hard it is to even book Angelic for an interview?? What make ya'll think they can get booked for a party? Ya'll sound dumb." All the girl did was let out a deep breath and roll her eyes. Her little entourage was looking lost not knowing what to follow next. At this point they were all looking at us and Que's mom.

Que's mom said, "Hold on, hold on, I have a slide!" She quickly set up a projector. Then she said, "Oh my gosh I'm so happy we have these." She was so excited to show the pictures. Before she played the slide, she said, "As you all know, Que and her friends whom you know as Angelic, met years ago in dance class. They were babies…well smaller babies."

Everyone laughed and we did too. That girl who was hating rolled her eyes and said, "Yeah, right. I wonder how they gone pull this one off." Then Que's mom said, "So I would like to share these photos with you all in honor of the birthday girl." Her guests cheered. Then she started to play the slides. It was nice to go down memory lane with Que.

It had been so long since we saw each other. This was the first time we were able to attend a public birthday party and without our moms! So this was the icing on the cake for us. We were able to see photos of us together during class, after class, before class, and during breaks. We had pictures of all of us together, and we had some with just me and Que or my cousins and Que.

My cousins even took some pictures with her by themselves. There was one with only her and Carmen. That picture was cute and funny, because they were clowning in it but were having so much fun. No one had ever seen us that small before, but we didn't mind. Even after seeing these slides, that one girl still had something to say.

She whispered, "It's probably photoshopped. They went all out for this party." Her little followers giggled quietly. Right after that, Que's mom played a video of us from dance class. She didn't record the video, it was recorded in class. We were on a break, and we all were clowning around. Me and Que even said each other's names in the video. It was so cute.

Then we all practiced a piece of the dance from class. At the end we hugged each other, and Que said, "This is my best friend, Camille." I said, "And this is my best friend, Shaquavia." Que had me in a neck hug while we said this, and we both were laughing. When I tell you that girl's mouth dropped! She let out a gasp so loud, people around her looked back at her to check on her. Everyone else was laughing and saying, "Aww."

Then her mom showed a video of Que being at my house for the first time. It was all of our first sleepover. Me and my cousins mouths dropped as we smiled. We didn't know she had that video. The way the camera was positioned, it didn't show my room much. It showed part of the wall behind us and some of the side of my bed, because we were at the foot of my bed.

We had one arm over each other's shoulder, and we were stepping with our legs bent. We were laughing and singing something like a theme song for a kids show. Then we looked at the camera and I said, "Sleepover!" Que repeated, "Sleepover!" Then we both said, "Our first sleepover!" We looked at each other and started laughing. You could hear my cousins laughing in the room. Next thing you see is me pointing behind the camera and saying, "Carmen turn that off."

Then the video stopped playing. Everybody in the room was laughing, except that girl. Then the last picture came up and it was a picture of me, Que, and my cousins from that same night. We put the phone on a timer and posed. It was a cute picture. Some of us had our peace sign with duck lips, some had a big smile with our eyes closed, some had a silly face on.

But overall you could see and feel the authenticity within the picture. Anyone who had eyes could tell there was so much love and fun in that picture. After that, that girl could not say anything else about them booking us. She just had to accept the fact that we really knew Que and that me and Que were best friends. During that last picture the words Happy Birthday Que came up on it.

We all said, “Awww.” We realized at that point, her mom had put that slide together for her before her birthday. She probably didn’t play it because of how sad Que was. But since we were there, and Que wasn’t sad anymore she played it. Que shed a few tears. I gave her a hug and of course everyone was saying aww again. Right after, Que’s mom sent her back to her room to put the pictures back.

That gave me and my cousins an opportunity to speak to her mom. When she came back out, her mom told her, “Que I’ll hand out the candy bags before everyone leaves.” Que looked sad and said, “It’s over??” Her mom said, “Yes baby, we gone wrap it up.” Que looked so sad. Her mom announced she was gonna hand out the candy bags, so everybody was waiting. Her mom gave us our bags first.

She said, “Camille and her cousins have to go, but Camille has another gift for you.” Everybody’s head turned and they got quiet. Que was excited as she said, “Another gift?? But you already gave me my gift.” I said, “Yep, one more.” Que said, “Oh wait!” She ran to her room. She came back in under a minute holding a gift bag. She handed it to me and said, “I almost forgot. I held on to your gift from this summer.”

I smiled and said, “Aww, thank you.” We gave each other a hug. She said, “You’re welcome. What were you saying?” I said, “Oh, you’re coming with us. We’re gonna have a sleepover like we used to!” She gasped and her eyes got so big. She turned to her mom and said, “I’m going to her house again?!” Her mom smiled and said, “Yes.” Que said, “Yes!” We both started to jump up and down as we held each other’s arms.

Everyone thought it was the cutest thing. We were genuinely happy. That girl knew everything was real at this point. Que said, “Wait, we’re leaving now?!” We said, “Yeah.” She said, “I have to pack my clothes!” I waved my hand like, “No problem." Then I said, "Girl, we'll go shopping." She let out a screech as she smiled and said, "Okay!" Que's mom said, "Say bye to your guests."

Que turned to everyone and said, "Thank you all for coming." She was smiling and had her hands clutched together in front of her chest as she continued, "Today has turned out to be one of the best days of my life! I'll always remember this birthday." Her mom then said, "Alright ya'll girls have fun." We said, "Thank you." On the way out me and my cousins said our goodbyes to everyone, and told them it was nice to meet them.

They watched as we all got in the suv. They came out in the yard just to watch us get in there. Then we drove off. Que's mom was so happy her birthday turned out so well. We were so excited on the ride home we forgot about that girl at the party. When we pulled up, Que was in awe as she looked at the house.

When we got out the car, she asked, “This is your house?” I said, “Well it’s my grandma’s house, but I live here for now. We’re supposed to move soon.” She looked at me quick and said, “Again?!” I laughed a little and said, “We’ll still be in this city. We not moving out of state again.” She held her chest and took a breath of relief. Then she said, “Oh okay good.”

We went in the house. Once we got to my room, we started to unwind a little bit. Que was so happy to be there, and we were so happy to have her there. We started to talk about the party and got our frustrations out about that girl. We felt a lot better.

We started to get ready for bed. We didn't plan to go to sleep, but we just wanted to get in our pj's.

My mom had got some clothes for Que for that night, after I called her to ask if Que can come over. Que was surprised I had her some clothes. After we took our showers and got in our pjs, we sat down in my room to have girl talk and chill. We didn't jump into anything heavy, because we never spoke about really personal things in front of Que before. But she did keep it a secret that the assistant wasn't our mom for a while.

I knew that because she told me her mom thought the assistant was my mom. We felt we could trust her, but we were moving slow with it. Only because it was new to us to speak personal around her. We all spoke about some stuff and not too long after, Que mention a boy she go with. We were all shocked she had a boyfriend too. She was in the same boat as us, her mom didn't know.

We knew for sure we could talk around her now. We trusted she wouldn't tell anyone, especially after experiencing some of the people she invited to her party. Plus she said she didn't trust anyone but us. She told us whatever we tell her or say around her is safe with her. She don't talk to anyone about things we tell her. She understood we had to be discreet.

As we pulled out the snacks, Alicia rubbed her ear as she looked upward and said, "You know, I been wondering where Shaun went. He haven't popped up lately." Without looking up at her, still looking down trying to open some snacks, I answered, “He’s home now, but he been busy in the studio.” My cousins got quiet for a few seconds. They all were staring at me with the same look on their faces.

They didn’t know what to think and they were confused. Then I heard Carmen very curiously say, “Camille, how did you know that?”

I paused and then looked up at her slowly like I saw a ghost.

Chapter 9

Keep Quiet

Everyone was still waiting for my answer. The room was so quiet you could hear a pen drop. I stared at all of my cousins as I slowly put a chip in my mouth and slowly bit down on it. Que was curious. She broke the silence and asked, "Who is Shaun??"

Without looking at her Carmen answered, "Her boyfriend." Que looked surprised as she lowly said, "OH." Carmen was looking at me the entire time. Then she said, "Camille??" I said, "Huh?" She sarcastically said, "Huh??" Then she asked again,

"How did you know that??" I let out a quick chuckle.

Alisha smiled at me and asked, "What did you do?" I smiled as I looked up to the ceiling, trying not to laugh. Then I blurted out, "Okay fine, I talked to him." They all smiled as they said things like, "OOOOH!" and "AHHHH!" Then we all started laughing. Cashae said, "Camille!"

I smiled and said, "What?! Ya'll told me if I'ma do it be careful. Soooo, I didn't tell anybody." Carmen pointed her finger and sassily said, "No, you be careful with yo mama not with us." She point towards the door when she said yo mama, then she pointed to herself when she said with us.

We all laughed again. Carmen then smiled still talking with her hands and said, "We gotta know these things, Camille. We gone be the ones that help each other out, when things get rough or if somebody get caught." Everyone including Que agreed.

I smiled and said, "You right. Alright. No secrets between us, and whatever goes on between us does not leave our circle…agreed?" I put my fist forward in the middle of us. They all smiled at each other and then put their fists together with mine and said, "Agreed."

We put our fists down. Almost immediately after, I said, "Good! Because I've been dying to tell somebody…he's really my boyfriend! Like, I like this boy so much. I like him more and more every day." They were so shocked to hear me confess this, because I've never admitted to liking a boy and in detail like that before.

They were happy for me. They smiled really big as I said this to them. Cashae smiled and whispered, "Shh, girl be quiet before yo mama hear you!" I covered my mouth and said, "Oh!" Que squinted at me and said, "Wait, yo mama here??" She was talking with her hands. She had both her pointer fingers pointed circling each other when she said that.

We all paused. I took a deep breath and said, "Yes, my mama here." She wasn't supposed to know that, and we all knew that. My mama told me she could come over, but she told us not to tell her she was there. This was because of the whole hiding they had kids thing.

Although we slipped, we knew Que wouldn't say anything. Even if she told her mom, she still wouldn't know who my mom was. Que said, "How come I didn't see her yet?" My cousins were looking on edge. I said, "She's not ready to expose herself to the public yet."

My cousins were so relieved I was able to explain it that well and off the top of my head. Que understood and said, "Oh! Okay, I understand." Cashae said, "Now back to you Camille…how did you talk to Shaun??" Alisha said, "Right! You were so scared to touch yo phone after you got in trouble about him last time."

Que looked at me and said, "You got in trouble?" My cousins filled Que in about what happened from the time I met Shaun until present.

Then Alicia said, “So not too long ago, Camille’s mom found the letter he gave her at the meet and greet. After we left, she confronted Camille about it. Then she found out Camille called him off the house phone. Her mama thought she was being sneaky, and Camille got in trouble.”

Que said, “Oh my gosh, that’s a lot. How much trouble you think you in?” Carmen said, “Let’s just say my auntie told Camille, if she find out she still have communication with him, she gone wear her behind out…but she didn’t use the word behind.” I took a deep breath and moved my hand up and down as I said, “Yeah.”

Que was so shocked. She looked at me and said, “Camille you bold.” I put my hand over my chest and said, “Me??” Que said, “If my mama said that to me, I would be terrified." I said, "I am. But I just can't seem to let him go. So we just had to find another solution…they doin it too!"

I was talking about my cousins when I said we. Que smiled and said, "I rather act like I'm not talking to a boy. My mama don't know about me dating." Carmen said, "It's not that easy for us. Our mamas know everything. Which is why we recently decided to keep each others secrets. Hopefully we do a good job of that."

Cashae was zoned in on me. She said, "Camille, you still never told us how you spoke to him." I turned to Que quickly and said, "I'm sorry Que…" They all were confused. Que said, "Why you sayin sorry??" I said, "I used your phone to call him." All their mouths dropped. My cousins started to talk at the same time.

They were saying, "Camille!" and "Why you did that??" They also said, "What if she get in trouble??" They were smiling when they said these things. Que was smiling too. I said, "I'm sorry. During the party I borrowed her phone and called him." My cousins were confused. Alisha asked, "When?? Because we were together."

I said, "I took it in the bathroom with me. I actually had her phone more than she did at the party. I guess she forgot about it." Cashae said, "That explains why you took so long!" Alicia said, "Oh I get it. Your mom can never check her call log." Carmen nodded her head in a yes motion as she said, "That was smart. I like it."

Alisha asked Que, “Would you get in trouble if yo mama found that on yo phone?” Que said, “No, my mama don’t check my phone.” We all gasped and stared at her. The room was like crickets in the air. Then she said, “Ya’ll mamas check ya’ll phones??” We all answered at the same time, “Yes! All the time!”

We were so caught up in the moment we didn’t realize how loud we were. A few seconds later my phone rung. Next thing you know, I was shushing my cousins as I picked up the phone. They all got quiet and was looking scared. I answered and said, “Hello?” Then I said, “Sorry Mommie.”

All of their demeanors sunk. Except Que, she was just looking concerned. Then I said, “Okay, goodnight.” When I hung up, I whispered, “Oh my gosh, how did she hear us? I hope she didn't hear what we said." Cashae asked, "What she said?" I told them, "She said to go to bed because we gotta get up early."

Alisha said, "Oh yeah! I forgot." Que said, "What's happening in the morning?" I said, "We takin you out for your birthday." Her mouth dropped, she was not expecting that. I continued by saying, "We're going shopping, we're getting something to eat, and my mom arranged for us to have a night out at the theme park."

Que's face lit up. She was so excited. She said, "Wow! Thank ya'll so much. I really appreciate it. Ya'll the best. I love ya'll man." We smiled and said, "Aww, we love you too." Then my phone rung again. My cousins got scared. Alicia whispered, “Dang! Yo mama calling again??” I looked at it and said, “No.”

I picked up and said, “Hello?” Then I said, “Heyy, huh?? You here?? For real??” There was a pause and then I said, “Why you didn’t tell me? Can I come in your room? …okay.” I hung up. My cousins asked, “Who was that?” I was still in shock. My face lit up. I smiled as I said, “Auntie Trice, she here!”

My cousins got excited and said, “For real?! Why she didn’t say anything?” I said, “I don’t know, but I’ma go see her. Ya’ll stay here with Que.” Cashae said, “We wana see her too.” So I said, “Okay we’ll go in two groups.” Me, Carmen, and Cashae went first. We were so happy to see her as she was to see us.

We gave her hugs and talked for a minute. She knew I had a friend over too. I'm sure my mom warned all of them because my grandma was there too, and we didn't see her at all. That was rare if that happened. I asked Auntie Trice, "Where you been?? We haven't seen you in so long!"

Auntie Trice smiled, she had the prettiest smile. Then she said, "I've been taking care of a lot of things Camille. It takes so much out of me. Ya'll have no idea." I said, "I understand. Well the twins coming in here next, but after that get some rest Auntie." She chuckled and said, "Ya'll too. I can hear ya'll in there."

We laughed and said, "Okay, sorry." Then we left out. When we got back to the room, Alisha and Alicia went to see her. I told Que, "I can't wait for you to finally meet our family. They all staying out of the limelight when it comes to us. But you'll meet them soon." Que said, "Okay."

Que was confused, but she was happy to still be invited in the house even though our family was there, and she couldn't see them. When the twins came back from Auntie Trice room, we had one last discussion before bed. I told them, "Listen, I don't wana lose Shaun's number. I've written it down twice, I don't want my mom to find the pieces of paper."

Alicia said, "So what are you gonna do?" I said, "I was thinking to assign ya'll with part of his number." They all said, "Part of his number?!" I said, "Yes, it's easier for ya'll to remember three numbers than to remember ten." So I assigned

Carmen and Cashae the first six numbers of Shaun's number, three numbers each. Then I assigned the twins with the last four.

We went over them, and they recited them. Carmen even saved the 3 numbers in her phone, she knew her mom wouldn't know what they were for. Cashae and the twins did the same thing. Carmen asked, "Wouldn't you need all of us to get the whole number? What if one of us don't respond?"

I said, "That's true. But this is only for emergencies. As a matter of fact, Que…" I took out a small piece of paper and handed it to her. Then I said, "Que, guard this with your life. Put it somewhere your mom would never find it. This is Shaun's full number. I can't give it to my cousins, because my aunties might find it and my mom saw the number before. I'm pretty sure she'll remember it or keep it on hand herself."

Que said, "Okay, I can do that." I said, "Thanks. If I ever need the number from any of ya'll, I would call or text and say number. Then you could give me the number you're assigned to. Que, I might have you call him on 3 way or something at times." They all said, "Okay." They were so shocked at how well organized I was.

Carmen looked at me admirably and said, "Camille, who is this girl? You changin." I looked at her, smiled slightly with my mouth closed and said, "So are you." She smiled at me impressed. She knew I was telling the truth, she couldn't deny it.

Alisha smiled and said, "Camille's always been a good girl." I smiled and said, "I still am…I just have a boyfriend." We went to sleep. The next day, we had so much fun. We showed Que the time of her life! She was so happy. After we went shopping, we went to dinner. Once we got back to my grandma's house, we were able to play runway with Que.

Runway was a game we made up. It's when you try on all your new outfits right after shopping. Que had a blast! She spent another night. We had breakfast and lunch the next day. We were able to watch a movie in the movie room and chill for a while before she had to go home.

Unlike all the other times, we rode with her when she was being dropped off. We had fun all the way to her house. Once we got there, we helped her take her stuff inside. She had so much stuff. Her mom said, “Oh my gosh, ya’ll spoil her!” We all laughed, her mom did too. Then we gave her mom some gifts for letting her come with us.

She was really happy. She cried and said, “Aww thank you. Ya’ll so sweet. Ya’ll didn’t have too.” She gave us a hug and then she said, “I wana get a picture of ya’ll coming back from the sleepover.” We all smiled and said, “Okay!” We all posed silly, and then regular and then cheery. She was snapping away.

After we were done, we all said our long goodbyes. Then we got back in the car to head home. Once we got back to my house, my cousins headed home too. We spoke to our moms and let them know how everything went that weekend. They were happy everything turned out great.

That night me, my cousins, and Que slept well, knowing that our secrets were safe within our circle.

Chapter 10

Revealed

Me, my cousins, and Que continued to have sleepovers and hung out whenever we could. Eventually Que met Lashae, and they bonded just like we did. We would all be together every other weekend in our down time.

Sometimes we hung out for weeks in a row. We were inseparable. Que's mom loved that for her, our moms loved it for us too. They were happy we were able to have fun with a friend and feel like normal kids for a change. Que still hadn't met my mom yet.

Some time had passed. We were still performing, making videos, and we were even doing interviews again. People grew more curious about who our parents were, but we were not giving in. Neither were our parents.

Our parents joined Auntie Trinity's tour. Alexi was on this tour as well. They were making big bucks. All of their shows were sold out. People really loved them and to have all of them on the same tour was epic! There were other artists on their tour as well, people loved them too.

That tour was lit. I can see why their shows were sold out. While they were busy touring, me and my cousins were busy performing, recording more songs, recording more videos, and doing more photoshoots. But in our downtime, we were able to do even more of what we wanted to do.

I took advantage and was able to speak to Shaun a lot more. We got even closer than we were before. I loved talking to him, he was so easy to talk to. He understood me best out of the people outside of my family. He always seemed to be in protection mode when it came to me.

I loved that most about him. I never felt that sense of protection from my dad. It was new and it was nice to have that. I never knew just how much I needed that. This drew me closer to Shaun. Auntie Trinity's tour was ending right before our birthdays. They had announced that they had a surprise for everyone at their last show.

So many people wanted to go, but the shows were sold out. A lot of people complained saying it wasn't fair. So our moms decided to allow the last portion of that show to be recorded live. This would allow everyone to see the surprise.

The people were fine with that. They anticipated the last show. So many talk show and radio show hosts were talking about it. They made it a big deal. So many people were waiting for it. Once they were done with the second from last show, the pressure was on!

Fans and viewers watched our moms closely. They didn't want to miss it. It wasn't until the day before the last performance, that our moms told us they want us there. We were shocked they wanted us there, I mean that was risky. Us being there in the back and not performing would cause suspicion.

But our moms told us not to worry about that. They also said they wanted to go somewhere after the show to celebrate the closing of their tour. They wanted us to go with them, they said it would be easier if we were at the show.

We understood. Finishing a tour was a big deal and they had been on tour for many months. We were happy to finish Alexi's tour after two months. We were happy to spend some time with our moms too. We didn't see them much during their tour.

The last day of the tour finally came. We were not supposed to ride with our moms. We were just supposed to go to the location of the show right before it was over. But because of concerns about the traffic and getting in there, we were told we would have to show up at the same time as the other artists.

We were told we had to stay there for the entire concert. We didn't want to stay the entire concert, but we were okay with it because we would be able to see our moms and Alexi. On that day we all got ready together. We got into a different car than our moms, but we all showed up to the venue at the same time.

They were able to get us in the building and in the dressing room they set up for us before anyone else saw us. The set up was comfortable. The room had places for us to lay down if we wanted to. We had a lot of things we were able to do in there too.

We mostly chilled, but we did take the opportunity to take a nap. During the show I even talked to Shaun. I called Que and she 3 way called Shaun. I told him who she was and why she called. He didn't mind. He was actually happy at how much effort I put into keeping in contact with him.

He felt like whatever it was we had between us was real. He told me, "I know we young, but I know real when I see it…and Camille, you as real as it gets. I feel like this gone be long term." I said, "Long term?" He said, "Yeah. You gone my girl forever." I smiled and chuckled a bit as I said, "Oh really?"

He smiled and said, “Yeah. I can feel it.” This whole time I was whispering while I sat on the couch in the dressing room. I had butterflies in my stomach the entire conversation. I didn’t even know what they were at the time. Que had put the phone down as soon as Shaun picked up.

She wanted to give us privacy. She told me she would check in with us every 5 minutes in case I wanted her. She did just that. When she checked in on us the next time, Shaun said, “Aye wait Que! Don’t put the phone down yet.” Que said, “Huh? What happened?” Shaun said, “I’m hearing an echo, you watching the tour too?”

Que laughed and said, “Yeah.” I was shocked that they both were watching it. Then Shaun said, “Yeah. I’m invested. I wana see what the surprise is." Que said, "Omgee, me too! They all my favorites! I just love Dynasty Chosen. I wanted to go to their concert, but my mama said I'm too young. Plus the tickets were sold out."

Shaun said, "I feel you. I love them too. Latoya my favorite." Que said, "Mine too!" I covered my mouth as it dropped. I couldn't believe my mama was my best friend's and my boyfriend's favorite out of the group. All I could think about is how could this play out. Shaun would freak out if he knew my mom already knew who he was and what he looked like.

Que would too if she found out she had been spending the night in the same house as my mama all this time. Also, knowing my mama knew her too would make her freak out. They had a full conversation with each other about our moms, not knowing we were their kids.

Que said, "If they ever have kids, their kids would be so cute." Shaun said, "Yeah they would be." I was just sitting there listening to them converse. Then music started to play, Shaun said, "Where that music coming from?" Que said, "I don't know, but that's Dynasty Chosen's song and it don't sound like a tv."

All I was thinking was uh oh. Shaun asked, "Camille, where you at? Is that yo background?" I said, "Oh yeah it is. I'm sorry." Que said, "Uh un! Where you at?!" I said, "Our managers had us doing some stuff today and we ended up at the concert." They both said, "What?!" They couldn't believe I was there.

Que said, “You are so lucky Camille!” Then she said, “Ma! Camille at the concert, and you said I was too young.” I heard her mama say, “And Camille is a superstar, they end up at places like that all the time. But they have security, something you don’t.” We all laughed a little.

Everything they were saying was all in fun. Shaun said, “You can see them?” I said, “No, we backstage.” Que said, “Did ya’ll see them at all?” I said, “We saw them getting out their car when we were pulling up.”

Que said, “I would have freaked out! Camille, you should’ve talked to them. Ya’ll never worked together before. If people found out ya’ll was in the same place, they would go crazy.” Then Que asked, “Do you know what the surprise is?” I said, “No, I didn’t even know I would end up here today.”

Shaun said, “So ya’ll not gone be able to see the concert?” Just as he said that Que said, “It’s on! I can see the tour!” This whole time they had been watching whatever was on that channel while they waited for the tour to come on. Shaun said, “Yes! I’m fina zone out a lil bit Camille.” I said, “That’s okay. I have to go anyway. Security just came in here, we have to go do some stuff.”

Que and Shaun said, “Okay, we’ll talk to you later.” I said, “Okay.” Then I hung up. Security said, “We need ya’ll by the stage.” We were confused. But we figured our moms wanted us to see part of the show from backstage. Security walked us up to the curtain where we could see the stage.

No one could see us there, but we saw our moms clearly. It was nice to see them perform in person. After they performed, the room cheered so loud. Our moms stayed on stage. Once the cheering died down, Beonca lifted her mic to her mouth and said, “We know what ya’ll waitin on, we still got that surprise for ya’ll.”

They started to cheer loudly again. They cheered so long our moms laughed. Latonya said, “This surprise is very special.” Trinity walked out on stage and said, “This surprise is well thought out and is near and dear to us.” Alexi walked out and said, “It’s been a long road for us all, but we figured it was time to share this with the world.”

Then Latoya said, “This is a big deal for us, and we want to share it with you.” Every time one of them talked the crowd cheered. They all had their own mics. Viewers were thinking all kinds of ways. But they were tuned in. We were waiting for them to tell everyone the surprise too. Everything got quiet. Then my mom said, “Ya’ll waited long enough…” She closed her eyes briefly and took a deep breath.

Then she said, “We have some birthdays coming up and we want to share them with you all.” Me and my cousins looked confused because we knew our birthdays were coming, but we didn’t know who she was referring to. We didn’t know where she was going with this either. Then she passionately said, “Please help us welcome to the stage, some people we love the most.”

They all spoke passionately. Trinity said, “Some people we cannot live without.” Alexi said, “Some people who have our hearts.” Latonya said, “Some people we’ve loved and known since birth.” Then Latoya said, “Please welcome to the stage, our mini’s, our babies…” Then they all smiled and said, “Angelic!”

We all gasped! We couldn’t believe they were doing this and now. We were stuck but we were moved by this. THE CROWD WENT WILD! While the crowd was still screaming, security told us to go on the stage. When we walked out, we were holding back tears and still looking surprised. Once the crowd saw us, they screamed even louder. We walked to our moms as they embraced us.

We also went to Alexi one at a time. To see us all together like that blew everyone's minds. They couldn't comprehend what just happened. Que and Shaun was like, "What?! Did they just say they, they parents?!" Everyone was shocked, the crowd gasped right before they cheered. They cheered and screamed for so long.

Then our moms looked at us and started to sing happy birthday to us. We cried as we smiled at them and wiped our tears. They sung slow but it sounded great! It was such a touching moment for us. It was more than just them bringing us on stage and singing to us in front of the world. It was the fact that they finally stopped hiding us and let the world know we existed.

The world knew who we were, but they didn't know who we were. It meant the world to us for our moms to do that. It bothered us for years that they decided to hide us and act as if they had no kids. But we didn't tell them that, because we always tried to make their lives easier. We knew they had us young and went through a lot.

We never wanted to add to the stress. This took a lot off our shoulders. They wiped some of our tears as they sung to us. The last line they sung was, "Happy birthday Mommie's baby, Happy birthday to you." As they finished singing, our moms hugged us, and we hugged them back so tight. Alexi walked over to me and my mom.

I turned to her and hugged her again. They both kissed me on my forehead when they was hugging me. Some people in the crowd shed tears from seeing how emotional we got on stage. Our moms even shed some tears. They could feel we were crying for more than the obvious. They knew they had to get us out of there soon. So my mama said, "Our babies everybody!" The crowd cheered again. Then our moms said, "Goodnight!"

We waved at the crowd and then we all started to walk backstage. The media started to talk about this immediately. They didn't know what to believe. They questioned the whole thing. Some of them thought that because everyone said we look alike, we were playing a joke on everybody. Others believed that it could be possible but didn't understand, because all these years they never saw Dynasty Chosen with kids.

The guy who did our first interview was lost for words. He sat there with his mouth open for so long as he held his head. He couldn't process the fact that he brought it up to us, and we did so well acting like we were not even related. Even the interviewers who interviewed our moms and Alexi were blown away. They had no idea we all knew each other personally.

Everyone was happy about the surprise, but they just didn't understand how this was. So of course a ton of requests for interviews started to come in right away. Que went to her mom looking shocked and said, "Ma, I think Latoya Lockhart is Camille's mom." Her mama knew how much she loved Latoya. She gasped and said, "What?! Why you think that?"

Que looked devastated and said, “Latoya just said it. It was the surprise…Dynasty Chosen are Angelic’s parents.” Her mom gasped and covered her mouth as she stared at Que for a minute. She was speechless. Shaun was stuck, still staring at the tv with his mouth wide open. His mama thought it was something wrong with him when she checked on him.

After his mom left the room, Shaun whispered to himself, “I had a feeling she had a famous parent! I can’t believe it…my girlfriend is Latoya Lockhart’s daughter. Is this a dream??” I have to admit, it shocked the world. After the concert that night, our moms took us out to dinner.

There were people in the restaurant that heard the surprise. We can tell by the way they kept staring at us. They couldn't believe we were all together. We had a nice time. On our way out we were saying stuff to each other, so people heard us interacting. We started to be seen with our parents, Alexi, our grandmas, and Auntie Trice over the next couple of weeks.

Some people thought we were dragging out "this joke" while others believed our moms were indeed our moms. We didn't do an interview just yet, but our moms had one coming up. We had an interview coming up around the same time. Que and Shaun did not hear from me since that night at the concert.

I guess I just didn't know how to start that conversation, especially after finding out my mom was both their favorite. It was kind of awkward. By the time the day of the interviews came, people witnessed all of us interacting with our moms, grandmas, aunties, and Alexi. They were able to hear how we spoke to them and how they spoke to us.

During our interview, the host said, "We have to clear the air…is it true that Dynasty Chosen, Trinity, and Alexi are your parents?" We all answered, "Yes." The host said, "WHOA! I need a moment." We laughed but he was serious. Once he collected himself, he said, "So please tell us who's your parent. Camille some people have heard you refer to Latoya and Alexi as your mom, can you clear that up?"

I smiled and said, "Oh, yes. That's because Latoya is my mom and Alexi is my God mom.

They're best friends." The host said, "Wow, that clears a lot up! We all said you all looked alike, but we had no idea you all knew each other personally! More less you all actually being mother and daughter!" I shook my head in a yes motion as I replied, "Yeeah." Then he said, "What about the rest of you?"

Carmen said, "Latonya is my mom." Cashae said, "Beonca is my mom." Alisha said, "Trinity is my mom." Alicia said, "And Trinity is my mom obviously, and to add to what Camille said earlier…Alexi is an auntie to all of us." During our moms interview, the questions were a bit more intense. But the host did ask, "Which member of Angelic are each of your daughters?"

Latoya said, “Camille is my baby.” Beonca said, “Cashae is mine.” Latonya said, “Carmen is mine.” Due to the nature of this interview, Trinity and Alexi was there too. Trinity said, “Alisha and Alicia are mine.” Alexi said, “They’re all my babies. So I’m an auntie to them all, but Camille is my God baby. She’s really my child, Toya just had her for me.”

They all laughed. Then the host said, “Wow, for so long we thought you ladies didn’t have kids and now we find out you do. Not only do you have kids, but they’re nine and ten years old!” He asked them why they never said anything, our parents explained to him their concerns for safety. They even told him we were almost always with them during the start of their career.

The host said, “Really? How? We never saw them with you.” Beonca said, “They were there.” Then the host looked surprised as he said, “The strollers! I remember, there were always strollers in your entourage! We all thought you allowed your employees to bring their kids to work. Were your babies in those strollers?!”

Our moms laughed and answered, “Yes they were.” The host was so shocked he could barely speak. He covered his mouth partially with his hand. His mouth was wide open as he stared at our moms. He was in deep thought. Our moms explained how they wanted to protect us and allow us to live a normal life.

He was shocked when he heard they put us in those strollers even at 5 years old to hide us. He said, “Wow! So they’ve been in plain sight this entire time. They’ve always been here!” Our moms shook their heads in a yes motion as they smirked and said, “Yep.”

He understood and all the listeners did too. The host then said, “Your daughters, in an earlier interview stated they were cousins. So if they’re cousins, what is your relationship with each other?” Our parents all said, “Sisters.” The host gasped so loud. He said, “We never knew this! I guess we never thought to ask because no kids were involved. But you’re sisters?!”

They all smiled and said, “Yes.” The host said, “Is there anything else you would like to tell us? Do you have any more kids?” My mom said, “Yes. I have 3.” The host was even more shocked, he said, "3?!" My mom said, "Yes. Camille is 10. I also have a 5 year old and a 5 month old." The host said, "What?! You practically have a newborn! You look great!"

My mom smiled and said, "Thank you." Then he asked my aunties. Beonca said, "Cashae is 9. I also have a 5 year old and my baby is 5 months old." The host said, "What?! You too with the newborn?? Wow you ladies look amazing!" Beonca smiled and said, "Thank you." Latonya said, "Carmen is 9 and my baby is 5 months old." The host was speechless. His mouth was hanging wide open.

Trinity said, "Alisha and Alicia are 10 and my baby is 5 months old." The host said, "All of you! All of you have newborns and you look great!"

They all said, “Thank you.” The host asked Alexi, “Do you have any newborns you’re keeping from us?” Alexi laughed and said, “No, I don’t have any biological children.”

The host then smiled and said, “So they’re not even the only child? They have siblings?! Wow! You all went from no kids to moe kids! This is the interview everyone has been waiting for. We’re finding out so much about Angelic and yourselves that we never knew before!” Both interviews went well. It cleared up the air. Now everybody knew that it was true, Dynasty Chosen and Trinity were our parents.

All of us were already well-known celebrities. But this made us all blow up even more. Our names and faces were huge among all celebrities. We gained even more fans. We all gained so much more attention and fans that we had to start traveling like our parents. Meaning, with security everywhere and being discreet. Those days of having playdates at them parks and arcades were over.

We were too big of celebrities now to even go out in public even if we were with security. Our moms didn't want us to go anywhere without them if it wasn't necessary. Now we understood why our parents kept us a secret. If people were gonna act like this when we were younger after finding out who our parents were, we were grateful they kept this secret.

We realized now that we had no idea what it was like to not be able to go anywhere. We started to see just how lucky we were right before we became famous. We complained about not being able to do what other kids did before, but we were still able to go to some places. Try putting us in a public school now. It couldn't happen. We didn't realize just how big we were until now.

It was nice to finally be seen with our moms and our family in public again. Everyone knew who our moms were, but they still didn't know who our dads were. I wonder what that'll bring once they find out.

Chapter 11

Face To Face

After two more weeks, I finally called Que. I honestly didn't know what to say to her. I didn't know how to approach her. Afterall, I had been missing in action for the past month. But she was my best friend and I missed her. So I called.

She answered in the quietest voice, "Hello?" I humbly said, "Hello?" She said, "Camille??" I immediately replied, "Que, I'm so sorry." I expected that she would be upset with me, but instead she replied with, "Camille! Omgee, why you didn't tell me Latoya Lockhart is yo mama?!"

I can tell she was all smiles as she spoke. I smiled and said, “I wasn’t allowed to tell anyone that all my life.” She went on to say, “What?! We sittin here talkin bout the concert waiting on the surprise, and ya’ll was the surprise! That’s why you was at the concert, did you know?!” She was so excited.

I said, “No! My mom told me the night before, me and my cousins had to go to the concert because they were gonna celebrate afterwards. We didn’t know until they introduced us that they were revealing the secret.” Que said, “Secret?”

I said, “Well yeah, that’s been a secret since before I was born. Nobody knew my mom, or my aunties were pregnant when they were. So they decided to hide it. When they had us, they were just starting their singing career and didn't feel the need to tell anyone. After a while they wanted to protect us so we could live somewhat of a normal life. So no one outside of our family knew they had kids."

Que said, "Wait, kids??" I laughed a little and said, "Oh yeah, I have two sisters. My cousins have sisters too." Que was so shocked. She had to be the only one that knew what gender our siblings were, because our parents never told the radio host if they had boys or girls, they only told them our ages.

Que said, "Wait, so there's more of you??" I laughed and said, "Yes, my mama have 3 kids." Que said, "Wow, so who is your dad?" I said, "Um, I don't know if my mom or my dad want that to be known just yet." Que said, "So your dad's famous too?!" I said, "Yes." She chuckled out of amusement.

Then she said, "Are your cousins dads famous too?" I said, "Yeah, they all are." Que said, "Omgee, this is so much. So your mom knew who I was this whole time??" I said, "Yep. She knows your name, she knows how you look, and she bought you those gifts I've been giving you. I only told her I wanted to buy you a gift, but she picked them all out."

Que was so happy. She couldn't believe that her favorite singer was the person that picked out her gifts all these years. She also couldn't believe that her favorite singer knew who she was for years! After a moment she said, "Wow Camille. I can't believe this, and I was sleeping in the same house as my favorite singer from that group. Like I was probably right down the hall."

I said, "You were two doors down from her." Que yelled, "Two doors?! I've always wanted to meet her, and I was only two doors down from her with no security around?!" I laughed and then said, "Well Que, I think it's time for you to meet my family. Do you think you and your mom can come to my house this weekend to meet my mom?"

Que got quiet for a few seconds and then she screamed, "Ahhhhh!" She covered her mouth. Then I heard her mom say, "Que?! Girl you okay??" Que couldn't talk, so her mama got on the phone. She said, "Hey Camille." I said, "Hi." Then she asked, "What's wrong with this girl?" I said, "I asked if you and Que was able to come to my house this weekend to meet my mom."

Her mom was shocked too. She knew who my mom was before she found out she was my mama, and she liked her and my aunties too. Her mama got quiet for a second, then she laughed and said, "Is that why…Girl, you know your mom is her favorite. As if being your best friend wasn't enough, Camille you got this girl over here losing her breath!"

We both laughed. I said, "I'm sorry. Que been wondering who my mama was for years and now that it's out, she can finally meet her." Que's mom said, "Okay that's fine, what day?" I said, "This Saturday. We all cleared our schedules to relax, and my mom thought it would be a good idea to have you and Que spend the day with us."

Her mom was listening as I continued to speak, "She's grateful to you to trust Que being here with me, even though you didn't know who my mom was. I didn't have a friend until I met Que. My mom said a person like you is a person that's loyal and trustworthy." Que's mom was honored to hear that my mom had all good things to say about her just by her actions.

I then said, "My mom would like to thank you in person." Que's mom said, "Aww that's so sweet, I would LOVE to meet your mom. Camille we'll be there, thank you for the invite." I said, "Your welcome. One more thing…" She said, "Yes?" I asked, "Can you please tell Que to call me back as soon as she gets over her shock?" Her mom laughed and said, "I sure will Camille!"

I said, "Okay. Thank you." Then we hung up. It wasn't long before Que called me back. We laughed about what happened earlier. I didn't want her to be too shocked, so I told her who all was going to be there. I also told her it was an all day thing, so our parents can bond. She was so excited. I was too.

Then I told her I needed to speak to Shaun. So she called him for me and put the phone down. We had a good conversation. He was super excited as well. I had to let him know that my mama knew who he was and that she did not want me dating. He was kind of bummed, but at the same time his infatuation with my mama was so great that it didn't affect him much.

He just had more questions about my mama and the fact that she was my mama. I only explained the situation to him and Que, because I felt them two out of anyone deserved to have their questions answered. They were the only two people that were close to me outside of my family. Shaun was clowning around asking when he could meet my mom and whatnot.

But I told him it wouldn't be a good idea. Because again my mom didn't want me dating and she knows how he looks. Shaun didn't know what to do. All he said was, "It's okay, we gone meet one day and she gone love me." I chuckled and said, "I hope she does." We spoke for a little while longer and then we got off the phone.

That weekend came so fast! I was nervous for Que. I had a feeling it would be a lot for her. My mom was home. My aunties, my grandma, my uncle, and Alexi was at our house. We was still living with my grandma. My cousins were there, Lashae was too. We was happy to have Lashae there. She was a well-known kid actress, so with her schedule and our schedule we don't be together as much as we would like.

But whenever we can we are together. Me Lashae were like sisters, really me and all my cousins were like sisters to each other. Me and Lashae just spent more time together in our earlier years, because her mom was so young and always had her at our house. It wasn't until we became a singing group, that I spent more of my time with my other cousins rather than Lashae.

But her dad and her mom kept her busy with acting by that time. So anyway, we all prepared for Que and her mom's arrival. All of the adults were in the living room. When Que and her mom arrived, security informed my mom. As they entered the gate, Que couldn't believe she was there. Sure she had been there before, but this time it was different.

Not only was she meeting my mom, but she was also meeting her favorite singer as well. Her mom was so shocked when she laid eyes on the house. She lowly said, "No wonder you said they were rich." Que smiled and nodded her head in a yes motion as she said, “Un uh.” Once they pulled in front of the house they slowly got out the car.

They waited for instructions. The security said, “Right this way ma’am.” Security led them to the front door. Once they were at the front door, my mama called me and said, “Camille, come get the door please.” I said, “Okay.” I came downstairs talking and laughing with my cousins. We walked past the adults and went to the door.

I opened the door and saw Que and her mom. My cousins were behind me, we all smiled. I said, “Hi Que!” I gave her a big hug. She smiled and gave me a hug back. I hugged her mom and said, “Hi!” Her mom hugged me back and said, “Hi, Camille!” I said, “Please come in.” They both hugged each of my cousins as they entered the house.

Then I led them to the living room. Once we got there, I said, “Ms. Johnson, Que…meet my mom, aunties, my uncle, and my mama. Everybody, this is Ms. Johnson and my best friend Shaquavia.” I was using my hands positioning them to each person I mentioned as I mentioned them. Then everybody said, “Hi, nice to meet you.”

I was smiling, clasped my hands together underneath my chin silently, and then bashfully said, “Ms. Johnson, this is my mom, Latoya.” I put my hands towards her while they were still clasped together.” My mom got up and greeted Que’s mom with a hug. Then I said, “This is my Auntie Beonca, my Auntie Latonya, My Auntie Trinity, and my Auntie Trice."

They all got up to hug her in that order. Then I said, "This is my Mama Alexi. She's my God mom. But she's my second mom." Alexi got up to hug her. Then I said, "This is my Uncle Gary, and this is my Ma Ma, my grandma." They all hugged Que too, she was so shocked. She couldn't believe this was all happening.

We spent some time downstairs with the adults. We talked and had fun. They all made Que and her mom feel welcomed. Maybe like an hour later, my mom said, "Cee Cee?" I said, "Yes?" She said, "Why don't you introduce Que to your sisters and cousins, and show her around a bit?" I was surprised she said that. I said, "Okay. Come on Que."

Me, my cousins, and Que got up and went upstairs. Although Que saw some of our house, she didn't see the whole thing. She only saw what we were allowed to show her when she came over before. We started to show her around the entire house and she was so shocked. She realized she only saw a fraction of the house before. Then we took her to meet Crystal and Camieka.

They were so cute and polite. I pointed to Crystal and said, "That's my little sister Crystal." Then I pointed to Camieka and said, "That's Cashae's little sister Camieka. They're 5." Crystal and Camieka waved as they both smiled and said, "Hi." Que said, "Hi. Aww I love them!" I looked at

Que and said, “I guess you all in now.” Que said, “Huh?” I said, “My mama told me to introduce you to my sisters and cousins…you gone be around more than you think.”

Then I said, “Come on.” We took her to another room. When I opened the door, she saw babies. I pointed out Careecia and said, “That’s my baby sister Careecia.” Carmen pointed at her sister and said, “That’s my baby sister Camesha.” Cashae pointed at her sister and said, “That’s my baby sister Canieka.” Alisha pointed at her sister and said, “And that’s our baby sister Aniyah.”

Que said, “Aww ya’ll really do have siblings and they so small.” I said, “You wana play with them?” Her face lit up as she said, “Can I??” I smiled and said, “Yeah!” So we stayed in that room for about an hour playing with the babies. Then Crystal came in asking if we could watch them in the back. So we went to the back and watched Crystal and Camieka play in the pool.

After about 5 minutes we all changed into swimsuits. Que didn't bring one, but we always had unused swimsuits on hand. We got in the pool and was able to bond with Crystal and Camieka. They loved Que. It made me so happy how everyone got along with her so easily. Of course we took more pictures. We had pictures with the babies, with Crystal and Camieka. We had pictures of us on the poolside.

We even had pictures of us kids with our moms. I made sure Que got an individual one with my mom. She was so happy. We were really making memories and we loved it! Our moms came out and watched us play in the pool after a while. They all seemed to really be enjoying each other's company. I was happy to see them all bonding. After we got out of the pool, we all had to take showers. Once we got out the shower, it was time to eat.

Dinner was amazing. We all sat together, and we talked about what we were grateful for. My mama and my aunties surprisingly talked to Que's mom about our secret. They told her the truth about why they hid their pregnancies and why they waited so long before they revealed it. I was shocked, but I guess they bonded enough for them to feel comfortable to talk to her like that.

They didn't go too much into detail but before we left that table, Que knew our moms had us young and she also knew they didn't want anyone to judge them for having us young. She knew that's why they kept it secret. Que started to feel compassion for us. She realized that the reasoning behind it could have taken a toll on us.

When we left the table Que talked to us about it. We told her how we really felt once we found out they were hiding us. I even cried, because it really bothered me for my mom to act like she had no kids. But I understood why. I cried tears of joy as I explained to Que how happy I was that she finally told the world she had a daughter.

Que hugged me so tight. She realized how alone I felt in the world, although it appeared I had everything. She just held me and allowed me to cry on her shoulder. My cousins cried too. We all were affected greatly by it, and our moms had no idea just how much. This was the realest conversation we've ever had with Que, with anyone besides each other. It was nice to be able to get it all out.

Afterwards we all went to chill with the adults again. We took pictures with them and whatnot. Then we all watched a movie in the movie room together. By the end of the night, my mom suggested that Que sleeps over being that my cousins were sleeping over too. Her mom was happy to allow her to. We stayed up extra late that night.

I spent a lot of time on the phone with Shaun that night. We spent so much time on the phone that

I video called him, and we all entertained him. We was clowning and dancing in front of the camera. He was engaging with us. We all had so much fun. He eventually traveled somewhere while he was still on the phone. Once he got there, I said, "Where are you?" He answered, "The studio." I said, "For what?"

He answered, "I'm a rapper." I said, "What?" He said, "You'll see me soon." Then I heard someone in the background lowly say, "Is that Camille?" Then Shaun looked at the phone and said, "I'ma talk to you later." I said, "Okay." Once we hung up, Carmen asked, "He said, he rap?" I said, "Yeah. But he never mentioned it before."

We continued with our night. We had so much fun. The next day when Ms. Johnson came to get Que, her and my mom greeted each other like they knew each other for years. I was happy to see that. They exchanged numbers the night before. All of the adults had Que's mom's number and she had all of their numbers.

I knew from this point on Que was gonna be around forever. Some time went past, and Que showed up to me, Alisha, and Alicia's 11th birthday party. That party was so much fun. My mom and my aunties treated her just like one of us. My grandma and my uncle treated her like that as well. It wasn't before long that Que was comfortable enough to feel like family.

My mom even helped Que's mom financially. She gave her the resources and a hefty donation for her to have her own business. Que's mom was making tenfold more than what she was before working for a corporation. She couldn't be more thankful to my mom for that. This made their life a lot easier. Which also meant that Que could hang out with us a lot more.

Que also attended my cousins birthday parties. Soon the family was used to seeing Que. Whenever we wanted to have a sleepover, Que was there. Her mom trusted my mom and my aunties one hundred percent. Now that they knew each other better, we saw each other a lot more frequently. Que even came with us to a couple of shows.

She would stay in our dressing room while we performed, and we would all chill in the dressing room during the down time. She loved it and we did too. This time around I wasn't going weeks without talking to her or Shaun. I was consistent with them, and this made our bonds stronger.

Chapter 12

Realistically

Some more time had passed. By this time Que was basically considered part of the family. Our moms were comfortable with each other and trusted each other with their kids. Although Que would have to come to our house mostly, we went to her house a couple of times.

Due to our fame we couldn't always go to her house. It was out of fear that someone might see us and there was no security there for us. The thing was we went over there to spend time together. So we stayed in the house which was okay with us.

When we did go to her house, we had so much fun with her.

It was a different scenery, so we were happy. Que and her mom moved to a different house than the one they were at before. She also dropped a bunch of those girls that were at her party that time we came. They were not her real friends and she realized that after that day.

She was still cool with a couple of girls from that party, but she basically only considered us and a couple of them her friends. She had some issues with some of the girls after her party. They were jealous and angry. But she didn't have to deal with it long, because shortly after those issues came about, her and her mom moved.

Que switched schools and started hanging out with us more at those times and we couldn't be happier for her. Speaking of moving, me and my cousins moved too. My mom got a place of our own for us, and so did our cousins moms. None of us lived with our grandmas anymore.

Our grandmas missed us, and we missed them. But we were all happy to be in our own homes again. The best thing about it was that we all lived close to each other! My house was the first on our block, Cashae's house was next to mine, and Alisha and Alicia's house was next to Cashae's house. Their house was the last house on the block.

Carmen's house was on the block in front of our street, directly in front of Alisha and Alicia's house. Her house was the last house on her block.

Lashae's house was on the block behind our street directly behind my house. Her house was the first house on her block. Lashae's block had more houses than our block. The houses were huge and took up a lot of space. We were lucky to be so close to each other.

We were all in home school still and there was a lot of talk about letting us start regular school. Everything was going great until after our 12th birthday. Me and the twins had our birthday party. We wanted to have it together, so we did. It was a great day. We had the time of our lives. Not too long after our party, my mom found something that was suspicious.

While I was out with my cousins, my mom went in my room and found a ring. She didn't recognize the ring. She examined the packaging which was really nice, but she still couldn't put her head around it. The ring was a pretty fine silver with the cut out initials SC on it. The initials were closed in a heart.

My mom was so confused. She couldn't figure out where it came from or who gave it to me. She called around and even had a jeweler look at it. Our jeweler confirmed it was 100% real. My mama had no luck finding out who gave it to me.

Once I came home, my cousins were still with me. We were smiling, talking, and laughing about the day we had. It came to a halt when my mama firmly said, "Camille." We all stopped instantly and looked at her scared. She pulled out the ring, looked me in my eyes and said, "Who gave you this??"

Our mouths dropped as we looked at the ring. Not even a split second later, Carmen said, "You know what Camille, I just thought about it…my mama gone want me home soon. I'll just walk." My other cousins agreed and said, "Yeah our mamas too, we'll walk with her."

Then they all ran out the house! I was left standing there shocked. My cousins all knew who gave me that ring. They just didn't know how to handle the situation. Especially when it involves my mama. They were supposed to get a ride home with my mama that day.

After they closed the door, my mama said, "I'ma ask you one more time…who gave you this?"

Honestly, I tried to think of someone's name with the letter S, but nothing was coming to me. Then my mama said, "Where did this come from?" I said, "The party." My mama said, "I don't remember this being opened at the party…. did Shaquavia give you this??"

Before I could answer, she said, "Well, that makes sense." She gave it to me and said, "Put it up." When she walked away, I took a breath of relief. What I didn't know was my mama was watching me as I walked upstairs. I thought it was over, but she was on to me. She just didn't let me know.

About a week passed and there was this announcement about a new rapper. When we saw it, we were getting prepped for a photoshoot. The tv was playing and the host introduced a rapper named woof. They said he was a new artist and that was his first professional appearance.

Me and my cousins happened to look up and to our surprise we saw Shaun! We instantly started to smile and giggle. Cashae looked at me and said, “Camille, you were right!” Carmen said, “I thought he was lyin.” Our stylist had no idea what we were talking about, they just smiled and laughed at our conversation.

I was so happy and proud of him. I knew he worked hard, and I knew his background. So I was happy he found something to keep him out of trouble. He performed and did really well. From that point on his career began to take off. Oddly enough we never told our parents we knew him.

He looked different from the time my mom saw him, so she didn't know it was him. Funny enough, Shaun ended up doing a feature on one of our moms songs. That's when they all fell in love with him. They thought he was so cute and full of talent.

The best thing about them working with him was that, I was able to finally see him in person after 2 years! Our moms decided to bring us to one of the shows he was a part of, so he could have kids his age to hang out with backstage. Those kids just happen to be us.

My mom told him, "I want you to meet my daughter. This is Camille." I smiled and said, "Hi." Then he smiled and said, "Hi." My aunties introduced my cousins afterward. Shaun told my mom and my aunties, “Ya’ll have some beautiful girls.” Our moms laughed and said, “Thank you.”

Once they were performing other songs, we all were in a room together. Me and Shaun stood up and immediately embraced each other. We hugged each other for so long. Once we let each other go, he looked me up and down and said, “Camille, you growing up.”

I looked at him smirking and said, “I see you are too.” We were smiling at each other. Carmen said, “Aww they flirtin.” I said, “Carmen shut up.” Shaun grabbed both of my hands and said, “I missed you so much Camille.” I said, “I missed you too.” Then he said, “You the reason I kept going at this rap thing. I felt like this was the only way I could get next to you again.”

I was shocked and said, “Really?” He said, “Yeah, you was my motivation…I don’t think yo mom noticed me.” I said, “I don’t think so either, otherwise we wouldn’t be in here together.” We all laughed. He said, “Let me guess, you still not allowed to date?” I smiled and said, “No.”

We laughed some more, then he leaned in and kissed my cheek. I was shocked he did that. My cousins were too. That was the most contact any of us ever experienced from a boy. Then he looked me in my eyes and said, “Thank you for sticking by me. No one has ever been consistent with me like that. I really appreciate you, Camille.”

I looked at him and said, “You’re welcome.” Too bad Que wasn’t there that day. But we all enjoyed each other’s company. We did speak to

Que while we were there. She said, "Ahh I'm so happy ya'll together in person!" We were able to spend the whole day together. We all loved it.

Our moms decided to have us at all the shows they had with him after that. As long as we weren't busy with our own shows and work at that time. So me and Shaun was able to spend a lot more time together. We loved every minute of it, so we were not going to reveal that he was the same person our moms moved us back to Miami for.

The song they did together was the number 1 song on the charts for a while, so there were a lot of shows, interviews, and appearances around the song. People talked about how quick they did a song with him when he came out, but took a long time to even acknowledge us.

That was something that was explained before. But our moms addressed it again. People waited for the perfect collab with us and our moms. What they didn't know was that we had already did a song with our moms. The song was a Christmas song, so it wasn't out yet.

We shot a video for it and everything. We just had to wait for the right timing to release it. We had another song with our moms as well that wasn't released yet. It was a cute song. The song and video was based off of us kids trying to be kids, but the parents are not approving of what we want to do.

In the end, it was kind of like a mother against daughter type scenario. How ironic. Our parents released that sometime after the feature with Shaun. People absolutely loved it. Soon we found ourselves performing with our moms for a while. This made all of our fame increase 100 times more!

Now Shaun was a hot commodity and our moms as well as myself and my cousins were more famous than ever. The option of being sent to regular school started to fade away. This upset us. It was the only thing we wanted and now because of the fame again, we couldn't have it.

We were once again fed up with this fame stuff. I decided to live as normal as I possibly could. I started to speak back to Shaun even more. Instead of just going through Que to speak to him, I started to sneak and call him here and there from the house phone. I even started to talk to him on my cell phone.

My mom was so busy, she wasn't checking my phone as often as she had been before. I made sure I didn't overdo it. Shaun and I became even closer. We started to be more comfortable with each other. We were young, but we were starting to experience what dating really felt like.

He felt as though I was the only one who had his best interest at heart, and I felt as though I was able to trust him with everything in me. We were a perfect match. We kept each other going. After my thirteenth birthday, Shaun and I were able to see each other again.

He was invited to our parties now and to other events we were at. Now that he was famous, we could see each other easily. We went to his birthday party as well. He turned thirteen months before me. His mom was familiar with us, and our moms were familiar with her. During this time when we saw each other, my cousins left us alone for a minute.

They left out of the room we were in. While they were gone, Shaun and I were able to have a heart to heart conversation. He talked to me about us and said, “Do you understand what’s happening between us?” I said, “No, but I feel it…and I’m willing to embrace whatever this is we have going on.”

Shaun smiled and said, “This why I love you, Camille.” I said, “Wow, that’s funny Shaun…I love you too.” He was happy to know I felt the same way he did. He then said, “Have you had your first kiss yet?” I said, “No.” He said, “Me either.”

Then he leaned in slowly. I smiled and leaned in towards him. We both leaned in until our lips met in the middle.

I couldn't believe it! I was experiencing my first kiss with someone I really cared about. I never imagined this would happen to me at thirteen, but it did, and we both loved it. We talked some more after that. We were both comfortable and didn't feel awkward.

When my cousins came back in the room, we did not tell them what happened. I waited until we got home to tell them. When I tell you they screamed so loud! My mama ran in the room to check on us. We had to play it off. After she left out the room, Carmen said, "See Camile?! Ya'll gone be dating for a while." Alisha said, "We told you that a couple years ago."

Cashae said, "Yep, first he got you that anniversary ring and now ya'll had ya'll first kiss." Alicia said, "I'm so happy for ya'll." I was sitting there in bliss. Lashae said, "Yep Camille, I think he's a keeper." I called Que and told her. She screamed too. She couldn't believe it.

It just felt like we were official now. In one of Shaun interviews the interviewer asked him, "Are you single?" Shaun smiled. We all expected him to bypass it or say no just to save face. But to our surprise, he said, "No, I got a girlfriend." We all gasped and were shocked he admitted to it.

I would not have been mad if he said no, because I know how this fame stuff goes. He could have lost a lot of fans by saying that. Surprisingly, his confession made him gain even more fans. Now it was a thing to try and find out who he was dating.

Fans started to pay attention to who he was around, but they had no luck. We were around him behind the scenes, so they could never suspect me or my cousins. Soon my mom started to notice a slight change in my behavior. It wasn't bad but it was familiar to her.

I started to remind her of herself at my age. When she was crushing on guys but tried to hide it. She grew concerned. She started to check my call log again. Since I was used to her not checking it, I didn't expect it. She saw one number that was dialed, not often but when it was dialed, she saw that I would stay on the phone for hours.

She saw that the number called my phone a few times too. When that happened the call would last for hours as well. She talked to her sisters, and they had no idea whose number that was. My mama said, “This number look familiar, but I don’t know from where.”

Trinity asked, “Is it her best friend’s number?” Latoya said, “No, the number isn’t saved in Camille’s phone.” One day we were all together at a private party, and the number conversation came up again. Latonya looked at the number and said, “You know what? I’ve been finding some strange things in Carmen’s phone lately. One thing I remember was a memo with three numbers on it. It had the second three numbers of this number on it. I asked Carmen about it, and she said she just like those numbers.”

Beonca then said, “Hold on, I found three random numbers in Cashae’s phone with the first three numbers of this number on it. I didn’t ask about it, I just thought she was being weird. Cashae is a weird child.” They laughed a little. But then Trinity said, “Now that ya’ll mention it, the twins had the last four numbers of this number in their phones. I mean it was weird. Alisha had two of the numbers and Alicia had the other two numbers.”

They were all shocked. My mama said, “I wonder whose number that is.” My mom then looked in her own phone. Next thing you know she said, “I know this girl didn’t!” Latonya said, “What?!” My mama yelled, “It’s that boy’s number Camille got in trouble for a couple years ago! The same boy I told her to stay away from.”

My aunties were shocked. Beonca said, "She still in contact with him?" Latoya said, "Apparently so! I'ma call Raquel. I gotta check something." Raquel is Que's mom. She called her and asked, "Hey, have you seen this number in Shaquavia's phone?"

After giving her the number, Que's mom checked Que's phone. After checking she told my mom, "Yes that number is in her call log. How many times did you see it in Camille's phone?" My mama said, "It's in her phone like 6 times." Que's mom said, "Well, I don't what's going on, but that number is in Que's phone over a hundred times."

My mom was confused as she softly replied, "What?" Until Que's mom said, "But the funny thing is, every time that number is in her call log, it shows Camille's number on the same call. I think maybe it was like a three way call, because it shows Que, Camille, and that number."

My mama was pissed! She said, "Are you able to find out how long this has been going on and get back to me?" Que's mom said, "Yeah, I'll check it now and I'll call you back." My mama said, "Thanks." After they hung up, my mama crossed her arms and started to pace in place from left to right as she continuously took deep breaths.

Her sisters asked, "What happened Toya?" My mama answered, "She been using Que phone to keep in contact with that boy…I'ma beat her a**." Trinity said, "How long she been doin that?" My mama said, "I asked Raquel to check Que's call log, she gone tell me."

Latonya said, “D*mn Toya. This sound real familiar.” She was referring to when my mama was younger and sneaking to still see my dad even though my grandma forbade it. My mama did not want to hear that. She looked at her with daggers and said, “That’s exactly why I’ma beat her a**. I told her if I find out she still in contact with him, I’ma ware her a** out…and I’ma do just that. She don’t know who she think she playin with.”

Beonca said, “But Camille a good kid. She hardly get beatins.” My mama said, “That’s the problem! Some things she do, I just talk to her about. But now she’s a teenager. She’s changing how she go about things, and I need to change how I discipline her.”

Just then my mom's phone rung. She picked up quick and said, "Hello?" She listened for a while and then said, "Okay, thank you." Then she hung up. She put her phone in her back pocket and started to walk fast towards the hall. Before she reached the hall, Latonya said, "Toya what happened?"

My mama looked at them and said, "Two years, this girl been doing this for two years and I had no idea!" Beonca said, "I understand where you comin from but please, calm down Toya." My mama said, "Beonca, two years. I didn't know. This sh*t scary. I'm not gone allow her to turn out like me."

She then ran up the stairs as she said to herself, "Where is she?" As she reached the middle of the stairs she yelled out, "Camille?!" When I heard my mama call me like she did, I knew something wasn't right. She scared all of us. Me and my cousins stopped playing and stopped talking. We all gasped as we quickly looked towards the room door. We were stuck.

A split second later my mama burst in the room. The look on her face was a look I've never seen before. She was zoned in on me and said, "What type of game you playin?" My mouth was wide open. I was confused. I answered, "No game in particular, we were playin random games."

She looked like she wanted to knock me out. She then said, "That's not what I'm talkin bout." We both had a stare off for a few seconds. Just as my aunties came upstairs and stood in the doorway, my mama said, "You still talkin to that boy?"

Me and my cousins were all so shocked. My eyes were the only things that moved at that moment. I looked back and forth from my mom to my aunties. She sternly said, "Answer me." I knew she had to know something if she was asking me like that.

So I softly answered, "Yes." My mom and my aunties were all disappointed, I can tell by their faces. My cousins were scared as heck! I was too. My mama let out a deep breath through her nose as she closed her eyes and tucked her lips in her mouth.

She opened her eyes, untucked her lips and said, "When I asked you were you still in contact with that boy, what did you tell me?" She was looking up at the ceiling with her hands over her mouth. I answered, “No.” Still looking up at the ceiling, she started to talk with her hands as she said, “And it’s been going on for two years.”

I was not prepared for her to say that. I had no idea she knew the length of time. My eyebrows raised in shock as my mouth dropped. I even gasped unexpectantly. Then she looked at me and yelled, “Get yo a** in there!” She pointed towards her room. I instantly pouted, covering half my face with my right hand for a split second before getting up.

I jumped up and walked past her and my aunties. As I walked to her room, my mom and my aunties stayed in the doorway of the room looking at my cousins. Trinity was the first to say something. She looked at my cousins and said, “Ya’ll knew.”

My cousins heads dropped. They knew they were caught. Latonya said, "Ya'll must really think we stupid. Ya'll got these random numbers in ya'll phones and tellin us crazy reasons why…oh I like those numbers, Carmen!" Beonca said, "I've been seeing those numbers a lot, Cashae!"

Trinity said, "They my lucky numbers, Alicia! Oh I have to remember what page I'm on in a book, Alisha!" All of them was so scared, but their mama's were pissed! My mama had her arms crossed as she said, "Que was in on it too. She probably did the most. Camille been using her phone to talk to him all this time."

My cousins were shocked she knew. There was a slight silence. Then my mama said, "As a matter of fact, I need to go get Camille a** together." My mama walked away fast. While she was gone Beonca said, "We tell ya'll this stuff for a reason. Ya'll do not need to be caught up with these lil boys."

Latonya said, "And now ya'll lyin for each other. This makes us think ya'll doing more than what we thinking." Trinity asked, "Are the rest of ya'll dating too?" My cousins quickly answered, "No." They were too scared to tell the truth, because they all were dating.

They also knew if they hesitated to answer, they would be found out too. Since their moms had no incidents of them being in contact with boys, they had no choice but to believe them. But they all were in trouble for helping me, including Que. After her mom found out what she had done, she got her phone taken and was placed on punishment.

My aunties were so mad at my cousins, that they took them home. Once they got home, they all got beatins. Meanwhile my mom talked to me first. She explained again why she didn't want me dating boys. She then addressed the fact that I had been lying to her.

That made her mad. Well, she kept her word. She wore me out with that belt! I had never in all my life gotten a beatin that bad before. Once again, I found myself in trouble for Shaun. He's all I ever really got in trouble for since I got older. I realized after that beatin, just how much more intense it was to get in trouble because of him as a teenager.

All of us got our phones taken and we were on close watch by our parents. Que couldn't come to our shows and events, because she was on punishment. Que ended up getting a beatin the same day she got on punishment too, because she knew she wouldn't see us for a while, and she threw a fit.

We didn't like this at all. This caused us to not appear happy whenever we had to perform, do a photoshoot, record, or shoot a music video. Work just seemed like work. We wasn't having fun at all. This caused us to start getting in trouble at work by our moms.

They would have to either call or show up where we were to get us to act right. It was never pleasant when they had to step in to correct our behavior. We would have to act like we were okay and hide the tears until we finished the project.

Homeschool was even worse. I would put my head down and cry in the middle of a lesson. I wouldn't listen to my teacher until my mom would pull me aside and go across my head. Then I would come back like nothing happened. This exhausted our moms.

They had to find another way to deal with all of this. One thing that went under their noses was that woof <u>was</u> Shaun. They still allowed him to be around us. When we first saw him again after we all got in trouble, we were shocked. He was escorted to our dressing room at the request of our moms.

After security closed the door, we all sat up and gasped. I nearly ran to him and hugged him. He hugged me back. Afterwards I smiled and said, "What are you doin here?" He smiled and said, "I perform today. How come you haven't called, or picked up?" I looked sad as I looked over to my cousins.

Then I looked back at him and said, "We don't have our phones. We all got in trouble and all of us are on punishment, including Que." Shaun smiled as he said, "Dang! What ya'll did??" I hate to tell him it's because of him, because then he'll feel bad. So instead I said, "It's nothing don't worry about it. They want us to focus on school and work more."

He said, “Well, at least I can still see you when we work the same shows or when we go to the same parties.” I said, “Yeah.” We all chilled together until it was time to go. As we all exited the dressing room, our moms were coming down the hall. Beonca was the closest to us.

She was right in front of the door. Before any of us saw her, me and Shaun was walking out the room. I was going right, and he was going left. He was holding my hand. As he started to let go, he smiled at me and said, “Bye Camille.”

I looked back at him, smiled, and said, “Bye Shaun.” When I said his name, Beonca looked confused as she did a double take looking at Shaun. That’s when I saw her. She looked at me as I looked at her. My eyes got big as I gasped quickly. I looked scared for a second because I didn't see her.

She watched me curiously as I walked down the hall. Her eyes were squinted and everything. My cousins were walking out the room behind me at this time. I was happy that we were still able to see each other, but I still wished we were able to talk on the phone.

We saw Shaun two more times at events after this. Then we had a house party. The house party was of course invite only. Other celebrities were there, and we were all having a good time. It was when me and my cousins saw Shaun walk through the front door, that we realized something was off.

We saw our moms greet him and welcome him in. They were hugging him and expressing how cute he was. As me and my cousins watched at a distance in confusion, I said, "I have a feeling they don't know that's Shaun." My cousins all agreed as they replied, "Un huh."

Then my mom pointed us out and told him to go to us. We played along, we smiled and waved at him as she did that. Once he got to us, we took him around the corner to talk to him and play with him. He immediately asked, "Where Que at?" Me and cousins looked at each other quickly before we all looked down.

Then I quickly looked up and said, "Remember we all got in trouble?" He said, "Yeah." I said, "We still on punishment. These parties are just business." He said, "Aw man. That's messed up. It's been like a month! What did ya'll do??" I still didn't want to tell him it was because of him.

So instead, I said, "To be honest, we got caught in a lie and our moms are big on being truthful." Shaun said, "Oh wow. Well, ya'll should always tell the truth especially to ya'll moms. They the ones that's gone back ya'll up for life. Always respect them."

We looked down as we replied, "Yeah, you right." It just so happened that my mom was passing by that area at that time. We didn't see her because she was on the other side of the wall. When she heard him say that and saw how we responded, she really wanted to keep him around.

My mom walked away to find her sisters after that. Carmen said, “Let’s go in the back.” We all said, “Okay.” As we started to walk away, Shaun grabbed my arm. I looked back at him curiously. Then he said, “I have something exciting to tell you.” I smiled and said, “What is it?”

He smiled and said, “I just bought a house.” I was excited for him. We were holding each other’s arms at this time. I jumped up and down once as I said, “Congratulations! I’m so happy for you!” He said, “Thank you, it’s on the block behind yours.” I was so excited that I had a late reaction to what he last said. But when I comprehended what had just been said, I paused.

I looked at him with a spooked look on my face and said, “Wait what??” He smiled and said it a little louder, “I moved on the block behind your house.” I immediately covered his mouth and said, “Shh!” I looked around to make sure no one heard him. I grabbed his wrist and said, “Come on.”

I ran with him towards the backyard. Shaun was so confused. I finally found my cousins in the backyard. They could tell by the look on my face that something was wrong. Carmen immediately asked, “What happened??” We all appeared nervous. Shaun asked, “Am I missing something??”

I looked back at him for a second. Then I turned to my cousins and said, “Shaun told me some exciting news.” They all looked at Shaun. I told Shaun, “Tell them the good news.” Shaun smiled and said, “Oh! I just bought a house!” My cousins smiled and said, “Oh! Nice, Congratulations!”

He said, “Thank you.” I said, “Tell them where.” I tucked my lips in as I looked down at the grass. Shaun was still excited as he said, “It’s on this block!” He pointed past our back fence. All of my cousins mouths dropped. I looked up at them. Carmen pointed over the fence and said, “This block?”

She did not break eye contact with Shaun at all. Shaun smiled and said, “Yep! My house is the second from the last house on that block. On the other side of the street.” When he said that, my cousins all said, “Shh!” He got quiet quick. He said, “Why is everybody telling me…” We all said, “Shh!”

Cashae said, “We all happy for you and we’re excited for you to be that close. But tell no one!" He said, "Huh?" Alisha said, "Don't tell anybody right now, especially our moms." He smiled and said, "What?? But ya'll moms love me." I looked at him, shook my head in a no motion, and said, "It's not a good time to tell them that Shaun. Just keep it between us for now."

He was confused but he said, "Okay. It's between us then." I said, "Thank you." We had to mingle a bit more, so we broke away from Shaun for a while. My mama finally got a chance to talk to her sisters. She told them what she heard Shaun say to us.

She expressed how much she loved Shaun. After that, Beonca told her what she saw that day we were coming out of the dressing room. My mom said, "I mean they're friends." Beonca said,

"What's the name of the boy you didn't want Camille to keep in contact with?" My mama said, "His name is Shaun."

Beonca said, "Do you know what Woof's name is?" My mama looked confused as she said, "Where you goin with this B?" Beonca calmly said, "You don't think Woof is the same person you been trying to keep Camille away from?" My mama said, "Why you sayin that?"

Beonca said, "All you have to do is pay attention. Their interaction with each other. I mean there's six of them and he takes to Camille most." My mama said, "It's not out of the norm for a boy to like Camille." Beonca said, "Didn't Camille say Shaun come down to Miami sometimes? That's how they got back in contact. Now this boy shows up and him and Camille are joined at the hip."

My mama was in deep thought. Beonca said, "The same boy Camille snuck in the house at that sleepover back in Chicago. He might look different now. Just like Andre did back then when he got older. <u>You</u> didn't even recognize him." Once she had my mom's attention, she said, "What's Woof's real name Toya?"

As she said that, Shaun was walking towards the door because he was leaving. My mom couldn't let him walk past her without stopping him. Once he got to them my mom called him over. He immediately smiled and thanked them for having him over. They told him he's welcome and it was nice to have him.

Beonca cleared her throat, my mama glanced at her and then back at Shaun. Then she said, "Um, Woof. I meant to ask you, what's your real name?" Shaun smiled and said, "Shaun Mace." My mom was shocked as she said, "Shaun?" He said, "Yes ma'am." My mama said, "Are you from this area?"

Shaun smiled as he replied, "No, I used to live in Chicago before I moved here." My mom's mouth dropped. Her and my aunties were stuck. He said, "But now I…" He thought about it. He was about to say he lived in Miami now and on the next block over. But he remembered what we told him.

Instead, he said, "Now I'm down here mostly." My mom and my aunties didn't know what to think at this point. Then my mama surprisingly said, "Well here, take my number. This way I can be in direct contact with you when we have events. The girls enjoy having you around."

Shaun said, "Okay!" He put my mom's number in his phone and left. Beonca looked at my mama and said, "What do you think?" My mama said, "Coincidence?" As Beonca looked at her sarcastically and let out a deep breath through her nose, my mama's phone notification went off.

She opened the text and said, "Oh Shaun just texted me his number." She paused for a second and then she frantically when through her phone. After a couple more seconds she said, "Oh my gosh!" My aunties said, "What?!" She said, "His number match the number Camille's been callin! …it's him!"

They all stared at each other silently with their mouths wide open.

Chapter 13

The Shift

After realizing Shaun was the same person she tried so hard to keep me from, she had no idea what to do. She felt a panic attack coming on. My aunties were no better, they were just as shocked and speechless.

My mom called her assistant over and said, "I need to lay down for a minute, can you please take care of everything while I do so?" Her assistant responded, "Yes of course Ms. Lockhart." My mom put her drink down. My aunties did the same and followed her to her room.

Once they got there, my mom laid across her bed as she freaked out. She looked at her sisters as she held her head, and said, “What do I do?” Her sisters opened their mouths but couldn’t speak. At best they could only gesture, “I don’t know.” with their hands and by shaking their heads in a no motion.

My mom looked out of it as she said, “For the first time in my life, Camille has me speechless. I really don’t know what to do. I mean I actually like the boy, but I had no idea it was him!” Her sisters sat down on her bed. Beonca said, “We all like him. It's just unfortunate it’s the same lil boy Camille been lying to you about.”

My mama sat up quick and said, “Do ya’ll think she been hiding the fact that it’s been him this whole time?" Latonya said, "The girl probably think you crazy for having him around in the first place. She probably thought you knew." My mama said, "But that makes no sense. If you on punishment for still being in contact with him, why the h*ll would you think I would have him around you?!"

Her sisters shrugged their shoulders as in, "I don't know." Once more my mama said, "I don't know what to do." She kind of said that in a whining voice. She continued in her normal voice, "She's a teenager now, and here comes this boy. She work, I work. I can't monitor her every second of the day, and now they work some of the same shows sometimes…"

Just as she got deeper into it, Trinity said, "Send her to your mom until you figure it out."

Latoya looked at her almost in tears and said, "My mom?" Trinity said, "Yeah. If you can trust anybody with Camille, it would your mom. She watch her close and never let her out of her sight."

Beonca said, "Yeah and we'll help you figure things out in the meantime." My mama was relieved. She took a breath of relief and said, "Thanks. I really appreciate ya'll…but I don't know if I should tell Camille or not." They all said, "Not!" My mom looked at them shocked. Latonya said, "Don't warn her. That way she has no time to think of anything to get around it."

Latoya said, "You think Camille would do that?" Trinity said, "I mean she has for the past two years. You told her she couldn't have a boyfriend, so she found a way around it to keep her boyfriend." Trinity's response was sassy, and she talked with her hands as she said the ending part of it.

My mom said, "Well, okay. What about work? She have to be with the girls." Beonca said, "After finding that number separated between them all like that, I think it's best you keep them separated while you figure this out. When they work, we can bring them together. Other than that, you and Camille have a lot to think about during ya'll alone time."

Latonya said, "Yeah, I agree. Camille is very smart, and she know how to work the people around her. Keep them separated for now and send her to your mom." My mom slowly reached for her phone as she said, "Okay. Hopefully this doesn't make matters worse." She picked up her phone and called my grandma.

My grandma picked up and said, "Hey baby!" My mom sounded like she wanted to cry as she replied, "Ma I'm sorry about this, but can you please do me a favor?" My grandma said, "Anything, what's wrong baby??" My mama said, "Can you please take Camille for a while?" My grandma was shocked as she replied, "What?! What's goin on??"

My mama explained, "Camille's been lying, she's got this boyfriend, she's not listening, she sneaking around, this is too much." My grandma thought about what she told my mom when my mom was taking her through it as a teenager. But she couldn't see herself telling her I told you so while she was going through something like this.

So instead my grandma said, "Of course I'll take her Toya." My mom said, "Thank you Ma. Just until I figure this out. My mind is messed up, because the same boy I've been trying to keep her from, is the same boy I've been having her around." My grandma said, "What?!" My mama explained everything to her that had happened and everything that was happening now.

Although my grandma knew it was gonna come back on my mama, she was still mad about me doing all that stuff. It really pissed her off. She never thought I would be doing things like this. After she got off the phone with her, my aunties asked, "What did she say?"

My mama looked like she was worn out as she calmly said, “She asked me when I want her to take her. I told her I’ll bring her tomorrow. But she said, no she coming to get her tonight.” Beonca said, “Uh oh, she mad.” My mom shook her head in a yes motion slowly. Then she shook her head in a no motion as she said, “I don’t know what else to do. My mama gone deal with her how she want to right now. Once I get her back, I’ll deal with her.”

Latonya said, “Hopefully by then she come to her senses. We all know yo mama don’t play.” My mama was staring into space as she slowly nodded her head in a yes motion, as she rocked back and forth. She didn’t want her mom to have to get to me, but she felt defeated.

Meanwhile, I'm still downstairs at the party with my cousins. We were having fun. In the middle of us playing, my grandma came in the house. My mom's assistant greeted her. Then my grandma spotted me. She walked behind me and said, "Camille?" I turned to look at her. Me and my cousins were shocked. We were happy to see her.

We gasped and smiled. We hugged her at the same time as we said, "Hi Grandma!" Well I said, "Hi Ma Ma!" She smiled, hugged us back, and said, "Hi my babies!" After a little small talk, she turned to me and said, "Camille, I need to have a word with you." That didn't sound good.

Me and my cousins smiles faded. I looked at them as I walked away with my grandma. She took me to a corner where no one was nearby. All my cousins saw was me looking up at my grandma as she spoke to me. They could only go off of our facial expressions and body language.

My grandma tried to be discreet, because she knew it was a party filled with celebrities and other people important to our careers. But one thing she did do was point her finger at me. When she did that, I was fumbling my hands underneath my shirt. She made me stop doing that immediately.

All my cousins saw was tears in my eyes and me trying hard not to make a crying face. After she stopped talking, I wiped my eyes as she watched me walk upstairs. My cousins was so confused. Carmen put her hands out, and looked around at our cousins as she said, “What happened?” Cashae said, “I know.”

They watched me go into my room for a while. Then they saw me come out and dart to my mom's room. When I did that, my grandma started to walk upstairs fast. I walked into my mom's room crying and said, "Mommie??" She took a deep breath. She had her hand on her cheek as she looked at me and said, "Yes, Camille?"

I asked, "Am I going with Ma Ma??" My mom dragged as she said, "Yes baby, you are." I started to breathe harder as more tears came down. I said, "Why??" My aunties took a deep breath and looked at my mom. My mom took another deep breath. Just then my grandma walked up to the opening of the room door.

My grandma heard me and said, "Excuse me? Camille, you do not question your mother." I looked at her and said, “Ma Ma, I just wana know.” My mama said, “It’s fine Ma.” My grandma said, “No it isn’t Toya. You allow her to do things like this. This is why she does what she do. She’s not your equal.”

My mom said, “I know she not Ma. But I can answer her.” What a lot of people don’t know is, my mama has a huge soft spot for me. My family knows it, but other people don’t. My mama looked at me and said, “Cee Cee, I have a lot to figure out. You’ve been doing a lot of stuff, and I have to figure out what I’m gonna do.”

I said, “It’s Shaun, isn’t it?” Everybody in that room was shocked I brung him up. They all looked at me at the same time. I was zoned in on my mom and said, “I knew it.” Tears started to fall from my eyes back to back. I continued, "I've been getting in trouble because of him for years and it wasn't my fault..."

My mom said, "But you continued to see him after I told you not to. You lied Camille, you're sneaking around doing things I don't want you to do." I coldly said, "You know why I did it Mommie?" She looked at me, everybody was quiet. I said, "Because I was getting in trouble for it. I kept getting in trouble for something I didn't do, so why not do it?"

All of them were shocked. My mama didn't know how to feel about that. She took a minute to collect herself and then said, "Eventually we would have found out it wasn't you, if you truly didn't do it. But because you went along with it, it caused you to continue to get in trouble…and I suppose you knew this whole time that Woof was Shaun??"

I looked guilty. I was looking around as I lowly said, "I didn't realize until tonight that you didn't know who he was." My mama said, "All this time. Camille, you normally tell me things. What happened?" She said that last part with compassion. I said, "Shaun…Mommie, Shaun happened. Ever since he came in the picture, we've been distant."

My mom said, "I agree and why do you think that is?" I said, "Because no matter what I tell you or what I tried to say, you don't believe me anymore. You automatically thought I was lying. That made it hard to tell you some things. Throughout everything, Shaun showed me he cares and he's there for me. I'm sorry Mommie."

My mom looked concerned and said, "Camille." I said, "It's just hard to finally have the love you longed for from a guy, just to walk away from it. I want to listen to you, but then that means I'll lose the best thing I've ever had from a guy. I don't have that from my dad. Mommie, I wish you understood."

My mom shed some tears because she too had daddy issues. At this point I've only ever seen my grandpa a couple hand full of times in my life, because of their issues. As she wiped her eyes she said, "Oh baby, you have no idea how much I understand. But I don't want you to fall for the first thing that comes your way, to fulfill what yo daddy should have. You understand?"

I said, “Yes.” She said, “Give me a hug.” I came to her, and we hugged each other as we both shed more tears. My aunties cried too. My grandma even shed some tears. After we hugged, my mama looked at me and said, “I just want the best for you. I don’t want you making the same mistakes I made.”

I said, “I know.” My mama said, “I love you.” I said, “I love you too.” She said, “You can still come to me and talk to me about anything. I know how frustrating and confusing this all can be. What I don’t want you to do is keep things away from me. Even if I don’t approve of them. Come to me so I can help you.”

I said, “Okay.” She said, “I have to figure it all out.” I looked at her and said, “So I’m still being sent away?" She shook her head in a yes motion and said, "Yes." I accepted it and said, "Okay." She said, "Be good." I got up and said bye to my aunties.

I walked out the room with my grandma. When I got to my cousins, I hugged them goodbye. I was crying and trying to explain to them what happened as fast as I could. They were confused. But as soon as I started to cry, I was pulled away and sent outside to my grandma.

No one wanted the guests to see me cry. The thing is my cousins cried too. They were immediately sent to my mom's room with their moms. My cousins were livid! Their moms had to explain to them what happened. They couldn't go back to the party because they wouldn't stop crying and looking mad.

My mom and my aunties had a lot on their hands at this point. They didn't even go back to the party until the very end, when they were saying bye to the guests. After the guests left, they were all in their feelings. They went home and my mom was in her room crying her eyes out.

She knew I needed discipline, but it was hard for her to see me go through it. My mama was tired. My dad was more active in our lives, but it was like my mom was raising us by herself. Thank God she had my grandma, her sisters, their moms, Alexi, and her brother. After leaving with my grandma, we talked about everything once we got to her house.

She was trying to pick my brain about everything. She felt like if Andre was there more, I wouldn't be that way over Shaun. In all reality, my grandma felt bad for me. But at the same time, she was big on discipline and knew I needed to listen to what my mom said.

After she talked to me, we went to bed. This was the worst! I knew I got in a lot of trouble because of Shaun, but being separated from my cousins and everyone else was terrible. I never knew things could get this bad. I couldn't help but feel like my mom was giving up on me.

She sent me away and that was not a good feeling. I've always felt loved with my mom and although I still did, I felt the only person that never made me feel alone in my life was Shaun. I had a lot to figure out and I didn't know what to do. Without my cousins to talk to, I didn't know my next move.

I just wanted to go home. I wanted this all to be over. But little did I know, this was just the beginning.

Chapter 14

Adolescence

I had been at my grandma's house for a few days now. I hadn't heard from my cousins, my mom, or anyone else. I was in total solitary confinement, and I hated it! I couldn't understand it. Here I was AGAIN being punished for yet another thing that wasn't my fault.

Well, I mean I take full responsibility for keeping in contact with him after being told not to. But I felt like I was being punished extra, because my mama didn't realize Shaun was the same boy from Chicago. During my stay at my grandma's house, all I had was time. Time to think and I thought about EVERYTHING.

My grandma talked to me about it every day. I was respectful and listened. Besides, she seemed pretty stern in what she was saying. It was like she had this talk before, she wasn't new to it at all. Me not knowing she told my mama the same exact things when my mama was my age.

She didn't have to yell at me because I wasn't questioning her. I listened and simply responded, "Yes ma'am." when it was time for me to respond. She even took a deep breath as she looked off to the side. We were sitting down. Her hands were pressed down on her thighs as she said, "Whew! That was surprisingly easier this time."

I looked at her and said, “Huh?” She looked at me and said, “Oh nothing.” Then she stood up and said, “Come on, let’s get you home.” My face lit up as I looked at her and asked, “I’m goin home today?!” She answered, “Yes. You have a show tomorrow.” I took a silent deep breath.

I was disappointed knowing I was going home only because I had a show the next day. I didn’t even practice. Nonetheless, I was happy to be going home. When I got home, I didn’t know how to feel. Did my mom not want me anymore, or did she really need to figure things out?

I was uncomfortable. I didn’t know what to think, or how to think. I just knew I felt out of place, like I was not supposed to be there. You wouldn’t think I would feel that way because my mama was happy to see me. She greeted me as if nothing happened.

She kissed my forehead, told me how much she missed me, and hugged me. I reacted how I always reacted to it too. I was happy to see my mom even under the circumstances. But one thing went under their noses. Due to the acting classes and acting coaches we've had for the past 8 years, we all learned to be actors.

In the acting world and in real life. I acted like nothing was wrong with me, when in reality everything seemed wrong. After my grandma left and my mom went in her room, I knew the only thing I wanted at that moment was to feel loved. At this moment in my life, I could only think about one person that could fulfill that need…Shaun, and that's where I wanted to be.

I closed my eyes tight as I rocked back and forth. I was sitting in the middle of my bed clutching my legs that was bent up to my chest. I cried silent tears. They were silent, but for whatever reason I felt they were the loudest tears I've ever cried.

The next day, everyone was getting ready for the show. We had to leave hours earlier than show time, because we had to do sound check and prep. My mom had everything together. But when my aunties showed up, she realized she didn't have everything.

Beonca asked, "You ready?" My mama was still doing some last minute rushing as she responded, “Yeah, just let me grab this bag.” Then Beonca asked, “Where’s Camille?” My mom’s mouth opened a little as she lightly gasped. She was looking like a deer in headlights.

After a brief moment of silence, she answered, “Oh my gosh. I haven’t seen Camille all day.” My aunties and cousins mouths all dropped. Trinity said, “But you did tell her they had a show today, right??” My mama said, “Yeah. That’s why she came home last night.” Then my mama turned her head slightly towards the stairs and said, “Camille?!”

They all started helping her put our things in the car. After making two trips to the car while they were still outside in the front, Latonya slapped her hand on her thigh. She looked at my mom and said,

"Where Camille at??" She was getting aggravated. My mama said, "I called her twice! Let me go check."

After my aunties heard my mama in the house calling me and looking for me, they all looked at each other and walked in the house to help her look. But as soon as they came in, my mama was coming from upstairs. She told them, "I looked everywhere, I don't know where that girl at."

This left them all in a state of confusion. My mama decided to call me one more time, "Camille!!" Right after that, I came running out of the kitchen. They all paused and looked at me. Latonya looked upset and confused as she said, "What the h*ll??" I looked a little nervous.

I started to walk towards them as I rubbed my hands together. I said, "Yes? Mommie, you called me?" I said that as if she wasn't screaming her heart out. I said the last part of that slowly as my eyes shifted from my mom to them, then back to my mom. This made their mouths drop even more.

My mom was looking at me very confused. Then she said, "Did I call you?! I'm sure the whole f**kin neighborhood heard me! Where the h*ll you been?!" I was shifting my eyes back and forth again as I answered, "I was in the backyard. I needed fresh air." The entire time I was still fidgeting with my hands.

My mama said, "You knew ya'll had a show to do today, and you wana be in the backyard acting like you can't hear nobody?! We gotta go and you not even dressed!" I was scared now. I walked towards them more as I said, "I'm sorry. I didn't know we had to leave this early."

Beonca shook her head in a no motion and sternly said, "We don't have time for this." My mama said, "Exactly!" She looked at me and with her arms signaled towards the door she said, "Go get in the car, you gone have to get dressed on the way there!" Me and my cousins ran outside and got in the car.

My aunties and my mom were looking at each other shaking their heads. Latonya squinted at my mom as she said, "The backyard??" My mama shook her head in a no motion as she looked up to the ceiling. She raised one arm all the way up. She waved it back and forth as she said, "Lord help me. She just came back. I don't know what to do!"

Then she looked at my aunties and said, "Let's go." They came out to the car, and we left. Since me and my cousins hadn't seen each other for days, they had us all ride in the same car. This way we could go over our performances and stuff. My cousins were pretty quiet outside of the performance talk.

I could tell they had a lot to say, but of course they wasn't gonna say it right there. One of our parents was in the car with us. But that did not stop Cashae or Carmen from staring me down. I caught both of them doing it at separate times. They both looked like they wanted to say something to me when they did it. But they knew it was not the time or place.

I wondered what they were thinking about. We did our show, and everything was fine. Some more time went by, and it became a thing for me to go missing randomly especially right before a show. My mom didn't mind me getting fresh air, but she did not like the fact that I didn't come when she called.

After the fourth time, I started to get in trouble for it. The trouble was scary. My mom would fuss me out, but the scary part came later when we got back home. I would get a beating. She waited to do this, because she didn't want me crying before a performance or an appearance.

Nobody knew. My aunties and my cousins only thought I got fussed at. I never told my cousins because I didn't want to get them involved. That would risk getting them in trouble. My mama was tired of beating me day in and day out for the same thing. So she decided to ban me from going in the backyard. That way she didn't have to worry about it.

The very next time we had to go somewhere, there she was calling my name again. Just a second after she yelled my name, she began to move faster as she mumbled, "You know what? I know she hear me, cause I told her not to go back out this doe." By that time she was at the back door with the door open looking for me.

She didn't see me, so she closed the door. She walked back up to her sisters and my cousins, who were all near the front door. She pointed her finger out of frustration and said, "Camille gone really make me hurt her. I done told that girl…" As she said that, I walked in the front door. Everybody paused and stared at me.

They couldn't believe I just walked through the front door. My mama said, "Where the h*ll were you??" With a blank look on my face, I calmly answered, "You said I couldn't go in the back, so I went in the front." Latonya said, "But we didn't see you out there." I quickly and calmly said, "Did you check the bushes?"

My auntie's mouth was left wide open. She looked confused and she thought to herself. Since they didn't check the bushes, they couldn't say I wasn't in them. My mama was over it. She pointed and said, "Now!" She didn't have to say anything else. I knew she was telling me to get my stuff so we could all go.

I hurried to grab my stuff and we all ran out the door. That same day, Cashae and Carmen both gave me the same looks they gave me the first time it happened. Only this time, they chose not to ignore it. During a break we had in between performances my cousins all went to the bathroom.

Except Carmen, she was moving slow as our cousins walked out of our dressing room. Once they were out of the room, Carmen threw her stuff down. She turned towards me quick and said, "Okay,

Camille what's goin on?" I looked at her shocked. I slightly smiled and said, "What you mean?"

She sternly said, "Cut the crap. You may have learned to pull one over on your mom, but not on me." I said, "Fine." Carmen asked, "What were you doing? Why were you outside?" I said, "I wanted to make a phone call. I didn't want my mom to know, so I went on the side of the house."

Carmen said, "Oh okay. That's believable. I just wanted to know." Later during that show, Cashae caught me as I was getting something to drink. She was getting something to drink too. She came up on the side of me and looked in my face sarcastically with her head tilted.

I looked at her and slightly smiled with my mouth closed and said, "What is yo problem girl?"

Cashae said, “Better question, what’s yo problem?” She pointed her finger in my face when she asked that. Before I could reply, she quickly asked, “What you was doin outside?” I looked at her because I was shocked she asked too.

She said, “Don’t lie either.” I laughed and said, “I went for a walk Shae. I needed to clear my head.” She looked me up and down as she said, “Mmm hmm. That explains why you ain’t hear yo mama callin you.” Then she walked away. I was relieved. After the show we all went home.

Little did I know, Cashae was spending the night at Carmen’s house. I’m guessing they didn’t bother telling me because I was in trouble already. Anyway, sometime that night I was brought up in the conversation. They immediately started talking about me disappearing often and not coming when my mama call me.

Carmen said, “Girl you know I had to ask Camille about it.” Cashae said, “When you asked her?” Carmen said, “At the show.” Cashae got excited and said, “Me too! She told me she went for a walk to clear her head.” Carmen looked at Cashae confused and said, “Hold up, what?! She told me she went outside to make a phone call on the side of the house.”

Cashae calmed down and was thinking as she softly said, “Maybe she’s talking about the first time then?” Carmen said, “I never asked her about the first time.” Cashae lowly said, “Me either.” After a few seconds, Carmen got loud and said, “Camille lied to us!”

She picked up her phone and started to dial a number as she said, “I can’t believe she would lie to us.” Cashae asked, “Wait who you callin?” Carmen looked at her with the phone against her ear and said, “Alisha.” When Alisha picked up the phone, Carmen filled her in.

Alisha ended up calling Alicia on three-way, so their mom wouldn’t hear Carmen telling them what happened on speaker. Alisha said, “I don’t know what Camille got goin on, but she better cut it out. She playin right in her mama face, and we all know Auntie Toya do not play like that.”

Carmen said, “Exactly! I put Camille on game when I told her how to sneak around or get away with stuff. But now she usin the crap on me!” They all started laughing. Alisha said, “You said she told you she had to make a phone call?" Carmen said, "Yeah."

Alisha asked, "When did Camille get her phone back??" Cashae and Carmen were both shocked. They said, "What??" Alisha said, "Camille hasn't had her phone since Auntie Toya sent her to Grandma Tam house that day." Cashae and Carmen were even more shocked. They both shouted, "What?!"

Alicia said, "Oh yeah. Mama did talk to Auntie Toya, and she said Camille can't have her phone." Carmen said, "That's why Auntie Toya was screaming her name instead of callin her phone??" The twins laughed as they said, "Yeah!" Carmen said, "I was wondering! I'm sittin there like, why don't she just call her phone??"

Cashae said, "So that makes sense. What if Camille got her phone and went outside because she snuck it." Alisha said, "Camille wouldn't touch that phone. She too scared of her mama. She even said it herself. She said she don't have her phone and she scared to touch it."

Cashae said, "Wait you talked to her on a phone or in person?" Alisha and Alicia both answered, "In person!" Alisha said, "Camille and her mom came to our house a few times since then. She told us out of her own mouth, my mama took my phone that day and never gave it back. I'm too scared to touch it, so I haven't talked to anybody."

Carmen said, "Dang! But it's been a couple months." Alicia said, "Yep, Camille never had her phone, Carmen. So she lied to you. Cashae, I don't know how true it was that she took a walk. But we all know…" They all joined in at the same time and said, "Camille is too scared to go off by herself! Right!!"

They were all confused. Alicia said, "Somethin ain't right. Camille tell us everything." Carmen said, "Whatever it is, I hope she alright." They all said, "Yeah." A few more weeks passed by, and my cousins did not confront me about it. My mom noticed that I wouldn't go missing anymore, because of this my cousins figured maybe I did take a walk that day.

While my cousins started to let it go, my mama got more suspicious. I still didn't have my phone. One random night, all of my cousins were woken up by their moms. Their moms were panicking. My cousins were ripped from their sleep. Their moms asked, "Do you know where Camille is??"

All of my cousins had the same reactions. They sat up fast, gasped, and said, "Oh my gosh, no what happened?!" Once their moms told them my mom didn't know where I was, they couldn't think straight. They were all at their own houses. Their moms said, "Come on we gotta help find her."

They all jumped up quick and made it to my house so fast. When they got there, they ran inside. My cousins were so scared they were crying. They all went to hug my mama at the same time. You couldn't tell if she was consoling them or if they were consoling her.

They hugged for a while, then my mama said, “It’s okay. It’ll be fine.” She started to calm them down and she was the most concerned, I’m sure. They sat down. My mama said, “I know it’s hard to think right now, but do any of ya’ll know where Camille could be?” They all shook their heads no.

It was a frustrating situation, nothing seemed to be helping. My mom didn’t want to worry my grandma or anyone else, but she panicked. After an hour of not finding me, she called my grandma, my uncle, my Auntie Trice, and Alexi. The only person she did not call was my dad.

I can understand why though, he can be a drama king at times. Once she called them, nobody was sleeping. They hurried to my house. Alexi was so scared when she got there, she was visibly shaking. She tried to hold it together, but when they thought they had a lead it fell through.

Alexi was sitting on the couch. She dropped her head catching it with her fingertips on her right hand. She was weak. She started to cry, thinking the worst but hoping for the best. Auntie Trice cried too she couldn't sit still. They all were crying at some point.

Uncle Gary told my mama, "I can't take this sittin down. I gotta go out there and look for her. Is there anywhere she go over here?" My mama said, "No, Camille don't go anywhere without us." Cashae then said, "Auntie, we asked her why she was outside last time, and she told us she went for a walk."

All of the adults lifted their heads up fast. Everybody was looking at Cashae. Then my mama said, "Oh wait!" She got up and ran out of the room. When she came back in, she had her laptop. She sat it on the living room table and said, "I found it weird for Camille to start disappearing and then all of a sudden stop."

As she pulled up the computer system, she said, "She haven't been giving me issues. She's been acting like the child she was before, innocent. So I installed a few cameras to see what she be up to." When she said that, Cashae and Carmen looked worried as they slowly looked at each other.

My mom pulled up the cameras. She was able to find four videos that showed me. As she played them, everyone including my cousins gathered around to watch them. They saw that I would tiptoe from my room, through the living room, and slip out the back door. This was in the middle of the night!

Once I was outside, the videos showed me jumping the fence to the other block. The videos also showed me coming back to the house, jumping the fence, and sneaking back in my room just before my mom wakes up. Which would be hours later.

They were all speechless. They couldn't believe I had been sneaking out! My mama said, "That's what she must've been doing on those other days, because she came in the side door instead of the main door. She knew I would be up and active. But on these nights, she knew I was sleep."

Uncle Gary immediately jumped up and said, “I’m searching the block.” He left right away. My mom said, “I don’t understand. Where is she going? Is it that block? Or is it a short cut to go somewhere else? And she staying out for at least 5 hours before she come back.”

They all waited. My mama would check in with Uncle Gary every now and again. Uncle Gary searched up and down that street a couple times, he called and told my mama, “She gotta be inside somewhere or somebody picked her up. Ain’t no way she came on this block, and we can’t find her.”

Just then my mama heard other men in the background. She said, “Who is that?” Uncle Gary said, “Some of the neighbors. They helping me out here.” As my mama sat on the phone saying to herself, "Why is she obsessed with that block?" She heard one of the guys say, "Oh yeah, Woof?! Yeah, he right there." That broke her concentration.

She immediately asked, "What did they say??" Uncle Gary said, "Oh, they talking about Woof. He got a house on this block and they fannin over it." My uncle laughed a little bit after he said that. My mama gasped as she stood up and said, "Omgee!" My uncle said, "Yeah, he bought the second from last house on my side of the block. He moved in round the time you had that party."

My mama could not move, she was barely breathing. She could not believe what she just found out. Everyone at my house was looking at her and saying, "What??" My mama stared straight ahead and said, "Thank you Gary. Ya'll can go home now.

I think I know where she is." My uncle was confused.

But my mama hung up so fast. My aunties said, "What happened?? Where she at??" My mama was still looking into nowhere as she said, "She better not be where I think she is." She grabbed her keys and firmly told all of them, "Stay here." She left out the door fast!

They all just sat there hoping for the best. By the time my mama got to the block, my uncle and the other men that helped him went home. That's exactly how my mom wanted it to be to keep matters private. She contemplated knocking on the door. She didn't want to disturb his mom's sleep, especially if she was wrong thinking I was there.

She then felt like she had no choice. She also didn't want me to know she was there if I happen to be there. So she called her agent and asked them for Shaun's mom's number. The agent gave it to her. She had rather take her chances calling than knocking.

Luckily Shaun's mom picked up on the second ring. My mom was nervous to find out if I was in there or not. Once his mom picked up, my mom introduced herself. After hearing her name, Shaun's mom said, "Oh Camille's mom! She's all Shaun talks about, she's such a sweet girl." My mom said, "Thank you. Have you seen her?"

Shaun's mom was startled. She said, "I'm sorry, I have never seen Camille outside of the parties and performances." My mama said, "You may not believe this but, I have reason to believe she's in your house." My mama explained what was going on.

Shaun's mom was shocked, but she was happy to help. She opened the front door for my mom. She told her, "Why don't we look together?" My mom said, "Okay." His mom led her to Shaun's room. Before she opened the door, Shaun's mom looked at my mom and whispered, "You ready?"

My mom took a deep breath and shook her hands as if she was trying to fling something off of them. She was nervous. She balled her hands up and placed them over her mouth as she shook her head in a yes motion. Shaun's mom slowly opened the door.

They both peeked in. Low and behold, they saw me laying in front of Shaun. He was sleep behind me, his arm was around my stomach holding me closely to his body. My mama took another deep breath, as she tilted her head back covering her mouth with both hands clasped together.

Shaun's mom was upset, but she could sense the fury coming from my mom. Instead of showing how upset she was, she consoled my mom instead. She rubbed her back trying to calm her down. My mom stood there for a good minute. Then she said, "Forgive me for what you about to see." Before anything else, my mama quietly stormed into the room.

She wasted no time! She didn't even bother waking me up. She threw them covers back, grabbed my wrist, and before I knew it, she snatched me out of the bed and out of the room. I just opened my eyes when we got on the stairs. I still didn't know what was going on, but I saw her.

She had me by the wrist. I gasped loud because it scared me. Shaun heard me and woke up in a panic. But his mama was right there to deal with him. He didn't know what happened. He just knew I wasn't there no more. My mama drug me all the way to the car, and when we got to the car she threw me towards it!

I looked at her and saw how pissed she was. I just opened the door and got in the car fast. I was breathing so hard after everything was making sense to me. I was in the back seat. She kept looking at me in the review mirror. She said, "Really?! Really Camille?!"

I was scared. She was mad. Then we pulled up to the house and I saw everybody's cars. I went crazy. I said, "Mommie please." Why I said that?? She turned around to me and said, "Please what?!" She started hitting me as she said, "You sittin there laid up with a boy I didn't even want you keeping in contact with!"

Those hits hurt! I was crying. I screamed a few times while I was getting hit. Then she said, "You thirteen!" She hit me one more good time as she said, "You f**kin thirteen!" I was crying so hard at this point. I was already sore from those hits. She got out the car, came around to my side, opened the door and said, "Now you scared to get out the car cause everybody here?!"

I was looking at her still crying. Then she said, "You gone get yo a** out this car! Everybody here inside crying thinking something happened to you, and yo a** at some boy house!" Her voice cracked at the end. A couple tears came out her eyes. She wiped them quick. Then she pulled me out the car with one hand.

Once I was out the car, she closed the door, pointed at the house, and said, "Go!" I started to walk towards the house. She unlocked the door, and I walked in. Everybody gasped. Of course they all ran to me and gave me hugs. They had no idea what they were about to hear.

Once they sat back down, they asked where I was and my mama said, “I found her at Shaun house!” My cousins gasped as their mouths dropped to the floor, my aunties mouths dropped too. They asked where he lived at. My mama explained how he bought a house around the time of their party.

She told them what she saw when she entered the room. She told them how she took me out of there, and how she had to jump on me in the car. I was embarrassed, but I was more scared. I was in front of my aunties, my mama, and Alexi, and they all were looking at me the same exact way.

They were livid! I covered half my face with my hands, closed my eyes, and started crying uncontrollably. My mama looked at me and asked, “Have ya’ll been doin anything?!” Through the coughing and crying, I shook my head in a no motion. I was able to let out a, “No,” through the gasping of air.

My mama said, “How am I supposed to believe that?? You been lyin and sneaking all this time.” I was still talking through the air gasping and wiping my tears as I said, “I…didn’t…we was…just sleep.” She looked at me and said, “Go upstairs!” She pointed towards the stairs.

I ran up the stairs fast. I was happy to get out of everybody’s faces. I couldn’t believe that happened. I really couldn't believe they were all at my house. This was bad. Meanwhile, they were all downstairs pissed. My grandma was shocked and lost for words. She shed some tears. She wiped them as she said, “We have to break this cycle. This can’t happen again.”

My mama was upset and overwhelmed. My grandma then said, “If you need her to come back to me to get further away from him, you can do that when you need to.” Alexi said, “Yeah, you can send her to me too. If I can help stop this whole pregnant at fifteen thing, I’m on bored. That wasn’t easy for none of us.” Trinity said, “I’m right by his house, but if you send her my way, she won’t get out of my sight.”

My mom said, “Thank ya’ll so much. I really appreciate all of ya’ll. I’ma take ya’ll up on those offers too. It seems like she’s getting worse as she gets older. I just have a feeling, I’m in for it. I’ma need all the help I can get.” They all said, “We got you Toya." My mama said, "Thanks, but first I gotta deal with her."

My mama didn't wait for them to leave. She came up to my room and wore me out! I know I said the other beating was the worst I've ever had, but that had nothing on this! I never experienced anything like that from my mama. But I guess she never experienced anything like that from me either. She switched up how she beat me, and it was way worse!

After that beating I wasn't so sure I wanted to keep up with Shaun anymore. I was barely able to take that beating. I just had a feeling if I didn't cut it out, I would have a lot more hands to deal with other than my mama. I felt like my aunties and

Alexi were probably waiting in line for me to do something else.

Sigh I had a lot to consider and even more to think about. I want to listen to my mom, but why can't I just leave that boy alone??

Chapter 15

Predetermined

After that day I was watched very closely. Not only was I watched closely by my mom, but I was also watched closely by my aunties, my grandma, and Alexi. My uncle kept his eye on me whenever he was around too.

I started to have issues with recording songs and cooperating with appearances and other work projects. My mom would have to chastise me on the spot. It got bad, because sometimes my mom wouldn't even be there and would have to travel to where we were for me to straighten up.

I wasn't doing this on purpose, but after being kept away from Shaun after the incident, I couldn't think straight. I wondered what he was thinking, and how he felt. I also missed how he comforted me when I needed it most.

Now that I was being kept away from him, I would just cry when I needed that comfort. I cried a lot more since then. I couldn't focus on anything. All I thought about was Shaun. Since I was having a lot of issues with work, my mom decided to keep me away from the parties.

When everyone gathered together, I would not be there. I would be sent to my grandma's house. My cousins were able to attend the parties and gatherings, but it wasn't the same without me. People would ask, "Where is Camille??" Between my cousins, my mom, and my aunties, they would say I was busy.

Eventually my cousins asked their moms if it was okay that they didn't attend the parties and gatherings. They got tired of people asking where I was, and they were not having fun anymore. All they thought about was everything we were going through behind the scenes.

So their parents didn't force them to attend the parties or gatherings. Instead, my cousins had rather spend their time alone and bored in their rooms. My actions affected all of us and I was too into my feelings to realize it. My cousins were fed up with the interruptions and unfinished projects due to my acting out.

But they didn't say anything. I could see it in their body language and faces though. The last straw was when we were in the studio together. They came in taking deep breaths as they put their stuff down. They had no idea how everything was going to go.

They were on edge. We started to warm up. After a minute, I walked away. I sat down in a chair in the corner and sipped my water. My cousins was glancing at each other as they continued to warm up their voices. I was looking at them and did not appear to have plans on getting up out of that chair anytime soon.

Carmen stopped and quickly asked, "Camille? You not gone warm up??" I calmly looked at her after taking another sip of water and said, “I’m comin.” They started again. I got up and stood with them around the microphone as they harmonized and went through runs.

Only thing is instead of joining them, I was looking at them. Cashae said, “Camille you not even warming up. You gone get in trouble.” I said, “My voice is fine.” They all shook their heads in a no motion and sarcastically said, “Alright.” Not too long after, the producer came in and we had to record our song.

Everything was okay at first, but then I had to take the lead and I missed the queue. The producer said, “That’s alright Camille. Let’s start from the top…here we go.” He started over and I did not hit the right notes. My cousins looked away in aggravation.

The producer asked, “Camille, are you okay?” I shook my head in a yes motion. He started over again. I did the same thing! He turned his microphone off. He said something to his engineer. Next thing you know, I saw my mama walk into the studio. My mouth dropped for a second.

They were talking. My mom’s facials looked confused, then concerned, then pissed. She pushed a button on the audio board and sternly said, “Camille. Hit the notes and do it right.” We all were looking at her. I was scared. She sat down and got comfortable. She stared at us as the music started again.

We did the intro with no problem. When it was my turn, I was hitting some notes that I didn’t hit before my mom came in. She knew I wasn’t doing it before, because of how my cousins and the producer looked at me when I did. They were shocked as if they didn't know I could hit those notes.

But right before my verse was finished, I did not hit a single note right. The same notes I hit before. I just stopped and stared at my mom. She was staring at me. I can tell she was beyond upset. She had her arms crossed and everything. My cousins all stared at her with their mouths wide open.

They were scared for me. She pressed the button again and sternly said, "Do it again." They started the track, but this time I messed the whole verse up. She let me finish it and then she stood up, pressed the button, and said, “Come here.” I already knew what time it was.

As I walked out of the recording booth and out the studio with my mom, my cousins started to whisper amongst themselves. Carmen had her hands stretched out with her arms down by her sides. She whispered, “She wasn’t singing.” My cousins said, “What??”

Carmen said, “She wasn’t singing. The only time she sung was her verse. She didn’t sing the chorus.” Alisha said, “Who?” Carmen lowly said, “Camille!” My cousins said, “Oh.” Carmen knew because I was right next to her.

Meanwhile, my mom took me into another room where no one was. She looked at me and said, “I’m not doin this with you today. I am tired of going through this same thing with you every time you have to work Camille! You sittin around worried about a boy and refusing to do what you supposed to do. I have stuff to do! I can't be coming to you every time you actin up!"

She saw I wanted to say something. She had her arm extended to the left with her palm up, because she was talking with her hands. She said, "What?!" I said, "My voice not warmed up." She said, "Don't ya'll go through warmups when ya'll first come in?!" She saw how I was looking down to the side.

I looked guilty and she said, "You didn't do warmups did you?" I shook my head in a no motion. She took a deep breath as she hit her thigh and rolled her eyes looking up to the ceiling. Then she said, "Let me tell you something, when you come in here you know what you have to do. When you choose not to, then you suffer the consequences."

I had tears in my eyes, I didn't want to be there. Then she said, "Now, you gone take yo a** back in there and hit every note you supposed to hit. You got one time, and if you miss one note Camille, I promise you, I will beat yo a** right there in front of everybody and you still gone finish the song afterwards. Do you understand me?"

A tear rolled down my face as I answered, "Yes ma'am." Then she said, "Let's go." When we went back in there, I looked like I wanted to cry. My cousins got up from their break and waited for me at the microphone. My mama sat down as she had before. The producer pressed the button on the audio board and asked, “Camille, are you ready?”

I looked at him and softly answered, “Yes.” The track started. I helped them sing the chorus and when it was my part again, I sung it correctly. As I sung my verse, I closed my eyes as tears flowed repeatedly from both of them. But I sang as if I wasn’t crying. My cousins were surprised.

The producer was even more surprised. He had no idea what my mama did, but he knew whatever it was it worked. I did not mess up at all. I was scared my mama was really gonna beat me in front of everybody. I was not willing to take that risk. Once the song was over, the producer and engineer clapped.

That was a wrap. My mom got up without saying a word. We all walked out the building with her and went home. Although I was being kept away from Shaun, my mom took this time to get to know Shaun's mom better. Even Shaun wasn't showing up to the parties like before. He didn't know how to feel after my mom caught me at his house, in his bed.

He felt like my mom didn't like him anymore after that. He couldn't bear to face her after his mom filled him in on what happened that night. It was awkward for all of us including my mom. Truth be told he got in a lot of trouble that night too. He was never supposed to have a girl in his room.

Sure it looked inappropriate and maybe it was, but Shaun and I knew why that night went the way it did. It was innocent. But that doesn't make what we did okay. We both understood that. After my mom checked me at the studio that day, I straightened up completely. I didn't want my cousins to feel burdened by me.

I chose to do my work and get it over with. It was easier that way. My mom noticed that I didn't have issues with my work anymore. I actually matured from all of the mishaps. I wasn't sneaking out anymore and I wasn't giving my mom, my aunties, Alexi, or my grandma any issues anymore.

After some time, it appeared that I wasn't thinking about Shaun much anymore. One day while I was out, Shaun showed up at my house. My mom opened the door. When she opened the door, she saw Shaun holding a bouquet of flowers. She slightly smiled with her mouth closed, took a deep breath out of her nose, and looked at him curiously.

Shaun looked up at her with his cute little face. He looked so innocent as he said, "I'm sorry Ms. Lockhart." He looked back down. You can tell he really felt bad about everything. My mom grinned a little more and said, "Come in Shaun."

Although she didn't like what happened, she still couldn't shake the fact that she took to Shaun. Shaun walked in and they had a long talk. By the time Shaun left, him and my mom was back hugging each other and laughing. They both felt a lot better. My mom never told me he came by.

Me and my cousins started to go back to the parties and gatherings. Shaun started to attend them too. We started to see each other more this way. Since we got in so much trouble before, we only spoke during these times which was frequently.

My mom checked my phone weekly as usual, and she did not find anything in my phone or call log indicating that I called or spoke to Shaun. My aunties checked my cousins phones and there was nothing in their phones either. No weird numbers, no secret text coding, nothing out of the ordinary.

My mama even started letting Que come back around us. Her mom would check her phone and they would find nothing. My mom was surprised and even more impressed with how maturely I was handling these things. She even asked me was I calling him, and I would tell her no.

There was a lot less conflict between us now, so she believed me. I straightened up right on time, I was working my way to no birthday party. But since I turned myself around, my mom decided to allow me to have one. Once my birthday came, me and the twins turned 14.

All of the people who helped raise us along with other family members were there. There were friends of the family, and also some celebrities that came too. Of course Que was sitting at the table with me and my cousins. We were all glammed up and happy. While we were enjoying the party, my mom said, “Camille, I have a surprise for you.”

She whispered in my ear. I smiled and turned my head towards her slightly. Then she smiled and pointed across the room. I looked up and I saw Shaun walking in. My smile was so big. My cousins mouths dropped too as they smiled and screamed a little.

I instantly put my head down and covered my face with my hands as I laughed. I couldn't believe he was there! I was so happy. His mom was walking behind him smiling. I got up and hugged him as he got closer. We both were all smiles. He handed me some gifts.

I turned to my mom and hugged her as I said, "Thank you Mommie." She hugged me back and said, "You're welcome baby." I sat down and Shaun stayed with me and my cousins the entire party. We were able to talk a lot and catch up. We were so happy to see each other on these terms again.

We all took pictures together and with our parents. Our dads were there too, all of my cousins dads included. We took pictures with our grandparents too. My mom even allowed me and Shaun to take some pictures together by ourselves. This birthday was a lot of fun.

At the end of the party, my mom told me, "I have to talk to you and Shaun." I said, "Okay." After everybody was gone, my mom sat us down. It was me, Shaun, my mom, and his mom. My cousins even left, but they went to get clothes in order to come back and spend the night with me.

First thing my mama said was, “Camille, do you have anything to say to Ms. Mace?” I looked at her, held my hands together and said, “Ms. Mace, I am so sorry for what happened that day. I’m sorry for sneaking in your house and disrespecting you by being in Shaun’s room like that.”

She smiled with her mouth closed and shook her head in a yes motion. I continued to say, “I know it’s like so long after, but I didn’t have a way to come to you and tell you. Please forgive me.” She hugged me and said, “Thank you for that Camille. I forgive you.”

Then my mom told me how Shaun came to our house months back apologizing to her. I looked at him so surprised. Then she said, “Camille, I know and understand what it’s like to have crushes and wanting to date. I also understand what comes with it. I admit I'm impressed with how much you've matured since last year."

I smiled because I was proud of myself too. Then she said, "For me I still feel like ya'll too young for dating. But I don't know what it is about Shaun, he tugged on my heart strings so long ago…" We all laughed a little. She continued, "And I looked at him as my baby. He's so lovable and respectful."

He was blushing. Then she said, "You both showed me and Ms. Mace that, you understood your wrong and you corrected it. Before I didn't feel like I could trust either of you. But after having a one on one with you and Shaun, I feel like I can. So with that said, Camille, I am going to give you permission to date Shaun."

We gasped as we smiled. She said, "But under my circumstances. If those circumstances are violated at all, you will not have my permission to date again. At least not before you're eighteen. Ya'll got it?" Me and Shaun said, "Yes ma'am." We couldn't contain our smiles.

My mom said, "Camille if you're dating, I rather know about it as opposed to me finding out you're sneaking around. So I'm willing to compromise my dating rule to help keep you out of trouble. Even after the trauma I went through as a teen. You have my trust, do not mess that up."

I shook my head in a yes motion and responded, "Yes ma'am." I knew exactly what she was talking about. Her being pregnant as a teen and having a baby by fifteen. For my mom to do this, I knew she cared a lot because that's something they're all afraid of.

That's something they spoke on from time to time. They want to break the cycle. They don't want any of us to have babies as teens. After our talk Shaun and his mom went home. My cousins came back to my house as Shaun and his mom was pulling off.

When they got inside the house, we went in my room. Carmen asked, "Was that Shaun we just saw leavin??" I smiled and said, "Yeah." Cashae asked, "What he was doin here??" I said, "My mom said she needed to talk to us." Alisha said, "About what?" I said, "My mom gave us permission to date."

The whole room got quiet. My cousins mouths were to the floor. Then they all screamed as they smiled. My mom was in her room and heard them scream. She smiled because she knew I told them at that point. I told my cousins how it all went down.

They couldn't believe it. They were so happy for me. We all felt like everything would be easier now that I had permission to date Shaun. I was excited to see how this all would play out.

What will come of this?

Will Camille make all the right choices now that she has permission to date Shaun??

Did Latoya make the right decision allowing Camille to date???

Find out what happens next in

Camille

-Chaotic-

Series 2 Book 3

Meet the Author

Kelonda Isom is a college graduate with a

degree in Broadcasting for television and radio. She graduated top of her class with a perfect 4.0 grade point average. She is listed in her college's Hall of Fame for her many accomplishments after graduating. She had the highest scores on all writing tests in school growing up. She has been writing Camille stories since the age of 12.

www.ingramcontent.com/pod-product-compliance
Lightning Source LLC
Chambersburg PA
CBHW070611310726
48982CB00001B/46

* 9 7 9 8 9 8 6 3 2 2 4 4 5 *